MARRIED
in BLACK

MARRIED *in* BLACK

BY

CHRISTINA CORDAIRE

DOUBLEDAY LARGE PRINT HOME LIBRARY EDITION

Crossings Book Club
New York, New York

This Large Print Edition, prepared especially for Doubleday Large Print Home Library, contains the complete, unabridged text of the original Publisher's Edition.

Published by Crossings Book Club, One Penn Plaza, New York, NY 10119

ISBN: 978-0-7394-9894-1

Printed in the United States of America

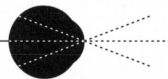

This Large Print Book carries the
Seal of Approval of N.A.V.H.

PROLOGUE

Spring 1861

"Virginia! I came as soon as I got back!"

Virginia Davenport ran across the deep carpet of the parlor to the stocky young man. Grissom, the butler, who had ushered him from the front door tactfully withdrew, leaving the door to the luxuriously appointed room standing open.

"William!" She greeted her guest warmly, fighting back the tears that his obvious sympathy brought to her eyes.

William Warner grasped both her hands in his. "You'll be all right, Vee," he used the name he'd called her since they were children, "Really you will. It's not the end of the world."

She sniffled once. "It certainly feels like it. Everybody knew how I felt about James."

"That's right—use the past tense. It's over, Vee, and good riddance. You just have to hold your head up and pretend that you don't mind a bit."

Oh, I should thank God for you, William Warner, Virginia thought. *You're just what I need.* "That's easier said than done when I keep getting all those pitying looks from most of my friends."

"Not all your friends."

"No. Not you and Dorothy, at any rate."

"Of course not. We believe it's your pride that's suffering more than your heart. The two of us think you've had a miraculous escape."

She tilted her head inquiringly, her eyes narrowing as she realized she might not like his answer about a miraculous escape any more than she'd liked his pointing out that she was mainly suffering from wounded pride. Frowning, she waited for it.

William threw back his head and laughed. "All right, I'll admit it. I think he's a conceited, self-centered boor. So does Dorothy."

Exasperated, Virginia snatched her hands away from him. "Then why didn't you tell me?"

William looked at her earnestly for a long moment before he asked softly, "Would you have listened?"

She spun away from him, the hem of her skirt swishing against his riding boots. "Certainly I would have listened! You two are my best friends in the entire world. Of course I'd have listened." She walked away from him and began to pace. "Yes. Surely I'd would have . . ." she paused.

"Maybe. Maybe I would have listened." When William didn't answer, Virginia laughed. "I wouldn't have, would I?"

William only smiled.

"Oh, William, why did I think he loved me?" She looked down at her clasped hands.

After a long pause, he said quietly,

"Because James gave you every encouragement to think so."

Her head snapped up. "What? Why do you say that?"

"Because I've known him all my life . . . and because my oldest sister was one of his victims, too." He took hold of her shoulders with gentle hands. "Vee, dearest, James was a consummate flirt back then, and time has only made him better at it." He tightened his grip as she started to pull away. "Wiser girls than you have fallen for his charming ways, you know."

Virginia frowned. "No, I didn't know. I didn't know any of this. What a silly fool you must think me." Her frown deepened. "What a fool *everyone* must think I am."

"No. I think you're quite wonderful."

She blinked away the unshed tears trembling on her lashes, uncertain now if they were more from vexation than hurt. "Well, I don't. I think I've been foolish past forgiving."

"Vee, I've noticed that people who truly are fools are not only incapable of admitting it, but also don't realize it." He held her gaze steadily with his own.

Finally, she took a deep calming breath as her pride came back. She gave herself a mental shake and stopped worrying about the opinion of those who pitied her. She wasn't the first girl to be a laughing stock, and she was perfectly certain she wouldn't be the last. She just hated being one. It did, as William had so carefully pointed out, come down to a matter of her pride being injured!

Smiling ruefully at her friend, she invited, "Shall we go out into the garden? I think I need to breathe."

Wordlessly, he went to the French doors that led out to the garden terrace. He held one open for her, his gaze adoring, while Virginia walked through it under his arm. It was a game they'd played ever since he'd grown tall enough for her to do it. For a great deal of their very young life, Virginia had been the taller of the two. Then William had spurted up, as most boys did, when he reached his first teen year. He was so proud when he passed her in height that Virginia had thought he'd pop.

That was when they'd begun this game of Virginia walking under his arm whenever he held a door for her. They laughed about it now, his laughter masking the way he felt about her. Then he followed her out into the sunlight.

Almost instantly, Virginia felt calmer. She loved to walk in the garden and this unseasonably warm day gave her an excuse. Her mother had the best head gardener in all of Boston, and the Davenports' garden was his masterpiece. Her father had spared no expense to help him make it so, and her mother had followed his lead in that. She continued to hire all the helpers her head gardener required and still bought every plant he recommended, as her late husband had always done.

As a result, the garden remained a glorious living picture at any time of the year, just as Virginia's father would have wished. It was beautiful even when it was covered in snow and had only red berries and glossy green leaves to rely on for that beauty. There were few who saw it without feeling envy or admiration at the results of all the effort.

This day was lovely and unusually warm for this time of year in Massachusetts, and Virginia was wearing the blue dimity gown that William had once told her he particularly liked because it set off the blue of her eyes. She'd worn it purely by chance, but now, since William had dropped in, she was glad that she had.

She was terribly fond of William. In fact, she loved him deeply as a friend and was really grateful for the support he offered.

William walked quietly beside her, just letting her calm down and come to grips with her problem. He knew that she'd always found peace in the refuge of her mother's garden and understood why.

Mrs. Davenport, always a very assertive woman, had become even more so since the death of her beloved banker husband. Christopher Langley Davenport's unfailing courtesy and good humor had always tempered his wife's comments and behavior, and she'd been welcome everywhere because of the regard people had had for him.

With the passing of her gentle husband and the resentment she harbored because of it, Claudia Davenport had become more and more domineering. Only the most stalwart of her friends still visited her. Everyone, even Claudia's friends, secretly thought that it must be difficult for Virginia to live under her thumb. They gave the girl a great deal of credit because she never complained.

Virginia had been so devastated by the news she'd received earlier in the week that she'd been sure she'd never recover. James McDermott, the man she loved, had become engaged to a girl Virginia only knew by sight—a cool blonde beauty a few years older than her own seventeen years.

For a while, Virginia had felt as if her life had ended. Now, thanks to her kind visitor, it seemed as if she'd survive and that there might be a chance for happiness, after all.

The sunlight filtering through the trees dappled the path they walked on and felt like a gentle benediction. Everything would be better—her wounded heart would heal. Virginia found her hurt lessening with each step they took.

He was a dear young man, well-thought-of by all her friends, and handsome as well. She and William had been best friends for as long as she could remember.

Now it seemed to her as if the Lord must have sent William, just when she was striving so mightily to recover from what she had thought of as her terrible heartbreak. She was grateful. William might not be as dashing as James, but he was kind and thoughtful . . . and he was at church every Sunday, something that meant a very great deal to her.

That had been something that had troubled her about James McDermott. He was quite cavalier when it came to his church attendance. Whenever she'd noticed he wasn't in his family's pew, she'd experience a little stop in her spirit. Church attendance was something that had always mattered to her. It had been something her beloved late father had insisted on, telling her that her week just wouldn't go right if she missed church.

And he'd certainly been correct about this week! The thought had a tinge of bitterness in it, so she thrust it out of her mind. She forced her thoughts, instead, to more pleasant recollections as she knew her father would have advised.

Christopher Davenport had nurtured his daughter in his faith so carefully, leading her by his own good example. Virginia didn't know how she would have survived his death if she hadn't had the faith of her father to cling to.

All her life, her father had been there for her. Always, he'd been the mainstay of her life—after God. And God came first because of what her father had taught her. He had led and grounded her in her Christian faith. Now he was gone.

She could hardly bear it.

It wasn't as if she could turn to her mother to lessen her grief. She and mother had a conflicted relationship. When she was younger, she had felt sad for herself; now that she was older, it made her sad for her mother.

Sometimes Virginia wondered if her

own closeness with her father might be at the root of her mother's distance. Virginia and her father had been bound ever closer by their faith, and it was a faith her mother didn't seem to share.

It had saddened her father that his wife treated church attendance as an opportunity to show off new clothes and greet her friends. To Virginia and her father, it had always been so much more.

William, she remembered, was always there in church. She had only to close her eyes to picture him in his place beside his mother and father, surrounded by his four sisters. Thinking back, she couldn't remember a time when he hadn't greeted her and stopped to chat for a while on the steps after service.

William had always been attentive to her, and right now she was even more appreciative of that in him. She'd never really been before—never really thought of how splendid William was. He had always been just Good Old William, her dear friend, and never anything more.

All her attention had been on the tall, dark James McDermott. In that, she'd been just like all the other girls. Dashing James, going from one scrape to another, had fascinated them, while faithful, steady William had been overlooked.

What an idiot she had been, not to see how much better William was! She turned her thoughts to her good friend, determined to put the perfidious James from her mind and heart.

William and she had sentiments in common. They shared thoughts and dreams. They'd done so since they'd learned to talk and could voice them. For instance, as Virginia did, he felt stifled by Boston society.

Of course, to be absolutely fair, though she'd always wanted more freedom, she hadn't longed so desperately to be quit of Boston until that devastating day she'd learned that James McDermott had become engaged. That information and the frequent pitying glances from those of her friends who had known how deeply she cared about James had given her an earnest desire to be somewhere else. Any place where she wouldn't have to see James and the girl he would soon bring home as his bride. She shuddered at the thought, and William's response was instantaneous.

"Are you cold, Vee?" He took her small hands in his large, competent ones as if to warm them. "Should we go back inside?"

She smiled at his quick concern. "No, I'm fine. Really I am." She turned to look him full in the face. "I've been so stupid, William. I'm having a hard time getting over that—that's all. Talk to me about something that will put James out of my mind, won't you?"

He released her hands and smiled winningly. "That's easy. I can always talk about the West. I don't bore you with all my talk about it, do I?"

"No, I think it's fascinating."

"Sometimes I get carried away. I forget not everybody is as interested as I am."

"Oh, but I am interested, William." She smiled brightly at him and suddenly knew that she wasn't just being polite in order to encourage him to divert her. She was really catching some of his excitement. When he spoke to her about his desire to go west, he made it all sound wonderful. "Tell me some more about the Indians and the scenery. From all I've heard, it doesn't sound a bit like our New England."

She led the way to one of the stone benches that bordered the extensive garden paths. William dropped down beside her.

"It isn't." He gestured to the soft blue sky and the trees that seemed to close them in. "It's not at all like it is here. The sky out there seems to burn, it's so vivid. It's wild and vast. The vistas seem to go on as far as the eye can see—way off and away, across grassy plains and hot, hostile deserts, and on to rugged mountains." His eyes sparkled with a sense of adventure. "It's difficult terrain. Not like here on our east coast where we can travel fairly easily. Why, you can only get across most of those mountain ranges by taking dangerous, rocky trails through steep passes."

He flashed a grin at her. "You'll find none of the rolling mountains, covered with acres of trees, that we have here in

New England. Anything gentle out there, they call hills. Their mountains are huge, towering piles of bare rock with almost nothing growing on them."

Virginia's eyes became even brighter with the excitement she felt at his descriptions of such a wild free country. Surely there, a body could escape the tight strictures of life maintained in her Boston circle. "What about the Indians, William? Tell me about them."

"There are all kinds of Indian tribes. Apaches and Navajos and Hopi. Sioux, Comanches, and Zuni . . . I have a book about them with excellent lithographs that I'll bring over for you to see the next time I come."

For the first time, Virginia saw the adoring look in his eyes. She was a little stunned by it. Why had she never noticed it before? Suddenly she realized that she would really miss him dreadfully if anything happened that William didn't come again.

"I'd love to see your book of Indians, William. I'm always glad to have you come. I feel so stifled here in Boston. We're so bound by convention, and you are the only person to whom I can say that." She looked at him earnestly, wanting him to see her sincerity. "I know there is so much to see and to do beyond the borders of Massachusetts that sometimes I feel as if my heart will burst with longing to escape."

Under his mop of sandy brown hair, William's face seemed to light up. "Aw, Vee, I had no idea you really felt that way. I thought you were only being nice, listening to all my ranting. I've been wanting to go west for the past two years worse than I can say." He locked his gaze on her, his brown eyes blazing with eagerness. "Glory, Virginia, wouldn't it be wonderful if we could . . ."

She returned his earnest gaze and wondered why she'd never noticed he was so handsome. He certainly was right now, with the light of his enthusiasm for the West in his face.

"Wonderful if we could what, William?" Her breath seemed to shorten as her heartbeat quickened. Somehow the image of James McDermott that she'd carried in her mind for the past year was beginning to fade.

"Wouldn't it be wonderful if you and I . . ." His voice faltered to a stop.

"If you and I what, William?" A strange feeling was building in her. She placed her hand over his where it lay on his knee, wanting him to finish his remark, the subtle excitement growing. "If you and I what?"

"If you and I might see it all together." The words were calm and intense. He regarded her steadily, his square, lean face still.

A long moment passed as Virginia thought about the implications of what William had said. His words had opened a whole new world.

Bees droned in the late afternoon sunlight. Somewhere in the neighborhood, a dog barked and was shushed to silence by its owner. A tendril of Virginia's dark hair blew across her lips as a breeze invaded the garden. As she pushed the wayward lock back into place behind her ear, Virginia saw the hope fade out of William's eyes and his countenance sadden.

Instantly, she realized that she didn't want to disappoint him. The love of her life had chosen another, and she was certain that she would never love deeply again. But surely a life of freedom and adventure with someone she had always liked and admired was preferable to being a lonely spinster here in her mother's house.

In fact, hadn't she yearned to see the very things that William had just described? Wouldn't it be wonderful, indeed, to be at his side to experience the freedom he talked so persuasively about?

She could picture the two of them standing together hand-in-hand on a tall hill, looking down on the smoke drifting up from the campfires of some peaceful Indian village. She was enchanted by the idea.

To marry a dear friend with whom one had dreams in common couldn't be a bad thing. After all, God had sent him to her in her hour of need; surely He would bless their union.

"William," she whispered.

"Yes, dearest Virginia?"

"Let us do this . . . together."

For an instant he was struck dumb.

Then he grinned. "You mean you'll marry me? You'll come west with me as my wife?"

Virginia touched his face gently. "Yes, William, I will." She smiled and leaned forward, intending to seal their promise with a gentle kiss. Instead, William swept her into his arms and crushed her to him for a kiss that was anything but gentle.

In his exuberant embrace, Virginia came to the conclusion that James Mc-Dermott might not be the only man in the world, after all.

It was a rather nice discovery.

Her best friend Dorothy Tate lost no time in telling all the cats who'd been talking about Virginia behind her back that Virginia had only pretended to be in love with James McDermott so that William would get up the gumption to propose.

Virginia and she got a lot of satisfaction out of the fact that they'd all believed her capable of such a thing.

William was hugely amused.

They were married in a lavish ceremony befitting a girl from one of

Boston's finest families and the son of one of its wealthiest merchants.

One week after that, war broke out between the North and the South.

CHAPTER 1

Spring 1866

Black! Black everywhere! Every single woman in Claudia Davenport's ornate drawing room was clad in it.

Virginia sat in the circle of women around her mother's silver tea service, balancing a plate of petit fours and a cup of steaming oolong, her mother's favorite tea. With all her heart, she wished she could be free of her own high-collared, black wool dress, but her mourning for William wouldn't end for six more months.

It wasn't that she didn't mourn for William. Their marriage had lasted four years—but in reality they'd had only a week together before the war broke out. No time to complete their honeymoon, and no time at all to start a home of their own.

Then, to her utter amazement, William had joined the army and she had been left to live with his parents while he was away. His enlistment had astonished her. Wildly disappointed that all their plans to go west seemed to have been knocked out of his head by the idea of preserving the Union, she'd put aside her feelings and tried her best to be supportive.

Not that she hadn't seen the necessity of keeping the nation whole. They were a big country, and she could understand that the world might need them to be a strong nation someday, not a divided one. It was only right that it remain a single entity.

She'd just been reluctant to give up her dreams, though—disappointed, too, that William had been willing to put all their plans aside, even for a war.

With an effort, she'd managed to hide her feelings from her new husband. Congratulating herself on being such a good wife, she'd sent him off with a brave smile after extracting many prom- ises that he'd keep himself safe.

William's letters were all she had, and she never failed to share them with her in-laws. She always skipped over the paragraphs that in which he spoke of their dreams of going west. After all, it would surely grieve them to think that William planned to leave again almost as soon as he returned from the army. In every letter she wrote, Virginia never failed to remind William of his promises to keep safe. It was almost as if she thought that there was the slimmest chance that he might forget that he was in danger every time he went into battle.

Poor William. He had made it through almost all the battles unscathed only to die in one of the last.

What a child she'd been! What a silly, foolish child to believe that promises could protect a man against gunfire. They hadn't—nor had her prayers—and now her dear William was gone, and with him, all her dreams of the west and the freedom they had hoped to find there. She was back under her mother's ample roof—and thumb—with no possibility of escape.

Many of her friends were in the same boat. She had only to glance around her to see it. Her best friend, Dorothy, who was sitting across the circle from her, had been the first to be widowed. Her wonderful Bradley had been killed in one of the early battles of the war.

Dorothy and Brad had had a small farm on the outskirts of Boston. It had been their pride and joy, and they'd been so happy working together to improve it. Then Brad had been killed and Dorothy's parents had insisted that she return to them as she was still too young a woman to be living alone. Since there were no children from the marriage, Dorothy had bowed to propriety and gone back to live with her mother and father.

Even James McDermott's beautiful bride was a widow now. Inconsolable, she'd gone back to Baltimore on the packet boat as soon as she'd recovered from the shock of the news of James's death.

The war had taken a terrible toll of the

young men who had marched out of Boston so bravely, certain that it would take no time at all to subdue the brothers and cousins turned enemies; enemies who didn't have even one single munitions factory in all their rebellious states. It was more than . . .

"Virginia! Mrs. Latimore is in need of more tea," her mother's sharp voice commanded, and with a little start, Virginia obeyed, glad to have her dismal thoughts interrupted. She smiled, put down her own cup and plate, and lifted the silver teapot.

Accepting Glenda Latimore's cup with her left hand, she asked, "Cream? Or lemon?"

"Cream and sugar, please, dear. Three lumps." Mrs. Latimore was fond of anything sweet. That fondness showed on her ample frame and made her one of the best cooks in their circle—especially when it came to deserts. That and her genial disposition caused her home to be one of the group's favorite gathering places.

Virginia did as Mrs. Latimore had

asked, and then looked around the circle of familiar faces. "Anyone else?"

Chloe Clarkson extended her cup.
"Just a warming, thank you." Her voice
always sounded so sad. Virginia could
certainly understand that and it made
her heart ache for Chloe. The pretty
young widow had been left with two
boys to rear, and already the strain
of making do and striving to make
ends meet was showing in her lovely
face. Chloe's plight tore at Virginia's
heart.

As she settled back in her chair, Virginia sighed. With so many men gone,
what hope did Chloe have of finding another husband to help her raise her darling boys? For that matter, what hope
did any of them have? The war seemed
to have stripped it from them.

To Virginia, from where she sat in her
mother's luxuriously appointed drawing
room, life looked bleak. Try as she
might, she couldn't forgive William for
going off and getting himself killed.

And, at night when she lay alone in
the silence in her lace-canopied, four-

poster, neither could she forgive God for letting him be killed.

Half a continent away, under a blazing blue sky, a lone rider sat his horse atop a rocky butte. From under the shade of his broad-brimmed hat, his cool gray eyes surveyed the landscape below him. Slowly, he turned his head one way and then the other and smiled with satisfaction.

At thirty-three, David Norris had achieved all he had set out to do. As he looked out from atop his big bay gelding at the rolling land that spilled away from the foot of the butte, pride surged through him. He owned it all. All the land as far as his eyes could see was his now.

Carefully acquired over the years he'd spent here in the west, vast sections of good grazing land were now his property. All Texas knew the giant Prodigal Ranch.

Away in the distance, he could see the sprawling house he had built to replace the small, dusty building that had been the heart of the ranch when he'd first arrived here.

The new house's many-paned windows glittered in the bright Texas sun. In his mind's eye, he could see the fine carpets and furnishings he'd imported for it and placed in it. It was a magnificent house, and it would serve him well in his ambition to become one of the men who guided the destiny of this vast, brawling twenty-eighth state.

He had the money to do it now. He'd earned it all. Nobody had given him anything. He'd earned it by long, hard hours in the saddle, first working as a mere paid hand for other ranchers, then while building his own herd and selling cattle from it. It had taken over ten years, but he'd done it. He'd done it, and it had paid off. Now he was rich.

And now that he had money, he intended to spend whatever was necessary on the lavish dinners and entertainments he planned for the wooing of the men who would further his ambitions.

Impressing those men to the point that he would be considered one of them was his goal, and he was content in the knowledge that David Norris had become an expert at achieving his goals long ago.

He was rich, and he'd be even richer when he got back from his planned cattle drive. His gaze went to where distance made it seem as if tiny horsemen raised clouds of dust as they worked miniature cattle, getting them ready for the drive. That sight brought a wider smile.

David was deeply satisfied with what he'd accomplished and with the men who worked for him. He'd chosen them carefully, as he did everything, weeding out the slackers and the incompetents almost as soon as they started working for him. Those left on his payroll were up to his exacting standards. Now he had almost sixty loyal men under his command to work his herd and to hold the land that he had claimed.

There was something else he needed for his plan, however. Something vital. *Someone* vital. A reigning queen to be the final jewel in Prodigal Ranch's crown.

He must have a wife. And not just any wife.

He'd given the situation a great deal of thought. None of the sunburned, hearty daughters of his friends on far-flung ranches would do. They made good friends who could ride well and herd cattle with the best of his men if the need arose. But he didn't want one of them for his bride. Nor was he inclined to pursue the lovely, dark-eyed daughters of the Spanish hidalgos who still held sway in some parts of Texas.

He knew just what he wanted, and he'd taken a great deal of care with the advertisement he intended to place in the Boston paper. He wanted a wife from his own culture. That meant the east, and she would have to be a good, Christian girl.

Strict morals were one of his first requirements. He had no intention of worrying about her behavior during the many times he'd be absent from the ranch.

Further, he wanted a beautiful wife—a wife with a peaches and cream complexion and grace in her every movement—a fitting mistress for Prodigal, a fitting mother for his sons.

He didn't think he'd have any problem procuring a wife. Sadly, he knew there must be many women in the east who'd be willing to come to a home as impressive as his was now that so many of them had been left widows after the War Between the States.

He was a Unionist, even if he hadn't seen any necessity of interrupting his plans for Prodigal Ranch to go and fight for it, so he'd prefer his wife to be a northerner. That was the reason he'd decided to advertise in Boston. He wanted an educated woman—someone well-spoken, who knew her manners and would make a gracious hostess and a fine addition to his achievement. He wanted someone who could work with him toward his ambition to be one of the men who decided the fate of the great state of Texas.

Smiling at that thought, he turned his horse away from the view he'd sat so long admiring. Picking his way along the narrow, rocky path that descended to the foot of the tall butte, he settled the big bay into an easy lope and started back to the distant ranch house.

As he rode, he reviewed his plan for the next step in perfecting Prodigal. A hostess for Prodigal, a mother for the sons he planned to have by her.

He wanted sons to share in the bounty of Prodigal. By the time they were old enough to need a ranch of their own, he was sure to acquire even more land, so each one could have his own spread to work. This wonderful woman he was searching for would give him his heart's desire. Sons to inherit all he had achieved.

Maybe it was time to ride into town and telegraph his advertisement to the Boston newspaper.

CHAPTER 2

"Dorothy, you can't mean it!" Standing in the sun on the sidewalk in front of the lending library, Virginia was rendered speechless by her best friend's brazen suggestion.

"I *do* mean it, Virginia. I think you ought to look at this newspaper advertisement. It's made for you. I wish I could do it myself, but Papa saw me looking at it and took it from me and read it. Now he strictly forbids me to answer." She giggled. "He's sure I'd get myself scalped, or end up as some Chief's favorite squaw." Dorothy smiled to take the sting out of her next words. "I know you're not really happy living with your mother again, Vee. She's . . .

difficult . . . since your father passed away. It's hard for any of us to go back home after we've been married. It was hard for me, but I knew my father was right. It just isn't suitable for a young woman to live alone, widow or not."

"I know, Dorothy. And, of course, I never had a home with William as you did with Bradley at your farm. William and I had not even finished our honeymoon." Tears threatened, but Virginia blinked them away. "His parents were so gracious to let me stay with them while he was away at war. They're the very dearest people, and his sisters are like the siblings I never had.

"After William was killed, they were even kinder, but I knew that every time they looked at me, they remembered their wonderful son." She gave a small smile at Dorothy's nod of understanding. "So there was never any peace for them when I was around. I couldn't stay and remind them of their loss. I love them too much. I simply had to go back to my mother's house."

"I understand. It was the same with me and Bradley's folks. I know they love me, but I'm a reminder like you, just the same. Every time they looked at me, I could see that little flash of pain they tried so hard to hide from me. I was just lucky I had my own parents to go to. Both of them." Very softly she added, "And that we love each other."

"Yes." Virginia knew that Dorothy was saying it must be hard for Virginia to live at home with a mother who didn't really even want her there, but she couldn't say it herself.

They stood remembering a moment longer, sighed, straightened their shoulders, and smiled tremulously, sharing their pain. Then Dorothy took a deep breath and looked seriously into Virginia's eyes.

"Dear friend, I remember how you always wanted to go west. It was all you talked about when you decided to marry William." She touched Virginia's arm gently. Her voice became sober. "Really, Virginia, can't you see that striving to realize your dream, even in this rather strange manner, would be better than staying here in Boston and becoming a dried-up old woman?

"You'd have a family. Children of your own. There's so little chance of that now in Boston. Here," she brought a folded piece of newsprint out of her skirt pocket. "Read it for yourself. The ranch this man describes sounds wonderful."

She stood closer to Virginia, unfolding the newsprint so they could read it together.

Thirty-three-year-old educated gentleman and rancher seeks a wife to share his life and achievements.

A 350,000-acre ranch in Texas with a large, well-appointed home currently staffed by a cook and housekeeper awaits the woman who answers this advertisement. The house has eight guest rooms in addition to the spacious family quarters. Many windows admit enviable views, and a wall of French doors opens to the terrace off the ballroom.

My requirements are that my wife be educated, attractive, an able hostess, and Christian. She will have a generous allowance, and I will pro-

vide her with gowns and the jewels to match.

 If she requires more staff to run the house, she will have only to hire them.

 Please write me a letter telling me about yourself and giving your reasons for considering this proposal.

 In addition, I further require a brief note from your pastor.

"See, Virginia. Doesn't that sound marvelous? His name and address are here at the bottom of the ad. The whole thing sounds like a fairy tale. Doesn't the house sound beautiful beyond belief? And there are two servants—a cook and a maid. And see here," she pointed, as if Virginia had not just read it and wasn't still looking at the advertisement, "he says you can have as many more servants as you want. And the man who wrote this must be nice, too, because he specifically states that the woman he wants for his wife must be a Christian."

 Virginia allowed that the man was probably nice.

"And he's a Christian. That matters a lot to you, I know."

Then a sad expression chased across Dorothy's face. "And wouldn't it be wonderful to get away from the feeling of mourning and grief that surrounds all of us these days?" There were tears in her eyes.

"Yes," Virginia had to admit, "yes, dear, it would be." She said a silent prayer for Dorothy's own loss, not wanting to remind her friend of her husband's death by praying aloud. Then she sighed, trying not to feel selfish at missing William and their planned escape to the bountiful west.

Dorothy swiped at her tears with the back of a gloved hand. After a moment of mutual silence, she leaned forward and hugged her friend, her red curls mingling with Virginia's dark hair. "I've got to go. I still have two errands for mother left to do. Take care." She turned and hurried away.

Virginia glanced down at the newsprint she still held. She started to let it fly from her black-gloved hand with the freshening breeze; then, after a slight hesitation she was at a loss to explain, she stuffed it into her pocket. Holding the brim of her bonnet against the rising wind, she turned and started home.

Arriving at the tall, austere house she'd grown up in, she was admitted by Grissom, her mother's butler. The large, dark-paneled foyer was dim, now that the day had turned gray and no sunlight filtered through the many stained glass windows.

"Mrs. Davenport is asking for you in the drawing room, Miss Virginia."

"Thank you, Grissom." *What now?* she thought, heading across the foyer to the wide hall. In the year since her father had passed away, her mother had become more and more controlling. Virginia's father had seemed to know this would happen and had asked her to be especially understanding about it. Loving her gentle father as she did and recognizing that his health was failing, she could not deny him a promise he asked of her. Sometimes, though, that promise was hard to keep.

Entering the oppressively opulent drawing room, she saw that her mother was alone. Good, at least she wasn't to be taken to task in front of a witness.

"Ah. There you are at last." Claudia Davenport folded the needlepoint she was working on for the kneeling rail at the altar of Saint John's Episcopal Church and dropped it in her lap.

"Was I gone so long, Mother?" Virginia was determined to stand up for herself, if only in this small thing. If she didn't, she'd eventually be ground away to dust, for her mother seemed always to be criticizing or attempting to dominate her. "I went to the lending library for a book."

"Well, you must have taken forever to find one to your liking. You've been gone three quarters of an hour."

Her mother's constant surveillance wore on Virginia's nerves more than ever now that she had had the freedom—however briefly—of marriage. She stifled a sigh. "I met Dorothy as I started home," she said and immediately regretted it.

"Oh? Had you made plans to meet? You didn't tell me."

There it was again—her mother's having to know what everybody was doing, her need to be in control of everyone around her.

"No, it was a chance meeting." *And how I wish I hadn't told you.* Wouldn't her mother ever realize that she was a grown woman?

"You don't have to tell me all your plans, of course," Mrs. Davenport said, as if she had read Virginia's mind. "But since you live under my roof, it would be a courtesy."

Virginia tried not to bristle. Though in the past, when her father was alive, her mother had been a lot gentler about it, heaven knew she'd been under her mother's thumb all her life. Right up until the day she married William. For a split second, longing washed over her the gentle, friendly guidance that had been her late husband's way.

Again she found herself wishing that he'd been a little less patriotic, a little more selfish—selfish for both of them. They'd have been safely in the west enjoying the wonderful freedom they both had wanted so much.

William hadn't been selfish, though. He'd been the brave, honorable man she'd always known him to be. Now, Virginia had to face life without him.

"Well, Virginia?" Her mother interrupted her thoughts.

"I'm sorry, Mother." At first, she was only voicing the response expected of her. Then she realized that she really *was* sorry. She was sorry for the death of the dreams she and William had shared, and, regrettably, she realized that she was becoming sorry for herself.

"That's better," her mother said and picked up her needlepoint, satisfied.

Virginia turned to leave the room, knowing she'd been dismissed. Her heart was heavy. There was no way she could please her mother, even if she tried. Her mother didn't want to be pleased; she just wanted to be the director of the lives around her.

Suddenly Dorothy's suggestion didn't seem so far fetched.

As she reached the doorway, Virginia felt a faint rustle in the pocket of her skirt. The newspaper ad! She still had it!

She hesitated in the deeply carpeted, quiet hall. The only sound was the faint hiss of the gas-lit sconces on the walls as she stood considering—assessing her situation, assessing her future. She didn't like what she saw. She didn't like it at all.

Everything that Dorothy had said came back to her with startling clarity. Dwindling away to become someone who was a mere shadow of herself seemed, suddenly, a very real possibility. It wasn't one she relished. In fact, it wasn't even a possibility she thought she could bear.

Surrendering to the truth of her friend's words, she admitted that now, in addition to possessing the newspaper advertisement, she also possessed a strong desire to use it to escape.

She walked firmly up the stairs to her room, planning her answer to the Texan.

CHAPTER 3

David Norris dropped the reins of his bay gelding over the hitching post in front of the general store and gave his neck a pat. He didn't bother to tie the big horse. He knew Crusader would stand until he came back for him.

As he stepped up onto the boardwalk, his way was blocked before he could take his next step.

"Hello, Norris." The words were delivered in a snarl. It was his nearest neighbor, Hal Broudy.

"Broudy," David acknowledged him with a curt nod.

"I wanna have a word with you, Norris." The man's hands were clenching and unclenching.

David tipped his hat back and re-garded him coolly. "Do you, now?" Placing his hand flat on the other man's chest he pushed slightly. "If you want to talk, you'd better move aside and let me get my feet under me. I'm not holding any conversations while I'm teetering on the edge of the boardwalk."

Broudy yielded with poor grace, stepping back so that David could move forward and stand firm. "It's about the land that you stole out from under me."

David's eyes narrowed. "Any chance you'd like to rephrase that?"

The man ignored the implied threat, and said heatedly, "This ain't the first time you've gotten in my way, Norris. I ain't forgetting how you hustled your herd into Abilene ahead of mine and got that fat government contract for Army beef. Not the way you bought the old, abandoned Gilbert ranch, neither. I had cattle used to graze there, and I don't like you stopping me.

"You keep getting in my way, Norris, and I'm here to warn you that it ain't healthy." He thrust his face forward as his anger grew. "Now you've crossed me again. Everybody knows I've had my eye on that section between our ranches for years now. I intended to buy it to add to the Rocking HB, and now you've snatched it for the Prodigal."

Two of Broudy's ranch hands had drifted over to stand casually behind their boss.

Wary, David leaned back against one of the posts holding up the roof that covered the walkway in front of the store. "Well, that can't be true, Hal, because," he went on, pretending not to notice the way the other man bristled at the suggestion that he'd lied, "I, for one, didn't know you or anybody else had an eye on that piece of land."

He smiled sarcastically. "Bit of advice, though. The next time you want something, don't wait so long to buy it."

Broudy colored. Anger blazed in his eyes. "You're blocking the expansion of the Rocking HB, Norris, and I don't intend to let you get away with it."

David straightened away from the post. "Well, now, there you're wrong again." He put a hand up to stop the remark that was about to burst from the other man. "First, I'm not blocking you on the other three sides of your ranch." He turned and walked slowly toward the double doors of the general store, saying over his shoulder, "And secondly," he grinned to add insult to injury, "I already did get away with it."

The doors of the mercantile swung shut behind him, leaving Broudy to sputter and rant to his two hired hands.

Inside the dim coolness of the store, David pulled the list of things needed for the ranch from a pocket and dropped it on the counter in front of Herb Johnson, the store's owner. Just as easily, he dropped Broudy and his complaints out of his mind. "I thought I'd give this to you so you could start getting it all together, Herb. The men'll be here with the wagons a little later."

Johnson shook his head at Norris. "I wouldn't go around making Broudy mad like that, David. He's meaner than a rattlesnake when he gets riled." The storekeeper's round face was full of concern.

David looked out to where Broudy

was hammering one of his hired hands. "I can see what you're saying." The grin on his lean face belied any anxiety about his neighbor. "Seems like I just can't get up any interest in staying on his good side, though, no matter how hard I try."

"Which you don't," Johnson told him.

"Afraid you have that right, Herb. Any mail?"

Herb Johnson gave up trying to warn his friend. "Yep. Your cubbyhole's getting pretty crowded. Glad you're picking it up. You know how Bess is about keeping the post office neat and tidy. Wouldn't want it spilling everywhere." He grinned at his friend. "I sure hope you brought saddlebags."

David went over to the corner of the store that served as post office to the town. He stared at the big desk topped with rows of cubbyholes.

"Great Scott!" Sure enough, his cubbyhole was indeed overflowing. Someone, probably Bess, had tied the letters into several bundles so that the mail wouldn't just fall out on the desk.

As he stacked the bundles into the

crook of his left arm, Bess arrived with a flower-printed sack. "Here you are. You'll need this." She handed him the feed sack and shook a finger at him. "I want this back, you hear. I'm making dishtowels."

"Yes, ma'am." He grinned at her lazily. "I surely will get it back to you. If not me, then one of the boys'll bring it in."

She handed him the sack and went back to what she'd been doing.

David smiled as he put the letters into the sack. It looked to him as if he'd have plenty to read when he got home.

A mild excitement filled him. Would he find the woman he sought in these letters? Someone to grace his table, entertain his guests, and help further his ambition to be one of the men who had a say in the way Texas developed? He had a secret ambition to be governor of the state one day; would she help him realize it?

More importantly, would he find the mother of the son he wanted to inherit all he had worked so long and so hard for? He hardly dared hope it would be that easy.

"Until next time, my good friends," he called out as he walked to the door. He turned, held up Bess's flower-printed feed sack, and grinned. "Thanks for the mail bag."

Catching up his reins, he swung up on to the bay gelding, tied the flower-printed sack to his saddle horn, and turned his mount toward home. He was eager to begin on the task of reading his mail.

He could have let the horse have its head and read on the way back to the ranch, but he wanted his undivided attention on the contents of Bess's future dishtowel. Though he told himself he was making a cool and calculated decision, in his heart of hearts, he sensed this was probably the most important decision he had made, or ever would make, in his life.

On his way back to Prodigal, he passed the four men heading to town with the supply wagons. One wagon was for whatever his cook Maria needed, as well as anything Teresa, the housekeeper, might require. The other, an even sturdier wagon, was for the feed and any farm implements the men needed, as well as the supplies for the cook wagon they'd want well-stocked on the mammoth cattle drive they were all getting ready for.

They stopped and talked for a moment, the men reporting on the few things that had come up in his brief absence from the ranch. He answered their questions about how he wanted those things handled, and after that short pause, the wagons rolled on, the drivers recognizing the fact that the boss was eager to get home.

Back at the ranch, dusty from his ride, David gave his housekeeper the sack of letters to take into the study and put on his desk, refused the supper she offered, and went upstairs. There he bathed quickly in the new, gold-appointed bathing room he'd had installed. As the dust floated away, he thought with pleasure of the stack of letters waiting for him on his desk downstairs.

Just the anticipation of reading them

gave him a feeling of satisfaction. He'd followed through on his inspiration to advertise for a bride, and, to his surprise, he'd received many more than a few responses.

He rose from the tub and toweled off. Then, wrapped in a luxurious, absorbent robe made of a fabric the French had developed called terry cloth, he padded barefoot straight for his library and the huge mahogany desk where the stacks of letters lay.

He hesitated before opening the first one, silver letter opener poised. What would he find? Would she be there, the woman he wanted to spend the rest of his life with? Or would he end up with a desk covered in disappointment when he was through?

Taking a deep breath, he began. The first envelope split with a little hiss as the opener slid through it.

He read, *I think I would make a perfect wife for you. I am fairly attractive if a little plump. . . .* Fairly attractive didn't appeal when you were looking for beautiful. Plump didn't appeal either.

He discarded the letter.

Surely you can't mean that you will give me jewels to go with each and every one of my gowns... Vanity-inspired greed seemed to leap at him out of that one.

It followed the first into the wastebasket.

Dear Sir, My late husband felt that I was a competent hostess. I am a good cook...

He wasn't looking for a cook. He had Maria. He was looking for a gracious hostess. Another hit the wastebasket.

I have never worked with beef cattle, so I hope you won't require that of me. My ma says to tell you I am a good, pretty girl... But not a sophisticated nor educated one. Wastebasket.

Though it seems a terrible way to get a husband, all that you said in your advertisement sounded so good that I decided to try...

He sighed and threw that one away, too.

Patiently he went through them, finding fault with each one. The hour was getting late, the wastebasket full, and David Norris was beginning to feel as if he might never find the woman of his dreams in the small pile of letters left on the desk. There were so few left.

He was almost in despair of finding her, and it was approaching midnight when he finally did. Near the end of the last stack of letters, he unfolded a single sheet of heavy white stationery and out dropped a picture of the woman who had written it.

She was perfect.

One of the new-fangled photographs, it showed a woman with a trim, petite figure. She had dark hair and wide eyes in a face as lovely as any he had ever seen.

He was so mesmerized by her beauty that the tall clock in the corner ticked minutes away as he gazed at her. She was lovelier than he had dared hope.

"Stop mooning and get the letter read, David," he chided himself aloud. Gently propping the photograph against the base of the oil lamp that lit the desk's surface, he eagerly picked up the heavy sheet of paper.

The first thing he noticed was that her penmanship was obviously that of a well-reared gentlewoman. He was pleased to see that she expressed herself clearly and concisely.

Dear Mr. Norris.

I find it strange to be writing to you in this manner. Indeed, I am rather amazed that I am doing so. I think the only explanation must be that my late husband and I had long dreamed of going west together. Now he is gone, and life stretches before me, challenging me to make something of mine.

As the east is blighted by the tragedy of war, your advertisement, given me by my very dearest friend, seems an opportunity for escape from it. I have six more months of mourning for my late husband William before I can do so, however.

I am 21 years old, five-feet-three inches tall, and slender. I have often acted as hostess for my father, a banker, who passed away just over a year ago. I am well educated for a woman, and I am, as you require, a Christian.

My pastor was kind enough to write the enclosed note in spite of being scandalized by my intention to answer you. As he is also a family friend, he knows me well and is correct in warning you that I can be stubborn.

David stopped reading to pick up and inspect the envelope. There he found a thin sheet of onionskin—the pastor's note.

Enclosed you will find a photograph of me.

Believing that this is the best I can do to answer you, I shall simply sign myself,

Virginia Davenport Warner.

David was staggered by the clarity with which she had written after reading the dozens of letters from the other women who had responded. He wondered if she had written the note many times until she got it just as she wanted it or if it had been her first draft. Looking into the eyes in the picture, he thought it just might have been the latter.

Almost immediately, he stirred in his chair, agitated. She wrote that she wouldn't be out of mourning, and thus couldn't be expected to travel, for six months. This would never do! That would put her trip in the dead of winter.

Impossible. Waiting for good weather would make it nine months before she could come to him. Nine months! A lot could happen in nine months. Especially to a girl who looked like—he glanced at her signature—Virginia Warner.

He picked up her picture again, gazed long at the photograph, and knew that this was the woman he wanted. This was his perfect wife. This was the woman he wanted at his side as he carried out all the plans he had made for them, and he had no intention of letting her slip through his fingers.

"Virginia." He said her name to see how it felt on his tongue. Then he breathed softly, "Virginia Norris." And at that moment his fate was sealed.

And so, far away in Boston, was that of Virginia Davenport Warner.

CHAPTER 4

David had rarely been so utterly exhausted in his entire adult life. By the
time the train pulled into the Boston station, he was ready to drop. Days in the
saddle, pushing his series of mounts
and himself to the breaking point, were
at last over. He hoped that he would
never again be faced with the necessity
of covering fifty miles a day on horseback.

Every bone in his body ached, and
every muscle complained. Without a
doubt, he had a new appreciation for
the short-lived pony express.

He'd never have been able to accom-
plish his mad ride if he hadn't been able
to arrange fresh mounts every twenty-

five miles ahead of time by telegraph. Nevertheless, it was something he was more than glad to have behind him, as was the discomfort of the three-day train ride from Kansas City that followed.

He was looking forward to the suite he had reserved at Boston's finest hotel. Crashing into the bed there after a quick supper, he promised himself that, first thing in the morning, he would implement the plans he'd carefully thought out during all those long, grueling days in the saddle from Texas to Kansas City.

He smiled sleepily as he congratulated himself on having come for his intended bride. By now she would have gotten his telegram warning her of his imminent arrival and had time to adjust to the idea of it but not time to stop him from arriving. He'd planned for that carefully.

By now her family would have had time to accept the fact that he was here to take her from them. He'd left them no room to doubt that he planned to marry her and take her with him back to Texas and Prodigal. That was his stated, earnest objective, and he had every intention of doing just that.

Winning her was part of his plan, too. Every step of his campaign to do so had been planned on his trip here. He had only to implement them. In his mind, he began to go over it all.

Sleep claimed him before he got beyond his intention to buy an extravagant bouquet of roses for his petite beauty.

The butler opened the door to David, looked a little startled at the number of roses he held, and ushered him in to the drawing room. There, Virginia and her mother awaited him. Virginia looked faintly apprehensive. Her mother looked as if she were ready to do battle.

David had sense enough to change his plan of presenting his bride-to-be with the bouquet of roses he carried. Not only did the Texas-sized offering look far too flamboyant even in this overdecorated, New England drawing room, but he decided it was also oversized for the petite Virginia.

She was even more beautiful than the photograph she had sent him. Her delicate coloring was all he could have wished for, and her dark hair shone with health.

He smiled at the mother and presented her with the roses instead. "For you both, Mrs. Davenport, an expression of my wish to honor the two ladies I am adding to my family."

Virginia's mother was completely taken aback. The set look of hostile disapproval changed to one of flustered pleasure. "Two ladies, you say?"

David fought to keep his gaze locked on the older woman. It was difficult. All he wanted to do was turn away to see and speak to Virginia.

Knowing he had to finish this battle first though, he concentrated on winning the good will of her mother. "Of course two." He smiled winningly. "Surely you know that I expect you to come to Prodigal as often as you have a mind to come and to stay as long as you'd like. You will always be welcome there, as I know how difficult it will be for you to do without having your daughter under the same roof with you."

Mrs. Davenport stared at him, her gaze traveling from the top of his sun-streaked blond head to the tips of his gleaming boots. Though the cut of his suit had a western flavor that was strange to her, it showed off the lean, masculine frame it clothed to advantage, and was certainly of the finest fabric. Its tailoring was impeccable, as well.

For a fleeting moment, she almost regretted the angry confrontation and resulting bitter words with which she had lashed Virginia when she learned of her daughter's audacious action. Her behavior in answering a newspaper advertisement for a wife was reprehensible, of course. It was certainly not what she expected from her properly reared daughter. And it was especially not what one expected of the daughter of a prominent and well-respected banker. She had been outraged!

Now, however, she was rethinking the situation. This man would certainly be preferable to some maimed survivor of the war—or having her only child wither away here underfoot in her home and before her very eyes.

Without even looking at her butler, she thrust the roses at him and ordered. "Grissom, find a vase for these."

The butler took the flowers and left to put them in water. David had noted the lack of the word 'please' and shot a glance at Virginia. She was watching her mother with a faint blush staining her cheeks. Had she noticed—and minded—her mother's curtness to a servant? David hoped so.

He turned in her direction and bowed. "I hope my arrival has not taken you by surprise, Miss Virginia. My telegram did get here safely, I trust."

Virginia turned her attention fully to him. Her eyes were a lovely dark blue, and he was both surprised and pleased. It had been impossible to tell their color in the photograph she'd sent, of course, and he'd simply assumed they were brown. Just now, the expression in them was a little wary.

For her part, Virginia was over-whelmed by this self-assured westerner who'd invaded her mother's den and disarmed her so easily. Tall and slender—surely he was every bit of six feet tall and perhaps an inch or two more—he seemed to tower over her.

"Won't you sit down, Mr. Norris?" she offered politely.

"Thank you." He moved to the nearest chair and seated himself.

Virginia sought desperately for something to say. "How was your trip, Mr. Norris? Was it difficult?"

"Yes." He looked directly into her eyes, his gaze bold. "I made it difficult in my haste to get here." His gray eyes said, 'to you,' as plainly as if he had spoken aloud. His gaze pinned hers as he promised her, "I shall make it gentler and far more pleasant when I take you back with me."

Virginia's breath caught and she felt her face flame. Why did his words sound so intimate to her? She tried to think of something that would put him in his proper place and wished, not for the first time, that the man had been required to send *her* a photograph of himself. Then she might have been much better prepared for the shock of having this blond Adonis turn up on their doorstep.

Mrs. Davenport said, "This is a most unusual situation, Mr. Norris. I'm not yet certain how I feel about it." She was trying to sound daunting, but the roses and his subsequent speech had done their work and taken some of the starch out of her.

"I can imagine, Mrs. Davenport. Please be assured that to have to advertise for a bride was not something I'd ever thought I'd do. Prodigal, however, is a very demanding obligation, and Texas has a shortage of the sort of women I would care to make mistress of my life's work."

"I take it Prodigal is the name of your ranch?"

"Yes, ma'am."

"Is it a very big ranch?" She tried not to sound bored.

"About three hundred and fifty thousand acres."

"Three hundred and fifty . . ." Mrs. Davenport was aghast. Her boredom gone, she managed to gasp, "Did you say three hundred and fifty *thousand* acres?"

"Yes, ma'am. Not as big as King Ranch, of course. They have eight hundred and twenty-five. Texas is pretty big. Over seventeen—nearly eighteen-million acres, they tell me."

Virginia's mother fanned herself vigorously with her hand. "Three hundred fifty thousand."

"Yes, ma'am." His lips quirked as if he were suppressing a smile.

Virginia tried valiantly to hide her own smile, even though when she'd read David Norris's advertisement, she herself had thought three hundred and fifty thousand had been a misprint, and had been certain he had meant three hundred and fifty acres, period.

Things must, indeed, be very vast in the west. She couldn't even begin to imagine a farm so large. It truly boggled the mind.

"That's an odd name for a ranch, isn't it?" Her mother tried to recover her poise. "The Prodigal son of the Bible is what comes to mind when one hears it."

"Yes, ma'am, I suppose it does."

When Mrs. Davenport saw that no explanation about the ranch's odd name was forthcoming, she asked Virginia to preside over the tea tray and changed the conversation to the very safe, time-honored subject of the weather.

By the time she had settled back in her chair with her cup, she was reconciled to losing her daughter to this obviously wealthy, perfectly charming young Texan.

That night, Virginia lay in her bed and tried to decide how she felt about the afternoon's events. Norris's arrival here in Boston had certainly foiled her plan of easily refusing him if she changed her mind during the six remaining months of her mourning period for William. He was here.

His coming had been a bold move certainly, and she wasn't quite sure how she felt about it. It was almost as if he'd come to Boston to throw her over his shoulder and carry her off by force.

She pushed her doubts away and

thought about the man she'd met today. She certainly couldn't fault Mr. Norris on his manners.

She smiled as she lay in the dark and recalled how incongruous her mother's delicate bone china tea cup had looked in his strong, tanned hand, but he'd been perfectly at home holding it, all the same. At least she wouldn't find herself married to a clod!

If she married him, of course.

She tried not to let herself think of his appearance, but the attempt was hopeless. He was so extremely handsome. Tall and lean and tanned, with his sun-streaked blond hair and silver gray eyes he'd turn women's heads wherever they went.

He was too handsome, by far, and that fact was sure to distract her from what she ought to be considering, just as it was doing right now. For instance, was the ease with which he'd subtly stood up to and charmed her mother going to be a problem? Without a doubt, it told her he was a strong man, but did it indicate a nature every bit as inflexible as her mother's? She really didn't want to trade one sort of tyranny for another any more than she wanted to marry a weakling.

She chuckled. She didn't have to worry about the latter! He was no weakling, that was certain. Her mother would have eaten him alive if he had been. She'd surely been ready to.

"Oh, dear heart." Virginia sighed and plumped up her pillow by punching it with her fist. Decisions were not her favorite thing, especially life-altering ones. "Well," she whispered into the dark of her room, "I think you've already made yours, my girl, so it is entirely too late now."

But was she going to have regrets?

Virginia turned to face the lighter rectangles of her bedroom windows. Even with the layers of fabric currently in style, a little light came through.

With all her heart, she hoped she wasn't making a grave mistake. After all, she didn't want to hop from the frying pan into the fire.

After a few more minutes of tossing, she fell into a fitful sleep.

CHAPTER 5

Virginia awoke refreshed in spite of her fitful night. She'd overslept, though, and was well aware how much her mother hated to have her arrive late at the breakfast table.

She was just rushing down the carpeted stairs when Grissom opened the front door to admit David Norris. Startled, she stopped midway down and stared. What in the world was he doing here so early?

David looked up and for a moment their gazes locked.

Virginia's breath was taken away by the intensity in his face. Then he relaxed and smiled, and she was left wondering if she'd imagined the look of determination she thought she'd seen.

"Good morning, Miss Virginia." He gave his hat to Grissom and walked toward the foot of the stairs without taking his eyes from hers. "I hope you will allow me to escort you to breakfast. Your mother was kind enough to invite me." Then he laughed, reaching a hand out to her. "Of course, you'll have to show me the way."

She liked his laugh. It was full and free, not like the polite, subdued laughter one usually heard in Boston's social circles. She found herself smiling back as she placed her hand in his.

A faint current like the new electricity seemed to tingle in her fingers at his touch. Startled, she glanced at his face.

David Norris looked as surprised as she felt. Then he laughed again, a rather triumphant sounding laugh, as if he'd found the solution to a puzzle or perhaps had won some valued prize.

It made Virginia a little apprehensive. Was she actually considered a prize to be won? Somehow, the thought that the tall man beside her might think of her as an award of some sort wasn't the comfort to her that most women might find it. To her, it indicated a possessiveness that might not bode well for the freedom she was hoping to achieve by marrying him and going west.

One thing was becoming increasingly clear to her, even in the short time she'd spent in the presence of Mr. David Norris. This man was no William Warner!

When they reached the dining room, Mrs. Davenport was already seated at the head of the long, highly polished, lace-draped table. Ignoring her daughter, she smiled pleasantly to David and asked, "Did you sleep well, Mr. Norris?"

Virginia was surprised at her mother's pleasant manner. Usually breakfast was a dismal affair. Evidently her mother was perfectly willing to be politely concerned about David Norris's welfare now that she had decided to accept this man— and his obvious considerable wealth— into the family.

Virginia had no way of knowing that her mother and David Norris had spent a good part of last night talking after Virginia had retired. They'd argued half the night about his intention to marry Virginia and take her back to Texas with him on this trip.

Mrs. Davenport had tried her best to change his mind. She'd told him that it was scandalous to think of Virginia marrying in the black of mourning for her late husband. She'd insisted it was simply not done to marry before one had finished the socially required year of wearing black.

David had countered with the fact that the trip back to Prodigal would be impossible in the dead of winter when Virginia would be able to put aside her widow's weeds and marry without flying in the face of tradition. He'd also told her that, since ranching obligations meant he couldn't stay to court Virginia, he had no intention of leaving anyone so beautiful behind to be courted by other men in his absence. "A sensible man doesn't leave a treasure unguarded, Mrs. Davenport," he'd told her.

The matter had finally been decided when Mrs. Davenport, flattered by the praises he gave her about the wonderful job she'd done in rearing so beautiful a daughter, yielded to his determination. Now she was quite in charity with David and not at all opposed to her daughter marrying this man. Her smiie had been almost friendly as she'd inquired about his night's rest.

"Yes, thank you," David told her. "The hotel is quite comfortable."

Mrs. Davenport smiled a tight little smile and signaled Grissom to begin serving. Virginia was quiet, amazed at the change in her mother. The Texan was a miracle worker. She sat watching David Norris as if by doing so she could tell what her future might hold.

David smiled at her as Grissom poured his coffee. "And you, Miss Virginia. Did you sleep well?"

Virginia decided that she would begin their relationship as she intended to continue it—with the truth. Even if it might be socially incorrect she answered, "I had a little trouble drifting off. I think I may have been . . . ," she hesitated, searching for the right word, ". . . rather overwhelmed by your coming here to Boston. I think I had been counting on a correspondence between us to get to know one another a little."

"I apologize if my haste has upset you. I'm afraid I'm not a particularly patient man, and I wanted to get you safely to your new home before the weather made the trip impossible."

Virginia thought David Norris looked like a man used to getting what he wanted, and, in light of his trip here to claim her, she thought he was quite used to getting it *when* he wanted it.

Handsome, rich, charming—and certainly dashing. He was all of those, but only time would tell if he would make a good life's companion.

"Tell us about your ranch, Mr. Norris," Claudia Davenport almost purred.

Virginia imagined her mother was gathering information to share with the group of women she called her friends. They were all interested most in material things, and she suspected that her mother would easily win their little game of one outdoing the other with David Norris's three hundred and fifty thousand acres.

"There isn't much to tell." He began.

"We run about sixty thousand head of cattle. It's pretty constant work what with the calving, the branding, and moving them from grass to grass. The low pastures are near the river so they aren't much trouble there. I have to say, though, that we sometimes do have trouble keeping the water tanks full enough for them in the high pastures."

"The high pastures?" Virginia's mother asked.

"Yes. We have part of a low mountain range on one side of Prodigal. They're hills, really, and the east side of it has slopes with good grazing."

"I take it that means the mountains run north and south?"

"Yes, ma'am. And the west side is steeper and catches the warmer winds. Makes it drier and less good for grazing cattle. Rather than slopes on that side, there are shelves that act like grassy terraces. It's harder to round them up there than on the east side, but we make use of the shelves as well as we can."

Virginia was curious. "How do you get water in the high pastures?" She could tell by the way her future husband looked at her that he approved of her question.

"We sink wells and draw water up into big, round stock tanks with windmills."

"Oh." Virginia could see that she would be learning a great deal when she got to the ranch David Norris had named Prodigal. She wondered if she would ever learn why he had given it such an odd name.

Mrs. Davenport asked, "How many men do you need for taking care of all those animals?"

"I currently employ about sixty, sometimes seventy-five or eighty."

Virginia saw her mother's eyes widen. Her father had only had thirty people in his employ, and his bank had been the largest in the state.

David and her mother talked on about cattle, discussing the problems of moving them and the dangers of working with them.

"I've heard of stampedes." Mrs. Davenport was saying. "Do they occur very often?"

David smiled mirthlessly. "Once is too often, believe me."

Virginia asked, "What causes them? Cows look so peaceful here."

"Thunder can set them off. A sudden sound like a pistol shot. A boulder falling off a cliff. Even a flash of light. Anything that gets them nervous and milling around can do it. Then one steer panics and starts to run and the rest just follow along."

"That sounds dangerous."

"A stampeding herd is an awesome force for destruction, I can assure you."

"What would happen if you got caught in a stampede?"

The expression on David's face became grave. "You ride like the wind and pray your horse doesn't fall."

Virginia could imagine the fate of the horse and rider who fell in front of those thousands of pounding hooves and didn't ask. She couldn't conceal her shudder.

David Norris saw it, and fixing her with an intimate look, he added, "I'll never let you ride into any danger, Miss Virginia."

She saw such a fierce protectiveness in his eyes, she was at a loss to decide whether it was something to revel in or a threat to the freedom she so avidly longed for.

She felt a little like a moth caught in a spider's web. David's strength of personality implied that things were liable to get well beyond her control. She'd made her decision, however, even if now it seemed to have been wrested out of her hands.

David Norris represented an escape from the grim reality of life in Boston and a chance to realize the dream she and William had shared, however. So she intended to ignore the tight little feeling in her stomach that things happening seemed to be spiraling out of her control. After all, most of the web was of her own weaving.

"Dressmaker! Why in the world do you want to know who makes my daughter's dresses?" Her mother's sharp tone snapped Virginia back to the present.

Obviously the subject of the conversation had changed drastically while she'd been lost in thought. Mrs. Davenport was astonished and not well pleased.

Virginia looked inquiringly at the man opposite her. Why indeed?

David answered easily. "While hoping not to offend your sensibilities, I would like to order clothes for Virginia for the trip to the ranch." He smiled disarmingly and gestured at their silk dresses. "While my suggestions can hardly compete with the impeccable taste you show in what I've seen of your wardrobes, I do feel that I know better what is needed on the long wagon trip after we leave the train in Kansas City."

Mollified, Mrs. Davenport allowed, "Well, that is very possibly so. While I find it an unusual request, I shall bow to your superior experience with wagon travel." After a delicate shiver to indicate that she was glad that she was not personally familiar with traveling in so rough a manner, she turned to give her permission to Virginia. "Virginia, you must take Mr. Norris to the dressmaker's. Lily may accompany you."

David's gaze sought Virginia's and she saw laughter in his eyes. The sight of it lifted her spirits. Maybe everything was going to be all right, after all. As she applied herself to her food, the knot in her stomach disappeared.

She found she was looking forward to going to Mrs. Fotheringgil's establishment with the handsome Mr. Norris in tow. It would be a great deal of fun to show him off—and after all, if he could leave her with the feeling that she was a prize to be won, she could certainly consider him a trophy to be exhibited!

She smiled at her mother. "Thank you, mother." She welcomed the chance for some time alone with this man who would soon be her husband.

CHAPTER 6

When she and David got to the foyer, Grissom was waiting. "Shall I call for a carriage, Mrs. Warner?"

Virginia had to repress a smile. Grissom always called her 'Miss Virginia'. She wondered why he chose to remind her of her married name now. Looking closely at him, she wondered if she detected a faint expression of disapproval aimed at David Norris.

Then Lily appeared with Virginia's shawl. Her cheerful, round face was glowing. No doubt she was glad of an escape from her duties and the chance to inspect her young mistress's husband-to-be up close.

Virginia was well aware that the whole

staff was abuzz with excitement over what they thought of as her audacity, not only in putting her future on the line by answering this tall Texan's advertisement for a wife, but by daring to do it in defiance of her mother.

Certainly some of them must have heard the storm that had raged when she had explained to her mother the meaning of David Norris's telegram. No one downstairs had believed that anyone could have that much courage. Virginia was glad to have proved to them that she did.

When Lily stepped forward to give Grissom the shawl to put around her young mistress's shoulders, the tall stranger smiled right into her eyes and took it out of her hands instead. "Thank you, Lily," he said.

Virginia was pleased to see that he not only noticed Lily, but even knew her name. Virginia had seen the by-play between her guest and her maid. She could see that Lily was obviously smitten with David Norris and his kind treatment of her.

David then turned to Virginia. "May

I?" he asked as he spread the shawl between his hands. In answer to the smile he saw in her eyes he returned one.

Her heart warmed toward him. Her doubts about the wisdom of her action in answering this man's advertisement were dissolving. She was willing to give him a chance.

Until now, she had to admit to herself, she'd kept the option of refusing to go to Texas with him alive in a prominent place in her mind. His kindness to a servant weighed heavily in his favor with her.

Then, when he put her shawl around her shoulders, he made the simple action seem like an embrace. When his long fingers brushed the nape of her neck as he straightened the cashmere of the shawl, Virginia could feel a tingle that ran all the way down to her toes.

Virginia looked startled.

David looked pleased.

Grissom looked thunderous.

"Would you mind walking?" she asked him when she had gotten her breath back. "The dressmaker's isn't far from Davenport House." She didn't add that the walk would give her that much more time alone with him out from under her mother's watchful eye.

Lily trailing behind just close enough to hear their conversation didn't bother her. The servants had always been her friends, and Virginia wanted them to share in her adventure as well as they might.

Grissom opened the front door for them, and as David gestured Lily out after her mistress, Grissom touched him on the shoulder. "I think you should know that I'm considered quite a good shot," he hissed.

With a grin, David followed the women out the door, chuckling softly at the butler's implied threat.

David offered his arm to Virginia, opened the gate to the street and said as if he'd read her mind, "I welcome a longer time to talk with you."

Virginia looked down at his well-polished boots. "But are those comfortable to walk in?" She was used to the round-toed, low-heeled boots of the men she knew. David Norris's boots came to a point.

David smiled. "They're really quite comfortable, I assure you. They're just designed for ranch work. The heel digs in while you throw the calf down to tie it so you can brand it, and the pointed toe makes it easy to catch a stirrup when you vault back on your horse after you've branded a calf.

"Oh." It certainly wasn't the most brilliant comment she could make, but until she learned more about cattle and ranch work, any attempt at an intelligent remark would have to wait.

The day was beautiful. Warm enough so that she didn't have to draw her shawl close around her, and with a breeze that stirred the leaves on the trees along the way without being strong enough to threaten the safety of her bonnet. Or, for that matter, threaten her escort's broad-brimmed hat.

She looked up at him a moment, then asked, "Is your hat different because it's designed for ranch work, too?"

His lips twitched as if he repressed a laugh. "No, ma'am. This one's for dress. The wide brim is for the sun. We have a lot of that in Texas. The low crown is so the wind doesn't take it. The wind can be strong there, too. It wouldn't do to go chasing my hat and leave my lovely lady standing."

He *was* laughing at her. Rather than feel piqued, Virginia laughed aloud. "Very well, then. What is your hat for ranch work like, or is your hair so sun-streaked because you go bareheaded in Texas?"

David took her teasing well, secretly relieved to see it. He hadn't liked her being so subdued in her mother's presence and was glad to see that she had a lively sense of humor, after all. "No, ma'am. I'm afraid that would be a good way to get sun stroke. For work, we still want the wide brim on our hats for sun, rain, and snow."

He had another bit of information he thought might amuse her. "Oh, and the crown is higher so that you can push the crease out of it and have a feed bag for your horse's grain in an emergency."

Virginia shot him a glance, eyes wide. "Are you telling me you'd let a horse eat out of your *hat*?" She was incredulous. Did she think he was joshing her?

"Drink out of it, too, if the occasion demanded it."

She regarded him a long moment then said, "I don't believe you."

Lily giggled behind them.

"Ma'am!" His free hand slammed to his chest. "I'm wounded. Cut to the quick. I'd never lie to you." He looked at her, his face solemn, but mischief danced in his gray eyes. "Why, in Texas, men have killed each other over being called a liar."

"Umm. Plenty of men have done the same here. Very foolish, we women think."

"Honor must be served." Now his eyes weren't laughing anymore, and the tone of voice was serious.

"Of course it must. But there are more sensible ways to serve it."

"Such as?"

"Calm, intelligent debate, for one." She stopped and turned to face him. "Frank discussion can solve most problems, don't you think?"

David was pleased. Immensely pleased. This was exactly the type of woman he wanted to preside over his dinner parties. For a moment, he envisioned her leading his guests in a calm debate, and the picture brought a pleased smile to his face. "Yes, I do think so."

They walked on.

Virginia was relieved. She'd had a quick vision of being in Texas, caught in a series of gunfights.

Up ahead in the next block, she sighted the tasteful sign of Miss Fotheringgil's Dressmaking Establishment. "There's our destination, Mr. Norris. I hope you won't be uncomfortable with all the women we may find there. Now that the war's over, better fabrics are appearing again, and everyone is eager for new dresses."

One side of David's mouth quirked up. He remembered all the trips he made as a boy to his mother's dressmaker. He thought he'd be all right with a flock of women now. He'd never seemed to have any trouble getting along with the fairer sex. "I'm sure I'll be fine," he told his bride-to-be.

Virginia made a small sound that indicated doubt, but as she obviously didn't intend for him to hear it, David pretended not to. Instead, he opened the door to the dressmaker's and gestured Lily in after Virginia.

A group of women inside the dressmaker's were fingering fabrics and commenting on their preferences. When they saw David, they went silent. Most stared in frank admiration, one with faint hostility at a male invasion of this female precinct, but to the last one, they were all curious.

Virginia acted as if she didn't notice anything unusual as the dressmaker came to meet them. "Miss Fotheringgil, my fiancé asks to be allowed to consult with you about my clothes for our journey to Texas."

Miss Fotheringgil seemed to stifle her surprise at news of Virginia's engagement. Clearly she didn't want any of the women present to realize that she hadn't known of it until this moment.

She tore her gaze from David Norris, looked directly at Virginia and nodded. Her tone was frosty as she said, "Of course, my dear Mrs. Warner. If something special or beyond my limited knowledge is needed, I'm sure I will be glad to learn of it."

Seeing her resentment, David didn't waste a moment. The last thing he wanted was to have the dressmaker and probably every woman present in the room annoyed with him. With his best smile he told her, "I'm certain that nothing would be beyond your ability, Miss Fotheringgil, much less the simple things I require. I've seen examples of your art, and they are lovely." He saw a thaw begin. "I'd like only to offer advice on the sturdier fabrics we in the west have found most serviceable for hard wear. The journey Miss Virginia and I will have before us when we leave the train at Kansas City will be long and difficult."

He smiled around the room at the others. "I have no wish to interrupt these ladies, however, and therefore must ask for an appointment at a better time for you."

There was a faint disappointment at his announcement. Everyone would have loved to hear what this tall, handsome man had to say about anything.

Miss Fotheringgil, however, wasn't going to lose the business she had already begun transacting with the several ladies and quickly told David, "I shall be free later this afternoon, and I have no objection to your returning then. Around five, if that would suit."

"Most admirably," David said with a bow. Turning toward the others, he bowed again, "Ladies, please forgive the interruption."

There was a chorus of replies, and even a sigh, as David opened the door and all but herded Virginia and Lily out it.

"Whew!" He made a gesture like wiping a perspiring brow. "You could have warned me."

Virginia grinned at this mild discomfort she was certain was only a pretense. "As you will recall, I *did* warn you, and all you did was smirk. However, you seemed to have been able to handle it well enough. None of them threw anything at you."

"True. I was fortunate, indeed."

Virginia burst out laughing then.

"What? No sweet, feminine comfort for a wounded warrior?"

"I do admit that there were more women in Miss Fotheringgil's today than I've ever seen in the shop before. I do not, however, see any wounds on you."

"Harsh. That was very harsh. I fear I have chosen a heartless bride."

"Alas. Sad to say, Mr. Norris, disappointment often comes to those who gamble with fate."

He stopped and regarded her seriously. "After seeing your photograph, my fate was sealed, Miss Virginia. There was no gamble left to me."

Virginia blushed at the sincerity in his voice. Her knees threatened to turn to water. Try as she might, she could think of no witty response to make.

"Yes," he said, stepping into the breech, "After seeing that poor wistful little waif in the photograph, I had no choice but to come and rescue her."

She turned an outraged face toward him. "Wistful waif!" She clenched her teeth on the rest of her sentence as David burst out laughing. "You aren't funny." Virginia pretended to sulk. "I was probably the only answer you got."

David had no intention of telling Virginia Davenport Warner that his mail box had overflowed with responses to his advertisement. Instead he made a silly remark. "No, I had an interesting one from a Romanian princess, but I declined when I read the dimensions of the cabinet she would require for her crowns."

Virginia laughed delightedly at his nonsense.

"And the cattle baroness from the Argentine interested me, until I read that she insisted on bringing her cattle and all her *vaqueros* with her. The logistics would have been terrible, you see."

Virginia answered, "Yes, I can see the dilemma. It would probably take ships and ships."

"Yes, and how do I know the vaqueros would get along with my own men? And I'd have had to enlarge the bunk houses to put them up."

"Entirely too much trouble."

"I'm glad you understand."

They went on this way, with David Norris proposing one absurd respondent to his advertisement after another, and Virginia making ridiculous remarks in response. Carrying on more than a little foolishly, they walked companionably back to Davenport House.

CHAPTER 7

Virginia wondered how David Norris's late afternoon appointment with her dressmaker had turned out—until she received the box two days later. It was one of the largest she had ever seen from Miss Fotheringgil's.

Lily peeked into her young mistress's room the minute Grissom left after delivering the box there.

Virginia saw her and smiled. No doubt the entire staff was just as curious. Even the dignified Grissom had lingered for a split second before turning away from the box when he put it down on Virginia's high four-poster.

"Come in, Lily. It'll be fun to have someone to open this with." She made a little face. "I'm sure it will be full of sturdy, unattractive things that I will have to wear on the trip to Texas."

Lily didn't need a second invitation. She ran into the room and hung over the box on Virginia's bed as if it were Aladdin's lamp. "Oh, do you really think he would choose ugly things for you, Miss? I can't believe he would do that. He was so nice and seemed so taken with you. I can't think he'd have had Miss Fotheringgil make anything for you that wouldn't be pretty."

"Umm," Virginia said noncommittally as she untied the ribbons holding the top on the box. "You saw how he ruffled Miss Fotheringgil's feathers. Even if he'd ordered robes fit for a princess, she might have decided to make my clothes even uglier than practicality dictated as her revenge."

She lifted the lid with a flourish. Both girls gasped. There were no sturdy clothes in the box. None at all.

Inside was a gown that looked as if it were spun of moonbeams. Pale blue, slightly shining, and tastefully ornamented, it was beautiful! On top of the dress was a gossamer veil in the exact same shade and on top of that, a folded square of heavy vellum. The note was addressed simply, 'Virginia.'

She opened it, suddenly breathless. It said, *Here is the wedding gown I wish you might wear. Black is not for brides, and it is past time we were married.*

Her heart seemed to stop, jump, and take up a faster beat. It was the first time the actual wedding had been mentioned, and she felt herself go weak at the thought. Until now, it was as if it were all only a pleasant dream of adventure. Now, suddenly, it was a reality.

The gown was a reality, too. A reality that she would have to inform David Norris was an impossibility. Not only would it fly in the face of tradition and good taste, but most importantly, she would not so fail to honor the memory of her dear William as to marry in other than the garments that spoke of her mourning for him. It was bad enough that she was being coerced by weather concerns to marry before her year of mourning was completed.

Lily was avidly watching her face, and

she knew it would be unkind not to share the note with the eager girl. "It's from Mr. Norris. He would rather I didn't wear black to our wedding."

"Oh, Miss Virginia," a wide-eyed Lily warned, "you'll have to appear at the last minute, then. You know your mother won't hear of that."

At that moment, Virginia's mother appeared in the doorway as if having been brought there by their thoughts. "Grissom tells me you have received a delivery from Miss Fotheringgil, Virginia."

Virginia stood quietly as her mother sailed to the bed and looked down into the box. She closed her eyes and waited for the uproar. Her eyes widened when all her mother said was "Quite lovely. Fotheringgil must have worked her staff day and night to finish a confection like this so quickly."

Virginia was surprised at her mother's lack of comment about the gown's color.

Again, as if she had read her daughter's mind, she said, "Mr. Norris informed me that as this was his wedding, too, he had no desire to have his bride look like a crow. A harsh, if apt, description, I think."

She cocked her head to one side. "That's a very forceful man you are marrying, daughter. I suspect that you're going to have your hands full." She fingered the material of the dress for a moment, then turned and looked at Virginia. "Did you order this when you went to Miss Fotheringgil's with him?"

Virginia shook her head. "Nor would I have. I have no intention of disrespecting William's memory by wearing such a dress." How could her mother consider, even for a moment, that she would do so?

"I'm glad to hear you express these proper sentiments, daughter. I was afraid that Mr. Norris's considerable charm might have clouded your usual good sense." Mrs. Davenport smiled one of her rare smiles. "You had better speak to Mr. Norris. As I said, he's a forceful man, and I suspect one who is used to getting his own way."

Virginia was taken aback by her mother's support. Until this moment, she'd been feeling that she was having to do without it. Hastily she asked, "May I send one of the servants to ask him to come to me?"

"As you wish, my dear. As you wish. In fact, I'll take care of it." Claudia Davenport swept out of the room with a smile on her face.

Virginia looked after her mother and thought that perhaps she planned to enjoy this first confrontation between David Norris and her.

Lily let out the breath she'd been holding and scuttled from the room.

Going to her dressing table, Virginia brushed her hair back and secured it with a ribbon that matched her dress. Then she took one last look at the magnificent gown on the bed, touched its softness with lingering fingers, and went down to wait for David Norris.

He arrived a little less than a half hour later, concern on his face. "Is everything all right, Virginia?"

Virginia led him out of the foyer to a small sitting room next to the larger parlor her mother always liked to use. It was as overdecorated as the other room. The windows were heavily curtained, first with lace, then with velvet swags and draperies. Knickknacks, albeit expensive ones, sat on every horizontal surface. The total effect was crowded and oppressive.

"I must speak to you about your generous gift, Mr. Norris. Please sit." She knew she'd never be able to say all she wanted to say with him looming over her.

He took the chair she indicated and watched her attentively.

"I want to thank you for the lovely gown. It's exquisite. In fact, it's the most beautiful gown I have ever seen." She hated the fact that her voice was not firmer. "I hope that someday there will be an occasion grand enough to do it justice"—she took a much needed steadying breath, and went on in a stronger voice—"but I will not wear it for our wedding."

He started to answer her and seemed to think better of it. He remained silent, realizing she had more she wanted to say, waiting for her to continue.

"It isn't just that it would be improper to wear such a lovely gown before my year of mourning is up, it's that I wouldn't think of so dishonoring my late husband's memory by doing so.

"William was very dear to me. We had known each other all our lives and we were best friends before we married. Our marriage was brief, but happy. I intend to wear mourning for him for the rest of my year out of respect for him and respect for our marriage."

Norris didn't comment.

"I hope you understand my feelings. As I wrote you, one of the reasons I responded to you was that William and I had had a dream of going west. It caused me to think that maybe God was behind my friend Dorothy's giving me your advertisement."

She took a little turn around the small parlor, wondering how she would make him comprehend.

"Will we be living with a ghost between us, Virginia?" His voice was tense.

Startled, she looked straight at him. Was he worried that she was contemplating marriage with him while still in love with her dead husband? The idea was extremely distasteful to her, though she imagined that if it were true, she would hardly be the first woman who had done such a thing.

She fervently hoped he didn't really think so. She was only holding William's memory in her heart, as anyone who had ever lost a loved one would do. William was no longer alive to hold her heart. She knew that she had to make David Norris see that, if there was any chance of them going on with their plans for a marriage.

"No." She frowned a little. "No, of course not. William is gone, but I revere his memory and always will."

David Norris took a long, careful breath. After a lengthy pause, he nodded his head slowly and said, "Understood."

She smiled, relieved that he really did seem to understand. She wanted to reach out and touch his cheek, but she didn't know him that well.

That thought struck her sharply. She didn't know this man well enough to touch him on the cheek, yet she was getting ready to marry him?

What a strange state of affairs! She gave herself a mental shake. Yes. Indeed, it was all very strange. War and widowhood had conspired to force a decision she fervently hoped she wouldn't regret. She was silent a long minute, digesting these thoughts, deciding whether or not she wanted to stop following this precipitous path.

She looked at the man seated in the chair. So far she had enjoyed his company. He was handsome and clean and appealing in every physical sense, but what was the main reason she was considering him—the real reason?

Closing her eyes a minute, she visualized her life as it was without William. She thought about spending the rest of it here in Boston, in the midst of all the grief that permeated much of the country since the tragedy of the war.

She had no illusions about what her life would be like under her domineering mother's roof. That had no attraction for her. There would be no place in it for her to be herself. She'd be forced into the mold society thought suitable for a young war widow, and pinned there by a rather unsympathetic mother's thumb.

She'd written David Norris that she faced the challenge of making something of her life. What chance had she of doing that here?

Taking a deep breath, she looked deep inside her soul, quailed once, and made her decision. She wasn't making it lightly. She knew she would never be able to turn back from it once she'd taken the next step.

Did she want to turn back? she asked herself. Quietly she heard the answer in her heart. No. The answer was no. A chance at freedom meant more to her than guaranteed safety.

Relieved finally to have settled her mind, she opened her eyes.

David Norris was watching her, and Virginia knew he was striving to read her thoughts from her facial expressions. There was a look of tenseness around his mouth. Virginia was glad to see he was truly anxious about what she might be thinking. It warmed her heart. She'd have been upset if it had seemed not to matter to him.

Firmly, she put her considerations aside and smiled gently at David Norris. "Are you sure you won't mind marrying a crow?"

David rose and took both her hands in his. He looked down at her for a long moment before murmuring, "Not this particular very beautiful . . . and very honorable crow."

Then, to Virginia's astonishment, David Norris pulled her to him, lowered his head and kissed her gently. Instantly, the last of her doubts swirled away in a vortex of heady senses.

Virginia and David were married less than a week later. David wanted a church ceremony, and he wanted it to be one they would always remember. He arranged it and made a staggeringly large donation to the church to ease the strain of having to get everything together in so short a time.

All of Virginia's friends hand-delivered invitations with enthusiasm, and on their wedding day, the church was crowded with well-wishers. Even William's dear, understanding family had come, putting aside their grief to graciously wish her well in her new life.

Thanks to them, and to David Norris, Virginia's second wedding was as lovely and as memorable as her first.

Since they were leaving almost immediately for the train, there was no further celebration for her to attend, however. Changing for the trip, she realized that she was standing in her room in her mother's house for the last time. She took a moment to look around the spacious room, wondering if she would miss it and all it represented.

Then she saw another huge dress box on her bed. She opened it, and began to lift out the things it contained. There were five bonnets of light-weight fabric with deep brims. Then there were blouses of soft, light material that buttoned down the front and had soft, open collars. Pin-tucking on some and embroidery on others made each one lovely.

Under them, she found simple skirts, not very full, and lacking the fashionable bustle women were beginning to wear. These were of a fabric she had never seen.

As she puzzled over it, Lily burst into the room.

"Oh, I'm so sorry, Miss Virginia. I meant to be here before you. I'm supposed to have all that packed. "Oh, dear."

Virginia smiled at the little maid. "We have time, Lily. Besides, I'm glad to have this chance to see my new clothes. Please, don't fret." She held up the skirt she'd been looking at. "Do you have any idea what this fabric is? I don't think I've ever seen it before."

"It's called denim. Grissom wears an apron of it when he polishes the silver. It takes a lot of rough use well. At least, so I've heard."

"Ummm." Virginia held a skirt up against her. The length was perfect. "So I shall need skirts that take rough wear." She tried to imagine it. She glanced at the little maid. Lily could hardly contain herself.

"Rough wear." Lily clasped her hands together just under her chin. She was ecstatic. "Oh, Miss Virginia, just think of the adventure you're about to have!"

Virginia smiled at the other girl's excitement. It was almost on a level with her own. She was going on an adventure, and she found she could hardly wait.

Time was flying, however, and she told Lily, "Quickly, I must get ready to leave."

Lily flew to help her change. The traveling suit that Virginia was wearing to the train was of an exquisite, very heavy, watered taffeta. It was black as night. David's wishes notwithstanding, that couldn't be helped. At least it was in the latest style, and unlike wool, it didn't cause her to itch.

As she dressed, her heart soared to think that this train trip was the last time she would have to wear black, at least until she arrived at her destination in Texas. None of the clothes she would wear on the wagon trip were black, thank heavens. She supposed denim only came in dark blue.

She pulled on her black kid gloves as she rushed down the stairs to find David waiting at the foot of them. He took her hand, and they ran together out into the bright, sunny day and through a double row of friends throwing rice.

They flung themselves, breathless with laughter, into the waiting carriage. The driver started the team, and, trailed by several carriages full of wedding guests, they headed for the train station.

Virginia was on her way to Texas. Her life was greatly changed, and one dream remained from it—at last, she was going to see the west!

CHAPTER 8

They arrived at the train station, escorted by a crowd of well-wishers. In
the two weeks he'd been in Boston, Virginia had watched with pleasure while
David made many new friends. In fact,
he and Virginia had been caught up in
such a whirl of parties—oddly quiet in
deference to Virginia's mourning, yet full
of joy for her future—that they had
hardly had any time to talk.

Virginia was happy to see that people
liked David. He had made so many
friends among her acquaintances. Many
promised to visit them at Prodigal. Now,
all of them were eager to wish the new-
lyweds *bon voyage*.

Laughing, David took Virginia from

the carriage, grasping her by the waist and swinging her down in a flurry of black skirts and petticoats. Followed by the others, they ran for the train.

If David hadn't thought to send Grissom ahead to hold it, the train would already have departed. As it was, the conductor was looking down at his big, gold pocket watch, then over at them, and shaking his head.

In spite of all the laughter, Virginia heard a loud hiss and looked toward the engine. There was a great cloud of steam as it prepared to leave the station. Suddenly, out of that cloud, a tall older man walked toward them. He stopped and regarded them steadily.

David froze. For a moment, their gazes locked. An instant later, David took Virginia's arm in a fierce grip to hurry her onto the train.

The conductor signaled the engineer. There was another great hissing of steam and the shining white cloud of it obscured the tall older man.

When Virginia looked back again to where he had been standing, he was gone.

David and she stood on the steps into the car, David holding her securely, his arm clasped around her waist. They waved and waved at their wedding party until the train had pulled out of the station. Then the conductor insisted they stop standing on the steps and go inside the car.

As soon as they were settled in their compartment, Virginia asked, "Did you know the man we saw down by the engine?" Her eyes searched his face.

His face was expressionless. "Why do you ask?"

"It seemed to me as if you two looked at each other with rather more than casual regard, and I wondered."

"Don't give it another thought." David took her gently by the shoulders and changed the subject. "Are you hungry? There's a new restaurant car, and it will be open for supper soon."

She looked steadily at him for a moment, disappointed that he was unwilling to share with her the truth of his reaction to the man on the platform. It would be uncomfortable, however, to start a quarrel on their wedding day, no matter how trivial.

It had been the tight grip he'd taken on her arm as he'd gazed at the man that had made her curious. That grip, though, might have meant no more than that he was eager to board the train. The conductor had obviously been anxious for them to do so. She decided that must be the case and smiled at him.

He returned her smile with one of his own. "This has been a very eventful day, for you, *Mrs. Norris*." He accented her new name just a little. "I propose that we have supper and then get to bed early." He moved close and put his fingers under her chin, raising her face toward his. "Does that suit you," he spoke the next word softly, gazing intently into her eyes, "wife?"

When Virginia answered with a breathless, "Yes," David swept her into his arms and kissed her.

Virginia felt a warmth rush through her that she'd never felt before. She ducked her head against David's chest so that he wouldn't see her confusion.

She'd never felt that way when William kissed her.

Seated in the dining car, Virginia slowly forgot the nervousness she'd felt when her new husband had called her 'wife'.

His kiss was another matter.

David was a gifted conversationalist though, and they spoke of many things. They had almost finished their meal when he said, "I hope you'll like living at Prodigal, Virginia. I know it will be very different for you."

"Yes, I expect it will. I hope it will." She smiled across at him. "I find myself looking forward to a new way of life."

He grinned at her. "I'm relieved to hear that. The west is a far cry from Boston. I'll try my best to make you feel at home, though." He leaned back in his chair. "I've chosen a horse for you."

Virginia gave a little gasp of pleased surprise, her face alight.

"Your mother told me you liked to ride, and of course, you'll need a way to get around. I chose a little mare bred and foaled on Prodigal. I named her Rosy so I'd have something to call her, but she's yours to name as you choose."

"I'd always heard it was bad luck to change the name of a boat or a horse."

"I'm not too much of a believer in luck," he said seriously.

Virginia's heart swelled. Obviously David was telling her that, like any good Christian, he believed in the Lord's blessing, not random chance. How good it felt to know that she had not un-equally yoked herself.

"Oh, dear. I didn't tell them to pack my sidesaddle with the trunks."

"Sidesaddle?" David chuckled. "Only women who live in big cities and ride in parks with their grooms trailing behind them ride sidesaddle in Texas, Bride. As you well know, once you dismount or happen to fall off . . ." he laughed to see the slanted glance his lovely wife treated him to at the intimation that she might fall off a horse ". . . there's no way to get back onto a sidesaddle without a mounting block or a groom to put you back up."

"True," she admitted, but added, not wanting to surrender so easily, "though I have one very athletic friend who can manage it."

"And I'd be willing to bet she's at least a head taller than you are."

"Ummmmm."

"I'll take that for agreement." He reached across the table and took her hand. "There are gates to open that you'll have to dismount for, unless you want me to send one of the men with you when you want to go into town. I'd be happy to do that, but I had the idea that you'd like to adventure a little on your own."

"Oh, yes, David, I would." She could hardly believe she was really to be given such freedom. She was elated.

"Well, most of the ranch is safe, as long as you stay where there are men working. They'll keep an eye on you. As for the rest, you'll have to wait for me to have the time to accompany you. For now, I want you home well before dusk," he chuckled at the look she gave him. "And I don't want you going beyond the butte in the middle of the ranch alone."

"For now we'll skip over the admonition to be home before dusk that we all had in our childhood," she told him pertly, then asked seriously, "The middle of the ranch? Can you give me some idea of what the middle of the ranch means in a measurement I can understand?"

"Certainly. I'll start with town." He picked up his fork and drew by pressing lightly on the linen of the tablecloth. "Here's town." He moved the fork toward her, leaving a long line of faint indentations in the linen cloth. "Then, five miles north is the house. The butte is another five miles northeast, and that's as far as I'll permit you to go unescorted."

Virginia clenched her teeth not to comment on his use of the word 'permit.' She'd have to see about changing that part of his vocabulary when she felt she had more influence over him. She settled for asking, "Just what are the dimensions of the ranch? That's already ten *miles*, David. Miles." She was wide-eyed.

"Prodigal is twenty miles, front to

back, and twenty-five miles wide, give a foot or two." He couldn't help smiling with pride.

"Isn't that a huge part of the state?"

At that he laughed out loud. "Bride, Texas is seven percent of the land mass of our country. You could drop New England into it more than a few times. My ranch is less than two-tenth's of a percent of Texas." He grinned. "You don't have to worry. We've left plenty of room for other people."

She smiled. "I guess I'm just used to New England. There we aren't in need of so much land to get our jobs done."

He smiled back at her and warmth shone in his eyes.

Now she was most eager to learn more about their destination. "Tell me about Texas."

His laugh told her she'd delighted him. How he must love his home state. She knew that she was going to love it, too. "Tell me," she pretended to be imperious, lifting her chin and making her words seem a royal order.

"Well," he began slowly, his mouth quirked in a lopsided smile. "It's big, ma'am," he spoke with an accented drawl. "Miiighty big."

"She cocked her head, to indicate that she was hanging on his every word, her eyes bright with interest.

"A rancher needs a lot of land out there. A great deal more than in the east."

"Why is that?" She really did want to know. After all, his Prodigal ranch took up more acres than most cities.

"Because in the east, an acre of grass might feed three head of stock," he was watching her closely to see if her interest was genuine and whether she would understand what he was talking about, "but it's the opposite in Texas."

"Oh?" She asked the question with a tiny frown.

"Yes, ma'am. A steer in Texas needs about three acres of grazing land."

"Why is that?" She was puzzled. "My late husband," she mentioned William with a faint blush, feeling a little disloyal, though she couldn't decide to whom, "told me that there are vast grasslands in the west."

"Yes, that's true." He nodded. "But

they're way to the north of us. They have a greater rainfall there than we have down south in Texas, so their grass is greener longer, and they haven't got the hot winds and the heat that bakes our land dry and makes it dusty much of the time."

Virginia's eyes were round with the new knowledge. "I'm so ignorant," she said with exasperation. She plunked her hand down on the table as if the gesture underscored her disgust with herself.

David smiled and reached for her hand. Holding it in his own large one, he stroked the back of hers with his thumb. "Then I shall take great pleasure in teaching you."

She blushed fiercely and laughed a small breathless laugh. "Well," she assured him, "you certainly have your very own *tabula rasa*." The way he held her hand made her feel as if she blushed all the way to her toes. She was certain he hadn't been talking only about Texas.

"My very own blank slate." He, smiled, obviously pleased at that thought. Relinquishing her hand, he signaled their waiter. At the same time he asked Virginia, "Would you care for dessert?"

"No, thank you."

David never took his gaze from her as he put his crushed linen napkin beside his plate and rose. Placing money on the table for their meal and a sizable tip, he reached for her hand with a slow deliberation that set her heart aflutter. He drew her to her feet and then close to his side. Leaning down, he spoke to her alone.

Very softly, he asked, "Shall we retire?"

CHAPTER 9

The next morning, Virginia was awakened by David's gentle kiss. The rocking of the train had lulled her senses, and she had overslept. He was standing, already fully dressed, looking down at her, smiling.

"So you're even beautiful when you first awake. I am, indeed, a fortunate man." He laughed then and told her, "I'll step outside so you can dress." He started to leave, then turned back, suddenly aware that there was no one to help her. "Unless, of course, you need me to serve as lady's maid."

Virginia shook her head at him. "If I need you, I shall call out." She sat up in the bunk, sheet clutched to her bare shoulders and her hair falling all around her.

For an instant, David just stood looking down at her. There was a flash of raw hunger in his eyes which he swiftly hooded. Then he said huskily, "I'll be just beside the door."

Virginia stared at the door as it closed behind him, remembering the look she'd seen in his eyes. It had caused her breath to shorten.

After a moment, she rose and used the water in the painted porcelain wall-hung ewer to wash as best as she could. She dressed as quickly as she was able, with the swaying and jolting of the train. Opening the door, she found her husband exactly as he said he'd be.

He smiled and guided her to the right. "We're lucky to be on this train. I think it's something of an experiment. We have a restaurant car to eat in, as well as Pullman's new car that gave us a bed."

"Wasn't this the train you came to Boston on?"

"Great Scott, no! That one was a nightmare. Only seats—hard wooden seats, I might add—to sit up in for the entire three days. Nothing for food the whole trip except for what the vendors sold us from trackside at the water stops, which happened only whenever the train happened to make one." He paused and looked down at her. "And I'd be willing to swear in court that their coffee was at least a week old by the time I got to it."

"Poor David." She laughed up at him. "I'm glad we don't have that to suffer on this trip."

He leaned down and whispered in her ear, "On this trip, I don't think I'd even notice."

The next two days flew by as they talked and got to know each other. Virginia got over any shyness she might have felt at having married a man who was almost a stranger, thanks to David's obvious delight in her. He complimented her continually—her manners, her disposition, her appearance. It became a matter of laughter between them as he did.

"My heavens," she finally exclaimed,

laughing, "next you'll be asking to inspect my teeth!"

That comment brought David up short. He *was* assessing her. He was inspecting everything about her. Wasn't he constantly comparing her to the image he had in his mind of the perfect mistress for Prodigal, his life's finest achievement? Wasn't he weighing her suitability to be the mother of his sons?

He had the good grace to be ashamed of himself. Resolutely, he shoved all that sort of speculation out of his mind. She was as perfect as he'd hoped she'd be, and he couldn't wait to show her to Texas.

He turned his thoughts to envisioning the gowns he'd order for her, and the jewelry he'd commission to be made to go with each one. If she still felt she had to wear black, then they'd be black. With the right dressmaker, even black gowns could be glamorous. He'd command them to be the most extraordinary black dresses the state of Texas had ever seen.

He knew just the couturier to whom he'd telegraph the measurements he'd gotten from her dressmaker. Gustave and his staff of seamstresses would make her the most envied woman in the state.

And he would be the most envied man.

They arrived in Kansas City amid the bustle and dust of a cattle drive arriving. Virginia stood on the walkway in front of their hotel and exclaimed, "My heavens! I don't think I've ever seen so many cows."

David cast an appraising eye over the herd being driven down the main street. "There're a lot more on Prodigal. About fifty thousand more. You'll get used to them."

Even as she shot him a startled look at the figure he'd quoted, Virginia heard the note of pride in his voice and slipped her arm through his. From all she was learning, he had every right to be proud. God had obviously smiled on his endeavors.

They walked the short distance to the

hotel. The lobby was spacious and re-
flected the new affluence of a railhead
town. The manager hurried forward, obviously impressed by the elegance of
Virginia's clothes and the number of
bags the porter had brought from the
train. "May I be of service?"

"Norris," David told him. "We have a
reservation."

"Ah, yes, Mr. and Mrs. David Norris of
Texas." He smiled fulsomely and hurried
to his long, polished counter to grab a
key from the cubby holes behind it.
"Here we are. Permit me to show you
your suite."

Once there, David tipped the man
who brought their bags and turned to
Virginia. "Is there anything you'd like?"

"Just a long bath and a nice dinner
that doesn't clack and rattle from the
rails under it, please."

He leaned down for a long, sweet kiss.
"I leave you to it, then. I'll see to our
travel preparations." He kissed her
again. "Hmm. A man could get used to
that." The next kiss was a little rougher, a
little demanding. He let her go with obvi-

ous reluctance. "I have to go. I'll be back in time to take you to dinner."

Closing the door to the suite behind him, he left Virginia staring at it, bemused by his kisses, and went to take care of three important matters. First, he telegraphed Virginia's measurements and an order for a number of gowns and riding outfits to the couturier in San Francisco whose designs he'd always liked. That done, he sent a second telegram to Bart Hastings, his ranch foreman, instructing him to arrange a dinner in honor of Virginia's arrival on Prodigal.

The actual date of the dinner would have to be set by telegraph later when they were closer to the ranch and could better estimate their time of arrival there, of course, but he wanted Hastings to alert the list of guests he'd compiled to the general time—surely within three days—to assure that they'd keep space on their calendars free to enable them to come.

He was fortunate in his foreman. Without a man like Bart Hastings, he could never have left Prodigal for so long. By the time he got back to the ranch, he'd have been away almost three months.

Instructions to Hastings seen to, David went to see about the third and most important thing on his mental list—his arrangements for the actual trip the rest of the way to Texas. He was pleased to see that the wagon he'd ordered had been built to his specifications—strong enough for the rough terrain they must cross, but light enough to make good time.

They had over seven hundred miles to go, and he had every intention of making the trip as pleasant as he could for his bride. That would be no easy feat, as some of the country still had hostiles in it. When there was danger of encountering any, he planned to link up with other wagons if and when he could, and make time alone when it was safer. The two teams of horses he'd bought were especially fine and would stand up well to the rigors of the trip.

He was impatient to get back to the ranch and his planned cattle drive now that he had secured a mistress for Prodigal.

The beautiful Virginia was his, safe from pursuit by anyone in Boston as he'd feared she might not have been if he hadn't put his plans on hold to go and claim her for his own. In addition, he had carefully made her his own in every way he could in the nights on the train, and he glowed with inner satisfaction to realize it.

Now he had to get her prepared for the arduous trip home. He couldn't wait to show her Texas.

They started out early the next morning. As usual, David had taken every care to start them off right. He'd even selected the clothes Virginia was to wear. He'd chosen one of the light-weight, deep-brimmed bonnets from Miss Fothering-gil's second box to preserve her creamy complexion, a soft-collared white blouse, pin-tucked from shoulder to waist, one of the almost-narrow denim skirts and something new.

Instead of the shawl women always

wore when it was cool, David presented her with a jacket made of the same denim as her skirts and cut like a man's. It had pockets that were actually useable, and was vented at the back shoulders to give her room to move freely when climbing up into the wagon. In case of cooler weather, it could be buttoned to the chin. That would leave her hands free instead of being occupied in clutching a shawl close around her for warmth.

"Oh, David. How unusual."

"Do you like it?"

"Of course I do. But I have no idea what to put into these pockets. There are certainly enough of them." She ran her hands down into two.

"Trust me. I'll give you things to put in them." He pulled her into his arms and lowered his head toward hers. She lifted her face for his kiss, losing herself in the warmth that flowed through her.

Virginia snuggled deeper into his embrace and put her head on his chest. "Oh, David, I wish this time could go on forever."

"Do you, my dear?"

"Umm."

David was getting used to the little hum Virginia made. He found it was oddly endearing. "You know," he told her, "I think I'm even beginning to learn how to interpret that sound."

She looked up at him, startled. "What sound?"

Laughing he picked her up and swung her around him. Setting her down again he said, "Widgeon. Are you unaware that you frequently say 'umm'?"

It was her turn to laugh. "Evidently."

He looked deeply into her eyes. "Well, whether you're aware of it or not, I command you never to stop."

She looked back, breathless. "Your wish is my command."

Suddenly David was breathless, too.

Waiting for David out in the sunshine of early morning, Virginia saw for the first time the wagon that was to be her home for the next month. It was really very nice for a wagon, she thought. Of course, being a city girl, she'd had very little experience judging wagons. The drays that had lumbered through the streets of Boston bore no resemblance to this rather elegant vehicle. While it looked quite sturdy compared to the buggies and gigs and such that she was used to, and she supposed it would have to be, it was far more handsome than any wagon she'd ever seen. It was painted a nice shade of dark green, and the seat was deeply padded leather with equally well-padded back rests.

In the bed of the vehicle, there were two large, built-in boxes with lids of the same water-proofed canvas that she had seen covering the luggage boots of stagecoaches. She could only suppose that they had been made that way to be lighter than wooden lids would have been. She guessed the things they would need for their trip were stored in the boxes. She had no idea what all that might be, though.

Lily had certainly been right when she'd predicted that Virginia was going on an adventure. She was only grateful that she was going on it with David.

By just looking at the wagon he had either chosen or designed, she was impressed.

She was grateful that he was strong and knowledgeable about the trip they were about to undertake. Most of all, she was grateful that she knew in her heart she'd be safe on this trek because she would be with him.

Her thoughts were interrupted when David reappeared. His clothes were very different from those she was used to seeing him in. He wore denim pants that had light areas of wear, and a jacket similar to the one she wore.

His hat was different, too. It was higher crowned, like the one he'd told her about that a horse could eat from, and there was a dark area at the band, as if he had worn it while working cattle and had perspired in it.

Low on his right hip there was a holster with a large pistol of some sort in it. It was tied down by a leather thong that encircled his thigh midway to his knee.

Virginia found herself staring. He looked rougher and manlier than he ever had, and she felt a warm shiver go through her that he was her husband.

He caught her looking at him and grinned. "Better get used to it. Courtin's done. These are my work clothes, Bride. You've married a cowboy."

She met him as he walked toward her. She was smiling up at him as she told him, "Yes, sir." She lifted her face for his kiss. "I married a cowboy."

CHAPTER 10

Starting out on the trip was a revelation to Virginia. She'd had no idea that civilization could disappear, as if they'd suddenly dropped off the edge of the world. That was the feeling she got when they were only a mile out of the city. The vast emptiness before them was awe inspiring.

David sensed that she was uneasy and tried to distract her.

"All right, Bride. It's time for you to name the horses."

"Me?" She looked at him in surprise. "Why not both of us?"

"Okay. Matthew, Mark, Luke and John. That ought to do it."

"David! I think that might be a little disrespectful, don't you?"

"What do you mean? Those are perfectly good names. Why should the horses think I'm being disrespectful?"

She punched him in the side, her uneasiness forgotten.

Having put her at ease, David grinned and told her, "Yes, that was a little disrespectful. Suppose you name them for me."

"All right. The one with the star on his forehead is easy. He'll be Star. The one with the blaze can be Blaze. It's not very original of me, but it's simple to remember."

"True, but there are still two horses to go."

"Yes." She gave the matter thought. "Lets name one Boston, shall we?"

"It's as good a name as any," he agreed. "And the last one?"

"Your turn."

"Then Luke."

She surrendered with a smile. "All right. One biblical name to go with the ranch."

David stiffened for a moment, then

leaned down and kissed her. "I named him after the town drunk."

Virginia looked so distressed that he relented. "No. We haven't got a town drunk. I just like the name Luke."

She looked at him steadily. "Good. Luke it shall be. Star, Blaze, Boston, and Luke." She gave him a mischievous look. "I'd no idea you liked the name Luke so well. We shall have to give it to our first child."

He looked at her, shocked. Clearly his teasing had come back to bite him. After a second, he rallied. "And if it's a girl? Don't you think she might mind?"

"That's no problem. I fully intend to have a boy first," she told him firmly. "I had meant to name him David after you, though. But if you prefer Luke . . ."

"Enough of your nonsense!" He looped the reins over the keeper and pulled her into his lap to kiss her breathless.

Unconcerned, the horses trotted on.

They spent their first night under the stars in what David called a bedroll, an exhausted Virginia held close in his arms. They had made good time. Almost thirty-five miles of the journey lay behind them.

David's idea of having two teams—one to pull the wagon while the other rested just following it and switching them out at mid day—made it much easier on the horses. Otherwise, they could never have made as many miles and have the horses last the entire trip. David alternated them trotting and walking and was careful to rest them ten minutes out of every hour.

Virginia was glad to see he was so considerate of the animals. Any carelessness or cruelty to animals had always distressed her.

The weather seemed to be on their side, too. Day after day, it was sunny and the roads, some of them little more than the country lanes around the outskirts of Boston, were dry.

When they drove across long treeless stretches they used the big umbrella David had had made for them. Virginia was certain that was for her sake, as

David's tan proved he was used to being in the sun.

Sitting what felt like forever was ex-
hausting for Virginia. Though she loved
to ride and spent hours on horseback
when weather permitted, she had never
traveled so long *behind* horses in her
life. Each night, David lifted her down
and let her stand, leaning against the
wagon, and watch as he did all the work
of setting up their little camp.

Then he'd fix them something to eat,
and when the bed—such as it was—
had been made, he brought her to it and
gently helped her out of her blouse and
her skirt.

"Oh, David," she told him with tears in
her eyes. "I'm such a drooping flower.
I'm no help at all."

He stopped her by the simple act of
kissing her.

She was grateful just to fall asleep in
his arms.

It took almost a week and over two hundred miles of travel for Virginia to be-

come travel-hardened enough to feel like her old self. Once she did, the laughter returned to her eyes, she was a veritable whirlwind around the camp in the evening, and nights were magical again.

While David saw to the horses, she put out their bedroll and then attempted to duplicate his skill in cooking over an open fire. She burned beans and coffee as if they had an endless supply, and was always contrite about her failures.

David was a good sport about it, eating all but the worst of it cheerfully. When he shot game, however, he was careful to cook it for them himself.

Virginia was grateful about that, to say the least. She had never seen meat in her life except when it appeared on a platter on a dining room table, and was afraid she might be tempted to become a vegetarian if she had to provide it herself.

"What will you do if I shoot something a little more exotic than rabbits, Bride?"

"Goodness. I shall eat it with pleasure, of course. Pheasant and grouse and quail are lovely."

"Not quite what I had in mind."

She started to ask him just what he was considering then changed her mind. "Surprise me," she said pertly.

She wasn't sure she liked his grin.

"That I certainly will," he promised her. "That's a promise. And you have to promise you'll eat what I bring home."

Recalling his grin, she ordered, "No mountain lions." They had heard one hunting in the hills a few nights ago.

"Nope." He was talking Texan again.

Virginia wasn't sure she'd covered all the ground she should, so she added, "And no coyotes." She looked at him seriously. "They look too much like dogs, David. I couldn't bear it."

"Virginia." He shook his head at her. "Nobody'd eat a coyote." He pronounced it cay-yote-ee, not cay-yote, she noted.

"All right then. Hunt what you will. I'll eat it."

David ducked his head so she

couldn't see his face. His grin this time was decidedly mischievous.

Two days later, as he went to hobble the horses for the night, Virginia heard a strange, dry leaf–rustling sound, almost like a baby's rattle. She saw David draw his six-shooter—she'd learned that was what his gun was called—then shoot at something on the ground.

The horses spooked and ran a little way off. David didn't seem to mind, and sure enough, they came back to their grain in a few moments.

Virginia smiled. The horses were as certain that David would keep them safe as she was about *her* safety with him. "What was it?" she called.

"Dinner." He held up his trophy.

Virginia looked at him in horror. "That . . . that's . . . a . . . s . . . s . . . snake, David!" She dropped the coffee pot.

"Sure is."

"Don't you bring that here!"

"Got to. Nowhere else to cook it."

"You are *not* cooking that thing over my fire, David Norris!"

"Where else, Bride?"

"Not here!" She backed away from him as he approached her eyes on the long, thick body of the snake.

"Now, Bride, just calm down." His reasonable tone did nothing to reassure her. She just stared at him as if he'd lost his mind. Nonchalantly, he sat down on a rock near the campfire.

Virginia retreated to the side of the wagon, ready to climb aboard it.

"I seem to remember you promised to eat whatever I brought to you."

Virginia still stared at the snake.

"And I recall you said to surprise you," he reminded.

She stared at him now. Surely he wasn't serious!

"So I've surprised you." He began to prepare the snake. "Maybe I've even shocked you a little." He stripped the skin from the snake and put on that easy Texas drawl again. "You being a city girl and all, I guess you're not used to foraging, but this is a real treat, I can assure you." He tossed some lard into their iron spider skillet and set it on the fire as he cut the snake into inch thick rounds.

Looking up at her he said very softly, "You promised."

Virginia bit back all the scathing remarks she wanted to make. She *had* promised, God help her.

Putting her hand over her mouth to keep from saying anything, she went, feet dragging, to where her husband was cooking *it*. She couldn't bring herself to say snake, even in her head.

Determined to be brave and to prove she was game, as her young male friends would have said, she asked, "What kind is it?"

David smiled approval at her. He seemed to have a very good idea what this move toward the campfire was costing her, and an even better one about the courage she was showing in pretending interest. "Rattlesnake," he said succinctly.

Virginia's chest heaved as she took a deep breath. She wasn't sure whether the breath was enough to bolster her sagging courage, but it was all she could manage. Hesitantly, she drew near her husband, her eyes on the iron frying pan.

Miracle of miracles, there was a rather delicious smell beginning to fill the air. With a gulp, she gathered her skirt and sat down opposite David.

With a glare she told him, "I'm going to be much more careful what I promise you in the future."

He'd won and he was gentleman enough not to rub it in.

When Virginia took a tiny bite of his offering, she was astonished to find it was as delicious as it had smelled when David was cooking it. She gave him a look that said he'd won that, too.

Again he was gentleman enough not to rub it in.

After long days on the trail, they were more than halfway home, and David was elated to be making such good time. Their rate of progress was due to the lovely weather they had been having.

None of the fords of the various rivers that they had crossed had been flooded by rains. The roads, tracks and open country they traveled were never mired in mud, and they hadn't been attacked by any hostiles. In fact they hadn't even seen one.

Virginia was certain that God was smiling on their journey. She thanked Him as they drove along, meaning also to thank Him in her nightly prayers. That, however, had become a problem. At first, fatigue had always pushed any thought of praying right out of her mind, sleep taking her quickly. Later, when she'd become used to traveling, it was David.

Tonight, David and Virginia lay under the stars and discussed his plans for Prodigal and for the state of Texas. Her head on his shoulder, Virginia turned her face to him. "You sound as if you want to be governor someday."

He tucked his chin in hard so that he could look down at her. "Would that be so bad an ambition?"

She thought of all he had accomplished in the building of his ranch and all the plans he still had for it. She thought of all the responsibility he carried because of Prodigal Ranch, and, try as she might, she couldn't understand why he wasn't satisfied. Why did he want to do more?

She didn't yet dare to ask him why. There was still so much she didn't know about him. He always changed the subject whenever she questioned him about his family and his childhood. It was this reticence about himself that made her hesitant about asking questions, now.

After a long pause, she said only, "I don't know, David. Politics is something I know so little about."

"Ah, but you do know how to be beautiful and charming, and you have a wonderful ability to put people at ease."

"What's that to do with you being governor of the state of Texas one day?"

"Everything, my Bride. You will be the lovely catalyst that will turn the gruff, old codgers who're attempting to run things down there into reasonable men. Then they'll be men who will, under your benign influence, give up their own selfish goals for the good of the state."

"Umm."

He looked at her with more than his accustomed seriousness. "I mean it, Virginia. With you as my hostess, I shall win every one of them to my side. Texas is a young state. Only twenty years old. There's room for younger men of ambition there. The prospect of becoming one of the men who guide Texas on to being the great state I know she's meant to be is there now, just within my grasp." He reached out a hand and closed it over thin air for all the world as if he'd taken something in it.

Virginia frowned. She wasn't at all certain she was comfortable with the ideas David was expressing. Being a charming hostess was one thing. She'd always dreamed of that, herself. Being a charming hostess in order to lull men into a state of mind that might make them more amenable to someone else's plans—even her own husband's plans— was quite another thing altogether. Leaders shouldn't be easily led, and she didn't feel at all right about being part of trying to lead them.

David sensed her resistance. He shifted, propping himself up on an elbow and looked down at her. "Don't worry, Virginia. I'd never ask you to do anything more than to be your own charming self." He smiled at her. "You need only to enable my guests to relax and enjoy their dinners in our home."

Virginia was quiet, digesting his analysis of the seemingly important role she would play in his life when they reached his home. She wasn't certain she relished it.

Slowly, sadly, the easy camaraderie of the past weeks paled a little. How could her wonderful new husband weigh part of her worth by how well she could charm his guests—guests he intended to invite so that he could influence them to his way of thinking?

The doubtful thought dulled the bright shine of her happiness.

Virginia hated it happening. Her heart ached with the sense of something beautiful about to be lost. She was wise enough, though, not to voice her thoughts. Not when she hadn't gotten to the depths of them for herself yet. She wasn't sure she completely understood, nor how she felt, and thus said nothing.

David was unaware there was any anxiety on Virginia's part was silent as well, but his was a silence of contentment.

They lay quietly watching the stars, neither speaking. David turned to kiss her and after a while, Virginia forgot her anxieties about the future, lost in the sweetness of his kisses.

Finally, as the stars shone brightly down, they both fell asleep, still wrapped in each other's arms.

CHAPTER 11

The weather changed abruptly. The next day dawned dim and dreary. There was an odd tension in the suddenly heavy air. The wide sky, always so bright and benevolent, seemed to grow sullen and oppressive, crushing down at them.

Off to the west of where they drove, there were towering clouds, dark and ominous, and the scent of rain was borne on the wind. David had already hitched up the first team and tied the second pair of horses to their customary place at the back of the wagon.

Instead of helping Virginia up into the wagon and starting them on their way, however, he stood looking at the sky in that direction for a few minutes. Then he scanned the terrain around them with such a serious face that Virginia became uneasy.

She looked from him to the clouds roiling in the distance. It looked to her as if the whole vast sky there were blackening, and bright spears of lightning danced through the darkest of the clouds. Distant thunder came faintly to them after each flash. Suddenly she was nervous. "Is everything all right, David?"

"Looks like we're in for some weather. Those clouds have a lot of rain in them. Wind, too." He considered the situation for a minute. "We might do well to find a sheltered spot and wait it out."

"Oh." Virginia was ashamed that her voice sounded so weak.

He turned toward her. "I've frightened you, haven't I?" He was at her side in a few long strides. "I'm sorry, Bride."

"It's just that I've never had to find a place to shelter out in the wilds before." She attempted to look calm and courageous, but the wind was rising, and she really hadn't ever had occasion to brave the elements. Storms didn't come up so suddenly in Boston, nor were sensible people ever out in them.

David swung her up in his arms, lifted her to her seat on the wagon, and got up beside her. Turning the horses toward a distant low bluff, he sent them into a trot, then into a gallop. The wagon jolted and bounced behind them.

"Weather moves from west to east," David told her, shouting over the rattle of the wagon as Virginia held on for dear life, "so if we camp there on the east side of that bluff, we should be protected a little."

He saw Virginia's eyes were round with apprehension and laughed.

"Don't read too much into this, Virginia. We could go on, but the horses could do with a little time off, and we'll be a lot snugger under the wagon than sitting up here on top in the driving rain."

The wind kept rising. The threatening clouds were moving toward them as quickly as they were approaching the bluff that David had chosen for their shelter. To add to their discomfort, great clouds of gritty dust now swirled around them so that they had to shield their eyes.

Peeping through her fingers, Virginia was relieved to see that they had almost reached the bluff. "Thank heaven," she murmured.

The horses bogged their heads down and shook their manes to indicate their displeasure with this change in what had been ideal weather so far. When they reached the slight overhang of the bluff, David told them, "Whoa," and they skidded to a stop. Only his quick application of the brake kept the weight of the wagon from slamming their breech straps into their rumps. He jumped down immediately to tend the horses.

The horses were too well trained to be really fractious under the hands of a skilled horseman. Sand and small pebbles were pelting them, though, and they danced a little in the boisterous wind.

David quickly unhitched them. Leading the first two, he gathered the second team from the rear of the wagon and led all four horses away to better shelter, close under the bluff. This time he didn't hobble them, though. He stopped with them between two sturdy trees.

"Virginia," he called over the rising whistle of storm wind, "bring me that rope from under the seat."

Virginia rummaged under the padded seat of the wagon and came up with a length of stout rope. Jumping down from her perch, skirts flying, she ran with it to David.

David had halted the teams close under the bluff where the wind was diminished. The stinging clouds of dust were blocked by it, as well, blowing over the top and around the sides of it, but missing their protected spot.

As a result, the horses had quieted down, no longer dancing as if to escape the sharp stings of the wind-borne pebbles. Nevertheless, David held their lead lines tightly as he tied the rope between the two trees and made a four-horse picket line.

"Safer for them this way than hobbled," he told Virginia.

She nodded as if she really knew what he was doing. She didn't though. In stormy weather, she was used to having her mother's driver put the horses safely in the stables at home while she was just as safely sheltered in the house. She certainly had never stood out in a terrible windstorm.

Grabbing her skirt, she tried to keep it from billowing in the wind with one hand while she held onto her bonnet with the other. She could hear David laughing at her efforts.

Then he was at her side and sweeping her up in his arms again. She grabbed him around his neck and buried her face in his shirtfront, clutching it tight in both fisted hands.

Holding her effortlessly in one arm, David snatched their bedding out of the wagon with his other hand and tossed it underneath. An instant later the skies opened with a great peal of thunder, and he rolled after the bedding with her clasped to his chest.

They were both laughing at the tangle they made. Then the slashing rain came pounding down on the wagon, and Virginia was more than glad they weren't out in it.

Twisting around to look at the horses,

she saw that they had their tails turned to the storm wind and their heads bogged down. Already rain was streaming off their sides and their manes and tails were sodden.

She was extremely glad that her new husband was so weather-wise. The thought that they might have been caught out in the awful slashing rain unnerved her. She turned to David and smiled.

David slid his hand around her neck, under her hair, sending little chills down her spine and brought her face to his for a kiss. She started to melt into him.

Just then, with a tremendous, searing crack, lightning struck a nearby tree. It split it from crown to roots and one smoking side of the tree fell toward the wagon.

Virginia shrieked and dove deep into David's arms. He held her against him so that his shoulder and his other hand blocked all sounds from Virginia's ears.

He couldn't stop her from feeling the

rumble in his chest, though. David Norris was laughing at his bride.

The next day, David wasn't laughing. He wasn't laughing at all. Roads that had been fine for so much of their trip were mud all the way up to the hubs of the wagon wheels. Streams and rivers that they had to cross were flowing deep and swift.

The horses, working hard to drag the wagon through the deep ruts of the roads, were getting tired out after only a few miles of such difficult going. All the ten minute rests and switching of the teams that David practiced for the horses' welfare made little difference in their progress now. The roads were impassable.

By the first day's end, they had gone no more than ten miles. David's disappointment showed clearly in his set face.

"David," Virginia said in an attempt to make him feel better about their lack of progress. "We've been making such good time. Surely a few slow days don't matter."

"If we only have a few, it might not be so bad." His expression was glum. "There's no guarantee that the weather won't be like this all the rest of the way, though."

Virginia wondered why it mattered so much to him. Was it because it was the one thing on the trip over which he had no control? She'd hate to think so.

She would dearly love to tease him by saying that that was the case, but decided it might be better not to. This was a new mood for David, one she hadn't seen before. She was so used to the confident, smiling David that she was at a loss, and she wasn't certain how to handle it. In fact, observing the frown he wore, she wasn't sure she could handle it at all.

She did try, of course, but it was useless. Nothing Virginia could say lifted his mood. When night fell, they made camp and went to sleep in strained silence, David rising now and then to study the night sky.

The next day was no better. They'd

not gone a mile before there was a tree that had fallen across the road. Evidently the storm had been more severe further south of where they had first weathered it.

Frequently, downed trees had to be moved off the road before they could pass. Every day it was necessary not once, but several times. David used the relief team to pull the trees aside, but each time they had to stop to move one made yet another delay in their trip.

Once Virginia asked, "David, isn't there anything I can do to help?"

"No," he'd replied so shortly that she didn't ask again.

Virginia wanted to talk to him, wanted to keep his mind off his difficulties, but she could think of nothing to say that might help. She could only sit there, useless and quiet, while David struggled.

At one river crossing the wagon had been almost swept away downstream. They'd been saved only because David, instead of insisting on making the weary horses fight to cross straight to the usual spot in the ford, had managed to

angle the lead team downstream to another low place in the river bank. With
the force of the water aiding them, the
team got them safely out of the river
there.

Virginia had clung to the back of the
wagon seat and prayed they'd be all
right as the horses bucked and clawed
their way up out of the river. When the
team had finished heaving the wagon
up onto the bank, they simply stood,
heads down and flanks quivering with
the Herculean effort they had made.

For his part, David got down and
slashed a path for them through the
heavy brush between them and the road
so they could get back on it. Virginia sat
in her place on the wagon seat and
watched him. He staggered with fatigue,
and she worried that the effort would
take his last bit of strength.

That night, she made the camp as
well as she could, attempting to spare
David. As she cooked, she asked,
"Would it do any good to wait somewhere until the roads are drier?"

"There's no way to know whether they
will get drier, Virginia," David had an-

swered, his tone curt. "It could just as easily rain again and make them worse."

With that, he threw the uneaten portion of his supper into the fire. Rising, he staggered to the place Virginia had put out their bedroll and fell into it.

He was asleep before Virginia had repacked the cooking things and come to join him.

As the days wore on, there were more places than Virginia could count where David had to jump down, slithering in mud, to help the floundering horses through deep miry spots in the road.

Sometimes there were great pits of mud where once the road had been, and David had to find a way to drive the wagon around them. There was no way they could ever have gone safely through them.

Virginia worried about David and about the horses. There were many times when David had to grab their shovel to dig the wheels out of ruts too deep for the horses to pull the wagon free of and forward.

Further, when digging wasn't enough to free the wheels so the straining horses could get the wagon free even more help was needed from David. Every sinew straining, he'd work with a pole to pry the wheel up and free.

Virginia could see the toll all this was taking on his strength, and her heart ached for him. When she spoke to him, he responded with grunts. It was obvious to her that David was exhausted.

Try as she might, nothing she could say persuaded him to let her help him in any way. She quickly learned that her offers of help only irritated him.

For miles and miles, they struggled through the storm-damaged roads. Night after night, she cooked, only to find David deeply asleep by the time the meal was ready. She was beside herself with worry for him.

Finally she turned to the one source of help that had never failed her. She dropped to her knees on the sodden ground. "Dearest Lord," she prayed, "I know I've been terribly remiss in my prayer life. I've let my new husband and the wonder of getting to know him take away time I used to spend with You. I'm so sorry, Father. I just . . ."

She took a deep breath and began again. "I know I've been neglectful of my prayers, but I also know that You are my Loving Father," a tear trickled down her cheek, "and I'm thanking You with all my heart for answering my hasty prayer and saving us at the river crossing."

She felt tears gather behind her eyelids. She was about to ask the very Father she'd so neglected for another boon. "I'm also asking that You make our way easier, dearest Lord. Please. For David, Lord. In Jesus's name I ask it, amen."

It wasn't much of a prayer, and it was certainly way overdue. She was truly concerned for David and terribly certain she should have done a much better job of praying for him, but she was so tired. So very tired.

Virginia was asleep before she could add any further self-condemnation.

The next day, by late afternoon, the roads were drier. The streams had calmed down as well, and the horses were finding the going a lot easier. David seemed a little more relaxed.

Virginia had been quiet out of consideration for the difficult time David had been having, but as the horses were making better time now, she longed for a conversation. "Thank heaven the roads are better. We're making good time again, aren't we?"

David turned and looked at her for a moment. "Not good enough. We still have a lot of miles to make up. We have to make it to Prodigal."

"Is there really such a rush?" She wondered how many hundred more miles it was to the ranch that was to be her home.

"Yes, there is." David answered her rather shortly again. "I've telegraphed my foreman to schedule a dinner party to introduce you to Texas."

"Surely the date of that depends on when we get there." She wanted to laugh as she said it, but for some reason didn't. She smiled at him instead, carefully not adding that the party could hardly be held without them. That dismayed her. It would have been a perfectly logical comment to make, but she felt somehow that it would anger David if she made it just now. That troubled her. She hated guarding her words.

Picking and choosing words had never been the way they'd talked to each other from the moment they'd met, and she was grieved that the ease with which they had always conversed seemed to have flown.

She looked at him a little anxiously. His face was still rather grim. Sighing softly, she resigned herself to a ride without conversation. It would be hard not to try to talk with her husband. She'd learned so much from him about the vast territory they traveled through.

At the pace David was setting now, conversation would have been difficult anyway, and she resigned herself to silence.

A moment later, one of the horses stumbled and almost fell. The wagon swerved, straightened, and went on. David never even slackened the pace.

Virginia felt the first real shock of fear since they'd begun their trip bolt through her. They could have been killed!

She was upset for the horse and frightened to realize that if the horse had fallen, they would have wrecked. One horse going down would have pulled the other with it, and the wagon would have flipped over the bulk of their fallen bodies. If that happened out here in the middle of nowhere, what chance would they have of anyone being there to help if they were injured?

Finally, even though she'd promised herself she'd not try for mere conversation, she was so concerned about the plight of their horses that she was having trouble not speaking up for them. David was pushing them harder every day. Even with the brief rests he still gave them every hour and the swapping out of the teams periodically, they were showing signs of strain. They were always lathered when he swapped them.

She might be willing to be quiet when it came to holding conversation to make the trip less tedious for herself, but she couldn't ignore the plight of the valiant horses.

"David," she spoke as gently as she could and still be heard over the rattle of the wagon wheels and the jingle of harness.

He turned his gaze toward her and asked with a quirk of his eyebrow what she wanted.

"Must we push so?"

"Why do you ask? Are you overtired?"

She was so tired she could have dropped, but pride would keep her upright on the wagon seat until the end of the trip.

The horses, however, were working their hearts out and she had to speak up for them. "No, this isn't about me. It's about the horses. I think they're losing weight. I think we're pushing them too hard."

"*We* aren't driving them, Virginia, *I* am." He regarded her coolly. "So suppose you let me."

Virginia's face flamed, and she gasped. She'd certainly been put in her place!

After a momentary confusion, she

wondered just where that place was to be. And she wondered, too, what had happened to bring about this very undesirable change in David.

CHAPTER 12

In spite of Virginia's voiced concern, David never slackened the pace. Miles rolled away under the horses' hooves as David drove them hard.

The horses grew gaunter, and under his tan, David's face was gray with fatigue. Virginia wondered again and again what had occurred to make this torture necessary.

After the way her husband had spoken to her when she had asked why they had to push so hard, she wasn't about to inquire again, she was too angry. His coolness had hurt, and his curtness had wounded her spirit. Furthermore, as far as she could see, he didn't care!

So she just hung on for dear life and hoped things would clear up when they reached their destination. She hoped, too, that in the meantime, she wouldn't be tossed off the wagon seat by the painfully frequent jolts and bounces.

With the absence of conversation came time for Virginia to think. Her prayer life was in a shambles. She was so weary at night that the time before sleep when she had always prayed for her mother, her friends, and her country, and most recently for her husband and her marriage, was non-existent. She needed to remedy that as soon as possible.

She had been tired during the first part of their journey, but now she was utterly exhausted. Almost before she reached the bedroll they shared, she was asleep on her feet, her mind blank as to prayer. Oblivion claimed her the instant her head hit her pillow.

This day, she hoped to do better. Before they set out, she stood by the wagon and breathed a short prayer that David would slow the pace so that she would have the time, free from the effort just to hang on, to remember the plight of her friends at home, at least. It seemed to her that every snatched moment of prayer on this trip so far had been totally selfish.

She was still seeking a reason for their breakneck pace, too. The time they'd lost to bad weather seemed to be the biggest reason for David's merciless haste. It was true that the weather had cost them many miles of progress, but she'd not been aware that they had some crucial deadline for reaching Prodigal Ranch.

The first few weeks of the trip had been relatively peaceful. They'd been grueling, yes, but David had been content to make thirty miles a day. She knew that was an impressive accomplishment for a wagon. The most important thing about the beginning of their journey was that they had been happy. With all her heart, she longed for them to be again, but it was impossible.

Now that he was miles behind whatever schedule he had set for them, David was driving all of them—humans and horses—beyond reason. And beyond endurance Virginia thought as she straightened her back for what felt like the hundredth time.

Finally, they topped a long rise. David called, "Whoa," and set the brake. The exhausted horses just dropped their heads and stood without moving a muscle, sweat dripping from them.

David stood, too, peering ahead and obviously thinking hard. After a long moment, he looked at Virginia as if seeing her for the first time since the storm. "You're tired."

Virginia nearly fell off the seat. She looked at him, incredulous.

Her new husband truly had a most amazing ability to state the obvious! She was ready to drop. She'd been ready to drop for days! Why was he only seeing that now?

David sat back down without further comment. Taking the lines up gently, he turned the team off the road and down a slight hill to their right. There was a stand of trees beside a small stream. After the heat of the road, the faint coolness of the little grove was like a balm.

David smiled at her. "This looks like a good place to rest, doesn't it?"

Virginia looked at him as if he'd fallen from the moon. What was *this* change? What had come over him? For days he'd been silent and . . . and horrible. Now did he think he could just smile and say something pleasant, and that would make it all right?

He reached up to help her from the wagon.

"I don't need your help," she said, turning her back on him and starting to leave the wagon by the opposite side. The side away from where he was standing.

"Nonsense." He took her by the waist and easily lifted her down.

Scowling, she purposefully didn't thank him. She just looked at him, stormy-eyed.

David didn't seem to notice. As soon as he'd lifted Virginia down from the wagon seat, David unhitched the team as if there were nothing wrong between them. He took all four horses over to the stream for a drink. After just a few swallows, he pulled them away and walked them for a minute or two. Then he took them back and let them drink, undisturbed.

Virginia was fuming. She could cheerfully throttle him! She couldn't believe he didn't know what he had done to her and to the horses over the last several days.

She also couldn't believe that they were setting up camp when it was only mid day. She was angry with her husband but at the same time, had to admit she was grateful for the circumstance. For that, she even managed a weary *Thank you, Father.*

She walked stiffly away from the wagon and sat on a large, flat rock beside the stream. Bowing her head, she apologized for her neglect and finally remembered Dorothy and Chloe and all the rest of the dear people she had left behind in Boston. She asked the Lord to ease the pain of the loss of their loved ones in the war. She especially asked Him to find a wonderful husband for Chloe to help her raise her boys.

She remembered little Lily and wonderful Grissom and all the other servants who had made her own life so easy for so long. Finally, she asked Him to keep her mother well and safe and help her to find some way to be happy. Then she asked Him to bless them all in some special way. And . . .

"Virginia!"

She startled and looked up to see David standing right beside her.

"Are you all right? You didn't answer me." His puzzled frown and the concern in his eyes began to warm her heart. She didn't seem to be able to stay angry; she never had been able to, no matter how many very good reasons she had.

Now, she found that she didn't really want to stay angry with David. With a huge sigh, she let most of her anger go and said, "I'm fine. I was praying."

David looked a little startled, himself. There was a long pause then he said, "I'll have camp set up shortly. You just rest."

"David!" She shot up from her seat on the rock. She realized she had not succeeded in letting *all* her anger go. A great deal of it had just popped right back up at his casual attitude. "I want to talk."

"About what?" She could tell he was truly puzzled by her forceful attitude.

"David, you nearly killed the horses. You didn't even seem to care that Luke stumbled and almost fell—which could have brought down Star and killed us, too. You didn't notice that I was so exhausted that I could barely hang on, and when I spoke up for the horses, you were cold and rude."

She stamped her foot. "Enough is enough. I want an explanation." She firmed her lips at him. "And I hope it's a good one, if you want me to be in charity with you again. Ever!"

David was clearly shocked. Evidently, he was unaware that she could be demanding and unpleasant. After the torture of the past several days, Virginia didn't care. "Well?" she demanded.

"I . . . I don't know what to say."

"Well, you'd better find something, David. I am thoroughly provoked with you."

He sat on her rock. Gently, he pulled her down beside him, ignoring her faint resistance. Taking her hand in his, he stroked the back of it. For a long moment he was silent. "I'm truly sorry, Virginia. I'm sure I was a beast."

She waited. It was a start, but it wasn't enough.

"You see, I had telegraphed Hastings, our foreman to go ahead with the list of preparations I had left with him for the party for you . . ."

"You'd left a list? How did you know I'd be coming back with you?"

He grinned. "I'm generally known to be pretty persuasive." Mischief danced in his eyes. "And I'm told I have a way with the ladies."

Her original anger was fading in the light of his teasing. She wasn't sure she didn't feel a new anger building. A way with the ladies, indeed!

"At any rate, there were two senators, four judges and various other important Texans invited to your party, and I was rushing to be sure we'd be at Prodigal before they had to leave for a very important gathering this month."

Virginia was torn and more than a little suspicious of his motives. She asked, "Was the party to honor me, David, or to further your political ambitions?"

He regarded her quietly.

"Well?"

"A bit of both, Virginia." He answered her honestly. "A bit of both."

She stared at him as seriously as he was looking at her. She was considering his answer. Finally she decided that honesty had won a victory on both sides of this little war she had started with her husband. And she valued honesty above jewels. So after a long hesitation, she smiled.

That night, for the first time in many days, David gathered her in his arms and kissed her sweetly. Relief swept through her. Whatever David had been enduring had evidently passed, and he was himself again.

The only thing she missed now was the way David used to call her "Bride." If only he would do so now, it would make her happiness complete. Even without that, however, Virginia was smiling as she mentally began to voice her last prayer of the day. She fell asleep before she had finished it.

The next morning, David grained the horses that he'd hobbled the day before so that they could graze. After a quick dip in the little pond made by the stream, he fixed them breakfast over the campfire he had banked the night before. He worked without his usual haste and seemed to be planning a leisurely day.

Virginia looked at him suspiciously. After all the awful, rushed days they had just endured, why were they suddenly in no hurry at all? "David." Her voice was firm. "Will you please tell me what is going on?"

He laughed. "We're here. We've finally finished our trip. The town is just over the next hill, and Prodigal's beyond it."

"Oh!" The single syllable held delight, wonder, and incredible relief.

David laughed again. "I thought you'd be happy."

She was. She was happy to finally ar-

rive at their destination and happy to
see that the man she had started the trip
with had come back. David's easy
laughter was like oil poured on the troubled waters of her spirit.

"I thought, too, that you might like a
chance to change into something a little
less . . . ," he hesitated and chuckled,
". . . utilitarian to meet your new neigh-
bors for the first time."

"Thank you, I certainly would. I can
bathe in this lovely little stream, and
then perhaps I can find something that
isn't all rumpled to wear." Eager to be
clean again, she headed for the water.

When she came back from the
stream, David was nowhere in sight,
but, laid out waiting for her was a dress
she had never seen. It was of expensive
muslin, cool and elegantly cut. The low
neckline was edged in ruffles, threaded
through with ribbons the color of her
eyes. There were even petticoats to
match.

There was also a parasol. Not a cum-
bersome umbrella like the one that
David and she had sometimes used in
the heat of the day, but a lovely dainty

confection. Its edge was also threaded with the blue ribbon, and a knot of them was clustered just above where her hand would hold the pretty toy. Where had David had this wonderful gift hidden?

She was smiling as she changed into the gown. Shaking her head in mute amazement, she supposed she would never cease to be surprised by her husband.

CHAPTER 13

It took no more than fifteen minutes to drive from their pleasant little camp beside the stream to the town. The hills they drove through were softly rolling, but in the distance, Virginia could see a mountain range.

David followed the direction of her gaze and told her, "The mountains you see are on Prodigal."

"But they're so far away!"

David grinned. "I can see you've got a real problem with understanding space in Texas. The New England states have you spoiled."

"Why spoiled?"

"Well, there you can visit in Connecticut by taking a little drive, here you'd spend days getting to Oklahoma."

"I'd hardly say it was a 'little drive' from Massachusetts to Connecticut."

David just smirked at her.

Virginia's heart warmed to the boyish pride her husband had in his state. No wonder he'd been in such a rush to get them here. Obviously he couldn't wait to show Texas off to her. The fact that he'd nearly killed her doing it had obviously never entered his mind.

Heaven knew there were certainly vast spaces between the scattered signs of civilization here in the west. She recognized in herself the fact that that may have intimidated her a bit.

No, it had very definitely intimidated her. She could tell by the relief she was feeling now that they were at last reaching a real town.

The stops they'd made at train depots for David to use the telegraph to keep in touch with his foreman had been just that—depots surrounded by a few shacks. They had done nothing to alleviate her hunger for the sight of groups of people.

She sighed. She was obviously going to have to do a lot of adjusting to make herself fit in this new landscape.

"What was that about?"

"What?"

"That sigh. Are you still tired?"

"How like a man," Virginia told him. "Not every sigh means one is tired, you know."

"But are you?" Concern shone in his eyes.

"Oh, David." She felt a rush of feeling knowing that she had forgiven him for all the abuse she and the horses had suffered on the last part of their trip whether she wanted to forgive him or not. After all, except for a little loss of weight, the horses didn't seem any the worse for wear, now that they'd rested at the camp by the little stream, and she felt as rested and eager to go on as they seemed. "I'm fine," she assured him.

The road ahead curved, and there, in a thick grove of trees, was a river spanned by a wooden bridge. The horses' hooves drummed as they trotted smartly across it. One of them whinnied, and there was a faint answering cry from over the next hill.

Once they'd crossed the bridge, Virginia found herself leaning forward. She'd caught sight of a faint wisp of smoke just over that hill, and now she was straining to see everything about the approach to the town as they drew near.

"Do you like it?" David asked. "The countryside, I mean."

"Yes. It's lovely." She turned and looked at him, smiling. "I was afraid it would be dry and dusty." She waved a hand to indicate the green of the hillsides.

David laughed down at her. "Oh, never fear: it'll be plenty dusty come full summer."

"Is it far to the town now?" Virginia was as eager as a child to see the town that would be a part of her life from now on. She didn't mind his laughter. In fact, she realized she'd been absolutely starved for it.

They breasted the hill at a brisk trot as the horses scented other horses and picked up their pace voluntarily. David

called, "Steady, boys," to remind them
that they were still under his control.
They flicked ears back at him and
seemed to settle down, ears pricked
forward again.

Virginia laughed. "They're as anxious
to get to town as I am, David."

"Possibly, though I hope you're less
headstrong about it." He tapped the
horses' bits with a light tug on the lines,
and the team was all business again,
their brief inclination to unruliness reluctantly abandoned.

Two minutes later, they were at the
edge of town, and David pulled the
horses down to a walk. "Easy, boys. We
don't want to raise a dust."

Ears flicked back at him again.
Champing their bits lightly, the team
walked sedately onto the main street.

The town was small, no more than the
single main street with several very
short ones branching off it. On their right
was a modest white clapboard church
with a tall steeple and red-painted double doors.

Surrounding the church was a patch
of green grass guarded by a white

picket fence. Tombstones marked its neatly kept cemetery at one side, and there was a long hitching post under shady trees on the other.

There were no trees on the main street, and therefore no shade. Since David and Virginia had spent such a leisurely morning in their little camp by the stream, it was approaching midday and the sun was beating down fiercely. Virginia was thankful for the meager shade of her small parasol.

Gazing around her with interest, she was glad to see at last the place she imagined she would come to attend church and to shop . . . if indeed there was any shopping to be done.

At least, she felt certain, there would be thread and ribbons in the little general store with the name 'Johnson's Mercantile' in gold lettering on a fancy sign over the door, and probably much more. It was on the left side of the street. As David had told her about the Johnsons who owned it, she looked forward to meeting them.

Further down on the left, there was the livery stable with a smithy next to it.

It was from the smithy that the faint wisp of smoke she had seen arose. Across from them were a two-storied saloon, and a low, adobe building that had 'Sheriff's Office' neatly lettered over the door. The barred windows there told Virginia the jail must be behind it.

As they passed the side streets, Virginia saw many modest houses with planted trees and gardens. The neighborhood engendered a feeling of quiet prosperity and pride.

Only a few people were on the street at first, but the sound of a wagon coming into town drew others. By the time David halted the horses in front of the general store, a sizeable crowd had gathered.

People! Virginia was delighted.

Thanks to David's excellent description of the Johnsons, Virginia recognized them as the couple who came out of the mercantile to meet the wagon. Her heart lifted as she saw that Bess and Herb Johnson looked really happy to see them.

"David!" Bess greeted him. "We're so

glad you're back." She offered Virginia a shy smile.

Herb stepped forward. "And this must be your bride." Smiling a smile that threatened to split his face, he turned his full attention to Virginia. "Welcome to our little town, Mrs. Norris. We've all been waiting for you."

Virginia didn't know what was expected of her, but her heart warmed at their greeting. She returned Herb Johnson's smile with a genuine one of her own. "Why, thank you, Mr. Johnson. Thank you very much."

Herb Johnson laughed. "Well, I guess David's described us, so, yes, I'm Herb Johnson, all right." He pulled his wife forward. "And this is my Bess."

The woman with the shy smile beamed at Virginia, and Virginia beamed back. Instant friendship blossomed between them.

Others stepped forward to welcome David home and to be introduced. Virginia was enjoying the enthusiasm of their welcome, exchanging pleasantries, and trying to fix each of them in her

mind when a group of horsemen galloped into town.

"Uh-oh." Herb Johnson was looking
at the new arrivals, but speaking to
David. "Here's trouble."

The riders stormed up the street to
where David had positioned the wagon.
Savagely reining their mounts, they
stopped beside it in a cloud of dust.

A stocky, barrel-chested man dismounted and stomped ahead of the main
group. He was obviously in charge and
had a mean look about him that made her
apprehensive. Virginia watched with a little trepidation as the other men slowly
dismounted to follow, and she moved
closer to David.

Ignoring everyone but David, the unpleasant man snarled, "So you're back,
Norris. It's about time. I been waiting for
you. We still have a matter to settle
about that last piece of land you added
to the Prodigal."

David met the man's glare with a
steely one of his own and answered
evenly, "I don't think so, Broudy. As I
told you the last time you brought it up,
the matter is already settled."

"Not to me, it ain't."

David regarded the angry man steadily for a moment and finally said, "This is not the time for this sort of discussion, Broudy." Then he turned away to introduce his bride to a group of older women who had just arrived, leaving Broudy to sputter.

Virginia hid her uneasiness and smiled charmingly at the ladies, saying how pleased she was to make their acquaintance, but her mind was on the belligerent man behind her. With a great deal of relief, she heard another man say, "That's enough, Broudy. Be on your way."

"So he owns you, too, eh, Sheriff?" Broudy delivered the insult in the same snarl he'd used to address David. "Guess Norris thinks he owns everything around here."

The sheriff stepped between Broudy and the wagon. "I said that's enough!" His tone brooked no argument.

Broudy spun on his heel and stomped back toward his horse. "We'll just see about that," he said threateningly.

Virginia, still smiling down at the others as if she hadn't noticed the vitriolic man's words, reached out and put her hand on her husband's arm.

David covered it with his own free hand. Then he smiled at their well-wishers, lifted the reins, and said, "We'll have a barbeque for the town as soon as we can. Then you can all get to know Mrs. Norris better. Right now," he turned and smiled at Virginia, "she could do with a little rest. It's been a long, hard trip from the railhead in Kansas and I want to get her on home to Prodigal."

Everybody moved back away from the wagon and called and waved good-byes. David signaled the team, and they were off. Virginia returned their waves until a bend in the road hid the friendly townsfolk from view.

"Oh, David, they were wonderful."

"Yep." He turned to look at her. "So were you."

Virginia had no answer for that, so she watched the road in silence. When she thought David wouldn't notice, she cast glances behind them once or twice to be sure the man called Broudy and his considerable group of men weren't following them. She was satisfied after the first half mile that they weren't. She let out one little sigh of relief.

David looked down at her and grinned. "Broudy won't bother us with the sheriff watching him."

Virginia refrained from asking whether the man would bother them if the sheriff were *not* watching. The west was not only vast, but also a little daunting.

Then all her attention fastened on the space between the ears of the two horses speeding them on their way. She was about to see Prodigal Ranch at last, and she could hardly wait.

Her first sight of the ranch house left her breathless. With its windows sparkling in the sunlight, it seemed to beckon to anyone approaching on the well-graded ranch road.

Back in Boston, when Virginia had read David's advertisement, she'd wondered if he had been bragging. Now that she was looking at the actual premises, she realized David had been modest in his description. The sprawling house was immense!

There were two women waiting for them on the wide porch that wrapped around the front of the house. One was as round as a butterball, the other tall and thin. Both were beaming. These had to be the cook and maid that the advertisement had mentioned and whom David had praised in their conversations beside their campfires along the trail.

David pulled the team up and a man ran to their heads to hold them. "Put them in the pasture nearest the house, Filipé," David told him. "They've had a hard trip, and we'll want to watch them for a while."

Virginia, suddenly shy, was glad the horses would be near the house. She'd just realized that, except for David, they were the only friends she had here on Prodigal. She was glad she wasn't going to lose them.

As her husband swung her down and led her proudly up the steps, the man quietly led the horses away. Virginia had a momentary sense of loss for the wagon that had been her home for almost a month. She gave herself a mental shake for being silly.

Then they were on the broad porch, and the two women greeted them. "Welcome home, *Señor* David!" the round one said enthusiastically. Then her curious gaze shifted from her employer to the woman at his side. The second woman said only, "*Patron.*" Then her gaze, too, was locked on Virginia.

David was quick to introduce them. "Virginia, this is Maria, my . . . no, *our* cook."

Maria bowed. "*Señora.*"

"And this is Teresa who keeps everything shining." Teresa followed Maria's lead and bobbed a curtsy.

Virginia smiled and said, "I'm so pleased to meet you at last. My husband has told me what wonderful care you take of him."

Both women smiled broadly and nodded their approval to David. They seemed genuinely delighted to see her.

Virginia was delighted, as well. The two women with their wide smiles were a far cry from the frequently dour ser-

vants she had so often seen in Boston homes. Already she felt she would be content with them.

A leisurely tour of the house followed. Every word of praise Virginia uttered was completely sincere. It was beautiful, and beautifully appointed.

The thing that pleased Virginia best was that David had chosen furniture from the Queen Anne and Empire periods. There were none of the heavy, dark, and ornate Victorian pieces like those that her mother had chosen for Davenport House.

"Oh, David," she told him, "I've not seen a house in Boston that was any finer."

David beamed at her. His pride in all that he'd done shone from his eyes.

"In fact," she went on, "I've had to keep looking out the windows at these wide Texas views as we went to assure myself that we are, indeed, in the west. "It's lovely, David." She looked up at him. "Thank you for bringing me here."

David leaned down and kissed

her gently. "You are more than welcome."

Two evenings later, it was time to dress
for the long-planned dinner party. Virginia was bathed and perfumed, standing in her corset and petticoats and
dressing gown as ordered. "David! What
are you up to? Why won't you let me get
my gown on?"

David, resplendent in his black formal
clothing smiled and put a finger to his
lips as if there were a secret about to be
shared between them. Then he opened
their bedroom door, and Maria came in
with a huge dress box.

Putting it on the bed much as Grissom had done with the box from Miss
Fotheringgil's back in Boston, she
smiled and nodded at Virginia and left
the room.

David stood watching. "Well?"

Virginia knew she was to open the
box, so she moved to the bed and removed the lid. The gown inside was
magnificent. Black *peau de soie*, it was

soft as a baby's skin. The bodice was tucked from shoulder to shoulder, the tucks crossing over her breasts. The neckline looked scandalously low.

Virginia lifted it from the box and held it against her. The bodice below the tucks was plain and fitted. From it, the skirt fell away in artful folds that swept up to the back to form the new fashionable bustle, then flowed into a short train.

It was a dress fit for a queen! Surely a master hand had designed it. And it was black. Quick tears threatened as Virginia's heart overflowed with this proof that David respected the fact that she was still in mourning for her dear William.

"David, it's . . . it's beautiful!"

David came close for his thank-you kiss. Virginia blinked back her tears and threw her arms around his neck to happily bestow it.

"Let me help you into it." He took the dress from her and suited his actions to his words, gathering the gown to drop it over her head.

Virginia emerged saying, "You do that

rather expertly, husband." Her eyes were teasing. "Where did you get such practice?"

"Did I tell you I had several sisters?"

"No, you did not."

He grinned. "Good, because it would have been a very big lie."

"So?" She cocked an eyebrow at him.

"Every gentleman is allowed a lady friend or two, surely."

"Not any more," Virginia told him firmly.

He swept her into his arms, crushed the breath out of her and kissed her. Then, his voice husky, he told her quietly, "Not anymore."

Virginia was giddy with happiness. "Oh, David. I do so love you."

"Good. Then you'll understand that I'm a jealous man, and you won't mind this." He went to the box on the bed and picked out a short length of gossamer black tulle. Coming back to her, he tucked it gently into the low neckline of her dress, covering the swell of her breasts.

While she stood in front of the mirror, he arranged the fragile fabric so that it made the daring neckline of her dress a great deal more modest without destroying the beauty of the couturier's creation.

"There." He stepped away from her, nodding his satisfaction with his handiwork.

"Much better," Virginia agreed.

"But there's still something missing. The gown is elegant, but rather plain, don't you think?" His eyes almost twinkled.

She looked at him inquiringly. "It's a wonderful gown, David."

"I had these designed for it." He reached into his breast pocket and removed a long black velvet-covered box.

When he opened it, Virginia gasped. Then he lifted the contents and fastened them around her slender neck.

Fire blazed from the tasteful waterfall of small diamonds that David had bestowed on her. Carefully, he put matching cascades in each of her ears.

"David! They're . . . breathtaking."

"No, Mrs. Norris. You're breathtaking. They are only jewels."

For the next few moments, even the

arriving guests were forgotten. Then sounds from the front of the house interrupted. David released her reluctantly.

"We must go down," Virginia spoke as if she were awakening from a dream.

"Yes." David took her hand, and they walked together down the sweeping staircase to the spacious foyer. They took their places at the front door to welcome their guests.

The party was beginning. Carriage after carriage arrived, some of their occupants came with carpetbags packed to stay overnight in the wing of luxurious guest rooms. After all, in some directions it took hours just to get off Prodigal Ranch and across their own ranches to their houses. Others, determined to return to their own homes after the festivities, came in vehicles more like stage coaches.

David and Virginia stood in the foyer, greeting them until the last one had been received. Then they all went into the sumptuous dining room.

Sitting opposite David a little later at the long table in the formal dining room, Virginia smiled at their thirty guests.

Clasping her hands in front of her, she waited for a quiet moment then requested, "David, would you please say grace?"

At David's insistence when she had asked him to do it, she'd always said the blessings on their trip, but this was David's home and David's party. There was no way she would usurp his place as host just because he'd said he preferred her voice saying the graces on the trail.

There were several surprised looks, but none like the stunned one on her husband's face. Her heart skipped a beat. Had she made her first social misstep? No matter. The Lord was going to be thanked for His provision at her table, regardless of who sat at it.

David gave a short burst of soft laughter, looked around the table as if he sought to excuse his wife's eccentricity, and bowed his head. His grace was brief but lovely to Virginia's ears, and she signaled that the dinner was to begin by shaking her damask napkin out at her side and placing it in her lap.

It was so nice to have David finally

say the grace. At their campfire meals he had always merely bowed his head while she did it.

Her guests followed her lead, and conversation began again, flowing easily through course after course. Even so, Virginia had a little difficulty being charming to one or two of the guests at first. She wasn't accustomed to the rough manners of some Texans.

"Blast you, Denham," one of them said. "I say we should have stayed a republic."

"Don't be a mule, Riley. There are lots of benefits to being a state."

"Yeah? And the first one was getting into the War Between the States, of course."

"Might have been bad timing, I agree. But . . ."

"Gentlemen," Virginia decided it was time to stop their argument and interrupted gently, "The war is over, and I'm certain you don't wish to sadden those of us who lost loved ones in it by discussing it just now."

The two men looked chagrined. Both

remember in a flash that she had lost her first husband in that war.

Riley offered, "Of course, little lady. You're absolutely right."

Denham added, "You just have to forgive us old war horses, Mrs. Norris. We tend to forget ourselves."

Virginia touched his hand. "We all do."

She wondered if David had known he had bracketed her with two men who seemed to persist in taking opposite sides of any issue. Though they never mentioned the war again, they treated her to their differing idea about raising cattle, fencing land, and hiring hands from south of the border.

By the time they had reached the dessert, she'd adjusted to their personalities and even found the conversation exhilarating. She not only smiled frequently but laughed low, ladylike laughter through a good deal of it.

She was exhausted, though, by the time the last of the departing guests were on their way to their own homes and those staying until morning had retired to the guest wing.

David stood behind her at the still-open front doors and slipped his arms around her. She leaned back against him, her hands resting on his where he had clasped them at her waist.

"David! Are you always going to have so many guests?"

"Did you mind?" He leaned forward and kissed her cheek. "I thought you were wonderful."

"Thank you," she said almost absently, "but if we are to do this again, I must see to it that we have more servants. We need a butler and at least two footmen to get so many people served."

She turned in his embrace and looked at him a little severely. "Didn't you see that Teresa was run off her feet?"

"No, I can't say that I did."

She gave him a stern look. "No, I don't imagine you did. You were so absorbed in your conversation with all the men within your range." She shook her finger at him. "Why, some of the women even had empty water glasses. There was no way one server could possibly keep up."

In her head, she began making lists of faults she would have to correct and staff they would have to find if this sort of entertainment was to be a frequent part of their life together.

David regarded his wife with a proud, possessive smile. "You absolutely charmed the two ogres I saddled you with. You kept the conversations going at your end of the table in spite of them. I think you even got those two to change their minds and agree on a point or two."

"You put them there deliberately? I should pinch you!"

"You were splendid with them." He kissed her cheek. "You're exactly the wife I wanted to preside over my dinner parties."

"I'm so glad, since I'm the only wife you've got."

Her comment brought a hearty laugh. Then he realized that his bride must be exhausted and merely said, "Let's get to bed, shall we?"

"Umm."

He laughed at that, scooped her up in his arms and took the stairs two at a time.

CHAPTER 14

In the late morning, Virginia was again standing at the double front doors. This time, after having seen them through a hearty breakfast, she was bidding the last of their guests farewell.

Truth be told, she couldn't be gladder to do it.

Most of them were nice people, of course—these men who David wanted to influence to permit him to help guide this vast state. A few of them were difficult, and one had been impossible.

After a lifetime of living with her mother, though, she'd been able to get along with the overbearing ones as well as those she found lovely.

She was looking forward to being

with just David, though. More than anything, she wanted to be alone with her
husband. Alone to get to know him better, alone so that he could know her better. Even though they spent a month on
the road together, they hadn't really discussed their goals as a married couple,
only his ambitions.

On the wagon trail, the focus was on
moving forward. Talk by the campfire
had been brief, and talk in their bedrolls
seemed always to devolve into something else.

Virginia felt they needed to set mutual
goals now that they were wed. They
hadn't, for instance, seriously discussed
children—beyond the comment he'd
made, as they lay under the stars, about
wanting a son to inherit all he'd built.

David had made that remark in passing, while he'd told her of his ambitions
for Prodigal and the state of Texas. A
son to inherit was essential, of course,
but she wanted other sons and daughters, as well. An only child herself, she
longed for a big family, and wanted to
share her hopes for one with David.

Too, she was curious about his shyness when it came to his faith. It was odd to have had to prompt him to say grace last night at dinner. Though David had been at his own table, possibly he'd been reluctant to make anyone who might not observe the custom in their own homes uncomfortable.

There was so much she wanted to discuss, she wondered if they would be able to find enough hours in the day.

Smiling, she turned to him. "I'm so glad they're finally gone, David. I have so much I want us to talk about."

David bent down and kissed her on the neck, just under her ear, and a tingle ran through her all the way to her toes.

"And I want to tell you how lovely and accomplished everyone thought you were last evening and how beautiful every man at the table found you. You were everything I hoped you'd be and more."

David pulled away and added, "I have something to talk about, too, Virginia."

"What, dear?"

"The cattle drive."

"The cattle drive?"

"Yes, I have a large herd leaving tomorrow. I postponed its scheduled departure so that I could go east to get you, but it can't wait any longer." He took her hands and looked deep into her eyes. "I have to go with them, Virginia."

"No!" The word just popped out.

"Yes." He gave her hands a little shake. "It's only for a month or so. Not forever."

"A month! But, David, we just got here."

"It'll give you time to get to know Maria and Teresa."

He said it as if it were only Maria and Teresa that she wanted to get to know better! Flabbergasted, she heard him go on.

"It'll give you time to hire any more servants you may think we need and to find your way around Prodigal." He was smiling, and she could tell that he wanted her to see it his way.

She couldn't see it David's way. She didn't want to! She didn't intend to. She could only see that she was about to be deserted by the only person she knew here in the vast west she'd been so eager to reach.

She'd been eager, too, to explore it. But she'd wanted to explore it *with* someone, not by herself! She wanted to explore it with a specific person. She wanted to explore with David.

And she wanted to get to know her husband better, here in his own special environment, not the cook and the maid!

Virginia could feel the beginning of angry tears and she didn't want David to see them. Moving to a window, she stood where she could keep her back to him.

"Are you all right?" he asked.

Wonderful! Not only was David leaving, but he'd taken leave of his senses. How in the world did he imagine she could be all right? She was a bride, for pity's sake—a bride who had been dragged at breakneck speed across half a continent, then inundated with thirty dinner guests, half of whom had spent the night, and now her husband was deserting her!

How could she be all right? And how could David think she would be? When they'd finally slowed down from their grueling rush through several states, and reached the place she was to think of as home, the person she was to make it a home *with* was going to disappear!

She blinked away the tears that threatened to spill over. They would probably mislead her dense new husband as to their nature. She turned to face him. "David," she said with deadly calm, "isn't there any way you could arrange to stay here with me?"

"No, Virginia," he sounded regretful, but adamant. "I have to be the one to negotiate the price for the herd. Bart Hastings would never be able to get a fair price for the beeves, and we've worked too hard to let that happen."

Virginia let the silence between them lengthen. She could see it was futile to try to change his mind. Minding it terribly, she capitulated anyway, knowing it was the wisest course to take. It wouldn't do to start their first quarrel on the eve of his departure.

Try as she might, she couldn't think of a thing she could do or say that would change David's mind anyway. She'd gotten a pretty good idea of how hard that could be on that last part of their trip when she'd tried to get him to spare the horses.

Squaring her shoulders, she moved off without looking back at him. "I'll go and talk to Maria about something for lunch."

"Good girl," he said.

She heard the relief in his voice and realized he'd known perfectly well how narrowly he'd avoided a scene. His comment made her angrier still. She felt like anything but a good girl, and fiercely resented him calling her one.

"I'm very proud of you," he told her again. He regarded her a moment, seeming to sense nothing of her frustration, "I'll be in for lunch after I've conferred with my foreman about the drive."

He was gone in an instant, his body following the path Virginia was certain his mind had already taken.

Tingle to her toes or no tingle to her toes, Virginia wanted to kick him in the shins.

David was gone the next morning before sunup. After one hasty kiss and an additionally hasty admonition to enjoy herself while he was away, he'd clapped his hat on his head and walked out of their bedroom without a backward glance.

Virginia sat up and stared at the door he'd closed behind him. She took a deep breath and tried to decide whether or not to throw something at it.

This was horrid. David was horrid. What was she supposed to do without him for a whole month?

She didn't know a soul in the entire state of Texas. How could he do this to her? How could he be unaware of *what* he was doing to her? Were men just impossibly dense?

Before she could decide what to do with herself for today, much less for thirty more of them, there was a soft knock at the bedroom door. Then an equally soft voice called, "*Señora*?"

Virginia bolted upright. "Yes?"

"It is Maria. I have your breakfast."

"Please come in."

Maria bustled in with a huge tray, set it over Virginia's lap, and beamed at her. "I did not know what you would like, so

I have cooked you many breakfasts."
Her grin widened. "Next time, you shall
tell me and the tray will be much smaller,
no?"

"Thank you, Maria."

Maria gave her a sympathetic smile
and looked for an instant as if she would
pat Virginia on the shoulder. Instead,
she folded her hands over her ample
midsection and quietly left the room,
shaking her head.

Virginia didn't want sympathy. She
didn't want to be lonely, either. Just because she'd never been left alone before, passing, as one did in her society,
from her mother's care to her first husband's, back to her mother when she
was widowed, and now on to David—
who had just deserted her!—didn't
mean she had to sit around and sulk.

Human company would help the situation, and she was going to find some.
She lifted the tray off her lap and placed
it carefully aside. Then she threw off the
bedcovers, jumped down out of the
oversized four-poster, and went to get
dressed.

A half hour later, she arrived in the

kitchen lugging the huge tray Maria had brought up to her.

Maria leaped up from the big preparation table at which she and Teresa were sitting over their own breakfasts. "*Señora!* What is this that you do?"

Virginia placed the tray on the table. She smiled and strove to keep a petulant tone out of her voice. She was mistress here, after all, not some unhappy child. "I am going to have breakfast with you two, Maria. I do not wish to dine alone!"

She plopped down in one of the chairs, and tears filled her eyes, in spite of her resolution.

Maria and Teresa fell over themselves getting to Virginia.

"Please, *Señora!* Don't cry." Maria put her arms around her employer's bride and gathered her close. To Teresa, she said, "It's the long trip and the big party—they have overwhelmed this little one."

Teresa nodded and stood beside the two of them, patting Virginia's shoulder. "Don't cry, Little One. He'll be back."

Virginia sniffed. "I know he'll be back,

I'm upset because he left. Why did he bring me here just to . . . leave me?"

"Men are like that when they have big, important business to do, *Señora*."

"Yes, that is right," Teresa chimed in.

"And the *Patrón's* cattle drives are big, big, business, you can bet." Maria was rubbing calming little circles on Virginia's back. "It is not that he did not prefer to stay with you. In fact, you know, this cattle drive was put aside so that he could go and seek you out, marry you, and bring you back here to us at Prodigal."

"Yes," Teresa assured her. "That is true. *Señor* Hastings, the foreman, has been like a bear with a very sore paw waiting for your husband to return and get on the way."

Virginia sat up straighter. What dear women these were.

Maria said, "Tea," and Teresa hurried to bring a cup.

Virginia sipped it and regarded her two comforters. "Thank you. You've made me feel much better." She offered a slightly tremulous smile. "Really."

"*Bueno*." Maria beamed at her. "Now

we must find things for you to do to make the time to pass, no?"

Teresa nodded vigorously. "*Sí!* There must be picnics and rides and such so that the time will seem to pass quickly."

"Yes!" Virginia agreed, smiling. Just looking at her two new friends' open faces made Virginia's spirits rise.

David or no David, she was going to enjoy getting to know these two very kind women.

CHAPTER 15

The next day when she came down for breakfast, Virginia ignored the shining silver and the gold-banded china waiting for her on the dining room table just as she had ignored them the night before. She went straight to the kitchen to eat her breakfast with the two Mexican women.

"Please don't waste your time setting a place for me in the dining room when my husband isn't here." She smiled to make certain Maria and Teresa didn't take offense at her words. "Unless you prefer that I eat alone, I'd really rather eat here with you."

"Ah." Maria and Teresa spoke in unison, "*Bueno*."

"Good." Virginia laughed. "In fact, marvelous. I really was hoping you wouldn't mind me eating here with you, and I'm glad you don't." She settled in her chair at the big preparation table with a smile.

Virginia was ready to go to work. In her hand, she carried a pencil and a long sheet of paper.

Maria and Teresa looked with interest at the paper. Maria hastened to put their scrambled eggs and bacon on plates she had warmed. Teresa brought the platter of buttered toast.

Virginia smiled her thanks, and when they hesitated, gestured for them to sit down with her. She was pleased to see that they bowed their heads and clasped their hands the moment they saw that she was going to say grace.

"Hmm. The eggs are delicious, Maria."

"*Gracias, Señora.*"

The three of them were silent as they enjoyed their food. Then Virginia studied her list and Maria and Teresa studied Virginia.

As they relaxed over their coffee, Virginia announced, "Now that my husband is away, I shall need to find two, nice-looking young men. Maria, Teresa, where do I find clean, healthy, reliable young men?"

Eyes wide with shock, the women exchanged startled glances. "*Qué?*"

Virginia didn't notice their appalled expressions as she was busy checking over the list she'd written last night of things to do. "Yes," she told them. "Mr. Norris didn't notice how hard you were working to serve our guests the other night at dinner, Teresa, but I did. I think we need at least two footmen to help you."

"Ahh!" The relieved exhalation came from the women simultaneously. Maria fanned herself with her hand.

Puzzled, Virginia looked up at them, saw they were not going to tell her why they had sighed, and then went on. "I think we must hire and train at least two boys to help you serve at table, because I'm certain that Mr. Norris has decided to carry out his plans to entertain frequently. We can hire more, if you think you can use them."

Both women nodded.

"I started out thinking we might begin training two of our cowboys . . ." She stopped, startled by the burst of laughter from her two companions. Looking from one to the other, she asked, "What is it? Did I say something funny?"

"*Sí!*" they answered in unison, bursting into fresh gales of laughter.

Virginia fought down a quick flash of annoyance. "Well, tell me what it is!"

"It is that you thought to teach cowboys to serve in the house at dinner parties," Maria answered with a wide grin.

"So?"

Teresa could no longer contain her mirth. She threw her apron over her head to hide it from her employer. Giggles escaped the fabric.

"Will you please tell me what is so amusing!"

Maria told her. "It is the cowboys. They would quit the ranch before they let you take them from their horses and make house help of them."

Teresa came out from under her apron. "And you could not teach them anything, anyway."

"Teresa!" Maria scolded. To Virginia she said, "You must excuse Teresa *Señora*. She thinks all cowboys are *estupidos*."

Virginia fought to hide a smile. "I'm sure they are quite knowledgeable about the work they do with the cattle," she said primly.

"*Sí*." Again they spoke in unison, Maria firmly, Teresa obviously under duress from her friend.

Virginia took refuge from her threatened laughter in consulting the list again. "We need some girls to help you with the cleaning, too, Teresa. This is a big house."

Teresa straightened, shaking her head. "I don't need help to keep this house."

Obviously, this was a matter of pride to her, and Virginia had no intention of interfering. "Very well. I shall leave that up to you."

Teresa was all relieved smiles.

"I do think, however, that you must have help at table when we have dinner guests and waiters to serve when we have entertainments of other sorts. One server can hardly circulate more than one tray, be it canapés or champagne."

Teresa was frowning. *Probably the canapés,* Virginia thought, but didn't take the time to explain the word.

If the frown was about the waiters, Teresa would just have to adjust. Virginia's mind was made up about that. She asked, "Do you know where to find the type of young man we can train to wait table?"

"*Sí.*" Maria, the quicker of the two, was ready to apply herself to the problem of more domestic help. She was eager to make the dinners at Prodigal remarkable in every way. Not just to please their *Patrón*, either. Now, too, she had extra incentive. Being loyal *to el Patrón* was good, but finding she was growing very fond as well of the lonely Little *Señora* was even better.

Virginia's offered friendship had won her heart. Her own children had all gone, and Maria was more than ready to adopt new ones, even if the new ones must never know.

Smiling expansively, Maria told Virginia, "I can show you where there are young men that we can cause to be clean and reliable, but the way is long, and Maria cannot ride *un caballo*—a horse. Is it that the *Señora* can drive?"

"I think so. Heaven knows I spent enough time watching my husband drive the wagon that got us here." She put her head to one side and considered the matter. "And back in Boston, one of my beaux had let me drive his gig several years ago. I think I remember enough to be able to do it again. I can only drive one horse, however," she warned.

Maria burst out laughing again. "Maria is not such a heavy burden that we will need more than one horse, Little One." She clapped a hand over her mouth, wide-eyed.

Obviously the term 'Little One' was the name by which she thought of Virginia. It certainly wasn't meant to come out, but it gave Virginia a warm feeling to know that Maria had a pet name for her. She hid her smile and didn't let her reaction show that she'd noticed it, though. Instead, she got down to the business at hand.

"Fine. Then that's settled. We'll leave tomorrow after breakfast, shall we?" She turned to Teresa. "The boys we hire are to be under your command until we can manage to get a butler . . ."

"A butler!" they exclaimed in unison.

"Yes, I shall write the advertisement tonight so that I can mail it if we go near town."

Her two friends burst into rapid Spanish. Virginia could see that they were much agitated. No matter. They needed a butler.

Since they were occupied with their own conversation, Virginia contented herself with debating the wisdom of sending the advertisement to her mother to place for her in the Boston newspaper. What better way to select a good one than to ask her mother to interview the candidates before Virginia went to the expense of sending for one of them? After all, there was probably not an experienced butler to be found in Texas. If there were, he would have been imported from the east and would no doubt be guarded like a priceless treasure by the family fortunate enough to have employed him.

After another moment of consideration, she decided that that would be a very good idea. Perhaps her mother or one of her friends might know of someone suitable. That would be infinitely better than hiring a perfect stranger. No matter how good references were, there was always the possibility that the applicant might not suit.

Of one thing, Virginia was certain: any one who earned her mother's approval would certainly have no difficulty gaining hers!

Looking over her list, she saw nothing else that she needed Maria and Teresa to discuss with her. They had finished their conversation, though, so she looked at them, awaiting whatever their decision might be. "Yes?" she encouraged.

"This butler. How much will he . . . ?" Maria stalled for lack of the word she needed.

"Interfere with the way we do things here at Prodigal?" Virginia supplied with a smile.

"*Sí!* Yes. That is it."

"Well, I think the three of us can keep him from becoming a nuisance, don't you?"

"*Sí!*" This time the word had no hesitation.

Virginia was glad they seemed content at that suggestion. They really did need a butler if David's grand plans as to various entertainments were to be carried out. Maria and Teresa would come to see that as well and would eventually appreciate his help with all the increased work, she was sure.

She just hoped that whoever the butler might be, he would be very good at diplomacy. Teresa had a distinct tendency to be prickly.

Virginia finished her coffee, folded her list and rose. She patted her stomach. "You are feeding me too well, Maria, I must get some exercise before I weigh as much as one of the steers."

Maria beamed with pride. She patted her own ample waist and told Virginia, "It is good to have a little meat on your bones. Men prefer featherbeds to beanpoles."

The slender Teresa frowned at her friend.

Virginia laughed. "That's all well and good, but I think I'll go for a ride this morning anyway. Whom shall I ask about a horse to ride, please?"

"Filipé is the man at the barn. He will know which horse *el Patrón* has chosen for you." Maria beamed at her.

"Good. I know there's a mare called Rosy, but I've no idea where to find her. While I'm out at the barn meeting Rosy, I'll make arrangements for our trip tomorrow morning, too." She was halfway out of the kitchen when she had a thought. "Oh! What do women wear to ride in here in the west? I imagine no one has a sidesaddle."

Teresa put her hand over her mouth to hide her giggle. "No, *Señora,* here we do not have the sidesaddles. They are for the grand ladies in big cities."

"Good. I didn't even bring my habit with me."

"No? Is it that the *Señora* does not like to ride the horse?"

"No, it's just that ladies all ride sidesaddle in the east. It always gave me a stitch in my side if I rode more than a couple of hours, but I love horses. I'm hoping it won't be difficult to learn to ride astride."

"How hard can it be?" Teresa giggled. "All the men here on the ranch can do it."

"Teresa, be quiet!" Maria flapped her hand at Teresa. She was the one of them clearly in charge. "Come, we will go see what is in your closet, *Señora*. With all the clothes the *Señor* has had sent here from the city of San Francisco, there will be something in which to ride the horse."

They seemed to know what they were talking about. Virginia hadn't looked for riding apparel in the dressing room closet yet. When she had first looked, she'd been a positively overwhelmed by the racks and racks of suits, gowns, and even ball gowns. Now that they were searching for something that she needed, Virginia was more than interested when Maria threw open the doors.

The cheerful twosome rummaged through the masses of clothes while Virginia stood and tried to take it all in.

David had spent a fortune! She was obviously going to be the best-dressed woman in Texas. And just as obviously, these dresses hadn't come from Boston. She didn't see a single fold of wool in the whole closet.

"Here! Here are the riding costumes, *Señora*." Maria pulled out and held up one. Virginia saw with interest that it had a slightly shortened skirt divided into two legs, very much fuller at the bottoms than the legs of a man's suit. There was a vest to match, and a shirt, reminiscent of a man's, hanging under it.

Teresa dove into the closet and came out with a pair of boots, ornately stitched, high-heeled and with pointed toes like those David wore. She beamed at Virginia, wanting her to approve.

Virginia did approve. David might have gone, but the proof that he had given her a great deal of thought hung in rows in the closet.

Some of the hurt went out of her heart. He did care.

"Where did all these clothes come from?"

"From a man who makes many grand ladies in San Francisco their gowns, *el Patrón* has told us. They came around on a ship into Galveston and then up here to us by stage." She grinned. "The boxes took up the whole stage coach, and the driver said it was the best run he had ever made. He said not one of the boxes complained to him on the whole trip."

Virginia laughed with her at the driver's not so subtle evaluation of his usual passengers. Then she stood and stared at the profusion of colors in the many dresses.

Finally her eye settled on an easily overlooked group of dresses at one end of the closet. They'd escaped her notice because they had been made in black fabrics. Her heart lifted. David had respected her wishes to finish her year of mourning for William when he'd had these gowns created.

He must have sent her measurements from Miss Fotheringgil's to the couturier's in San Francisco the moment he got them. Heaven only knew what bribe he'd offered to have so many gowns made so quickly that they'd gotten here before she and David arrived.

Virginia was humbled by this proof of David's thoughtfulness. Her heart was lighter than it had been since before David told her he had to go with the cattle drive. Even absent, he had not forgotten her.

She laughed with delight and reached for the unfamiliar clothing Maria held out to her. Now it was her job to stay occupied until David returned.

She'd begun by tackling the tasks involved with the running of the house. In doing so, she'd come to realize, from their discussion of the butler, that she'd have to approach any changes cautiously. She didn't want to risk offending the two women who had been running Prodigal ranch house up until now.

In addition to those tasks, she could begin her explorations of the ranch. She held the garments they'd found in front of her and spun around once in front of the mirror and her new friends.

"Praise the Lord, I'm about to become a cowboy!"

CHAPTER 16

The next morning, as planned, Virginia and Maria went out the front door to where an open buggy waited. Maria carried a basket of food big enough to feed an army.

Virginia helped Maria settle her burden in the back of the buggy. "Maria, are you afraid we'll starve on this drive?"

"Ah, no, *Señora*," Maria instructed. "We must take a gift to the headman of the village. It is the way to show respect. Without respect, you will not get the best boys from him, I can tell you."

Virginia was glad Maria knew how things worked in Texas. She'd certainly be at a loss if she'd had to do this without her.

Maria settled beside her, Virginia carefully drove the big gray gelding that David's head barn man, Filipé, had hitched to the light buggy. Filipé stood watching them for a while, then turned and went back to the barn.

Evidently he thought she was doing all right, but even with Maria's solid presence beside her, Virginia was a little hesitant about her ability. As she drove the buggy, her confidence grew, however, and by the time she got to the gate at the road to town, she was quite comfortable.

It was only four miles to the village. Maria assured her it was down a lane a little off to the west just before the town.

"*Señora*," Maria prodded when they'd been driving no more than five minutes, "I can see that you drive very well, but we must go a little faster if we are to get this thing done and be back for supper, no?"

"Yes. You're right, of course." Gingerly, she swung the tip of her driving whip out over the gray's sleek back. She didn't even touch the horse with it, but he broke into an easy trot immediately.

"*Bueno*," Maria settled back against the seat, satisfied.

Almost half an hour later, she indicated what was little more than a pair of ruts that led off to their right. "We must turn here, *Señora*."

Virginia stopped the buggy and gave the reins to Maria. "Here, just hold these while I get the gate." Virginia led the horse through and closed the gate behind them.

"Having the road fenced off is a lovely idea, Maria, but I can certainly see why everybody rides astride out here. Having to open gates would be a real chore for anyone riding a sidesaddle."

She climbed back into the buggy and walked the horse, negotiating the turn into the little lane Maria indicated carefully. Except for a mild bump when the right rear wheel failed to clear the rough edge of the rutted little road, all went well.

Another few minutes brought them to a small, dusty village. Maria told her where to go, and when to stop. It was a good thing, because Virginia was busy looking around her.

She'd never seen anything like it before. Adobe houses stood side by side, with low walls around tiny gardens in the front.

Laughing children ran along beside them, giving up for the moment the games they had been playing in the street. Their bright eyes were filled with the excitement of seeing a visitor come to their village.

"Whoa, boy." Virginia halted the buggy. She was afraid that with so many children running and jostling each other, one of them might fall under the wheels.

Maria got down and led the horse to a place under a tree and tied him there in the shade. Virginia sat enjoying the antics of the excited children until Maria gestured for her to follow.

Virginia got out of the buggy and was immediately inundated by children who clung to her, crying out greetings and welcomes in words that she couldn't understand. She smiled and nodded and returned the hugs with enthusiasm.

What a far cry this was from her own reserved culture. How wonderful to experience such warmth.

Maria extricated her, scolding good naturedly and flapping her hands at the children to send them away, laughing, tan legs flashing. Then she grabbed Virginia by the hand, snatched her basket from the back of the buggy, and plowed across the square before the crowd could regroup.

They went to the most prosperous looking of the houses. There a dog gave up basking in the sun to lift his head and let out a single *woof*. Duty done, he put his shaggy head back down on his paws.

In response to his bark, a man appeared at the door. Maria presented him with the basket of treats she had brought, and it disappeared instantly into the house behind him.

After a rapid exchange with Maria, the man stood aside and invited them in with a bow. Virginia and Maria took a moment to let their eyes become accustomed to the dim interior. It was pleasantly cool after their drive in the hot sun.

Their host called an order to a youth just outside his door. Then he offered them something to drink.

Virginia had hardly finished the cool, fruity concoction when four young men presented themselves. Maria turned to Virginia and asked, "Which two would you like to have come to work at Prodigal, *Señora*?"

Virginia felt totally at a loss. She had never hired servants before. Back in Boston, her mother and Grissom had always done it. She'd imagined she'd have to do it once she arrived at Prodigal, but she'd certainly never dreamed she'd have to try it in a foreign language. Mustering as much dignity as she could, she told Maria, "Perhaps it would be better if you chose."

Maria talked with the four boys for a few minutes then indicated two of them. The other two looked so terribly disappointed that Virginia didn't have the heart to leave them out. "Take all four, Maria."

The cook was startled, "We don't need four, *Señora*."

"Nevertheless, we will find things for them to do. Perhaps they will do as gardeners."

Remembering the formal garden at

Davenport House, Virginia knew she'd love to have a larger garden than the one Prodigal currently had. That one was just around the terrace outside the ballroom, filled with flowers that scented the evening. She wanted to add more and to surround David's house with gardens that would be worthy of the house itself.

She turned away from Maria and spoke to the village headman. "All four, please."

He grinned and said, "*Sí, Señora.*"

There were smiles all around. The four boys all but turned cartwheels as they left the house. They and the whole crowd of waiting children escorted them to their carriage.

Children with flashing smiles ran to them from every corner of the village. Virginia was amazed at their number.

"*Gracias, Señora,*" the headman beamed. "These are good boys. They will work hard for you."

Virginia smiled down at him, "Thank you. I'm sure they will."

Suddenly someone in the crowd called out, and two girls ran up with bouquets of wildflowers so large that Virginia was sure someone must have gone to pick them the instant they'd arrived. She told them, *"Muchos gracias,"* and smiled as they laughed at her pronunciation.

Dogs and the smallest children were called out of the way of the buggy's wheels, and the older ones ran beside them as they headed for the lane leading out of the village.

In spite of the chaos and Virginia's fear that it might cause her to lose control of him, the gray behaved as if he had nerves of steel and trotted steadily through it all.

They were sent on their way with many smiles and good wishes, she was certain. Her only desire as she drove away was that someday she'd be able to understand them.

Virginia turned to Maria as soon as she was sure she had the gray under her control and headed in the right direction. "That was lovely, Maria."

Maria smiled, pleased to hear Virginia's sentiment.

"Because of you, it went very well. Thank you."

Maria laughed. "But now you have four instead of two to train, and you have no Spanish." The thought vastly amused her.

Virginia grinned at her and turned the tables. "Yes, but I have you and Teresa to speak Spanish." She smiled and shrugged sheepishly. "Besides, I couldn't bear to leave the other two behind."

Maria beamed her silent approval of this newly come mistress of Prodigal.

They turned right when they reached the road that led to the ranch house and went instead into the town—which, in reality, was only a little larger than the village they'd just left.

Driving straight to the general store, Virginia gave the driving lines to Maria. "Here, you hold the horses, Maria. I'm going to mail the letter to my mother."

"*Sí*," Maria replied, taking the lines as if they were made of tissue. "But don't you be long. Maria is not a driver of the horses!"

Virginia entered the mercantile and

headed for the little post office in the back corner. Virginia was glad she'd finally made her decision to write to her mother asking her to procure a butler for the ranch. Choosing a butler long distance would have proven a very difficult proposition. She only hoped her mother would agree to help.

Bess Johnson greeted her so effusively that Virginia had no doubt the other woman was glad to see her. "Oh, I'm so glad you've come. Won't you have a cup of tea?"

"I really can't, though I'd love to," Virginia said earnestly. "May I come again when I haven't got Maria with me? She's worried that she won't get home in time to fix supper if I tarry." She proffered the envelope in her hand. "I only came to mail this letter to Boston."

Bess looked disappointed, but it was getting to be late afternoon, and she seemed to understand. She took the letter and told Virginia, "I'll take care of this and I'll put the charge on the ranch account. Is that all right?"

"That's fine. And I really will come for tea," Virginia assured her. "I'd truly love

to, and it won't be long before I can."
She smiled at the other girl, glad to think
that she might be making a friend. She
added ruefully, "I just have to learn to
ride western style first. After driving today, I realize that I much prefer the
horse under me rather than out in front."

"Very well, I'll try to be patient." Bess
walked her to the street and smiled and
waved as Virginia drove off. "I'll see to it
that your letter gets out on the very next
stagecoach, and . . ." she raised her
voice to a shout that Virginia might hear
over the noise of the buggy's rattle and
the horse's hoof beats ". . . I'll be hoping
that you learn to ride western style
quickly!"

The next morning, Virginia arose, determined to keep her promise to Bess.
Right after breakfast, she went out to
the barn to apply herself to the business
of learning to ride western, while Maria
and Teresa taught the four young boys
the duties they thought were fitting for
them.

The boys had walked from the village before sunup, obviously eager to work at the big house of the *patrón*. Under the heavy mops of their shining black hair, they greeted Virginia with grins that almost filled their faces.

Though she had no idea what they'd been telling her, she was able to recognize effusive compliments no matter what language they were offered in. Laughing and thanking them, being careful not to try it in Spanish this time, she was relieved to escape to the stables.

Filipé politely inquired, "How did the *Señora* do with the gray? He is a good buggy horse, no?"

"He was wonderfully kind to me, Filipé, thank you. Never once did he give me a moment's worry. Not even with the dogs and children running along beside us in the village."

He smiled and nodded, satisfied with her answer. When Virginia didn't turn and leave the barn, he looked at her inquiringly. "Is there something else the *Señora* desires?"

"Yes, there is." She felt a little foolish

asking, as she was considered an excellent horsewoman at home. She wasn't at home now though, and she needed his help. Putting her pride in her pocket she asked, "Would you be able to teach me to ride astride, please? I've ridden all my life, but only sidesaddle."

"With the greatest of pleasure, *Señora*." He bowed. "Do you wish to begin now?"

"Have you time?"

He nodded and went to saddle a horse for her, Virginia trailing after him. He chose an older horse, a big blue roan. He swung a heavy western saddle onto him and had the horse tacked up in minutes.

Virginia tried to watch how he managed the straps that held the saddle on. It looked a lot more complicated than the buckles that fastened the girths on her sidesaddle.

He saw her interest and told her, "You will let Filipé do the saddling for a while, please. The latigoes must be just right. Too loose, you fall. Too tight, perhaps you get bucked off." He grinned as if he'd made a joke and led the roan out into the sunlight. "I think we begin in the corral."

Virginia could stand being treated like a child if she could just be taught to master riding astride quickly. Already, she could taste the freedom it would give her. Not the least of that freedom would be going into town for tea with Bess Johnson.

"This is the way you mount." Her wiry instructor put a foot into the near stirrup, grabbed the saddle horn and swung effortlessly into the saddle. Swinging down as easily, he said, "You try."

Virginia stepped forward, copied his movements and was in the saddle, smiling. It felt strange sitting astride the horse instead of being perched high on his back. She felt as if she were a lot more in contact with her mount. She liked that and was certain she would quickly become accustomed to the new position.

"Very good. Now dismount, please."

Virginia thought a moment, then stood in the stirrups. Cautiously she brought her right leg over the horse's rump to the near or left side of the horse and reached for the ground with her foot. Immediately, she was falling backwards.

Filipé caught her and put her back on her feet. He was chuckling. Obviously he'd known she'd fall. "*Señora*, while the men are tall enough to leave the foot in the stirrup, you must kick your foot free and drop off, because you are not so tall as they."

Virginia said, "Let's try again." Without waiting for his reply, she slipped her left foot into the near stirrup, grabbed the horn, and rose, flinging her right leg over the horse's back. Losing her balance, she fell into the saddle with a thump.

The patient roan gave a grunt and turned his head to regard her reproachfully. Chagrined, Virginia asked, "What's his name, please, Filipé?"

"Ranger."

Virginia stroked the roan's satiny neck. "I'm sorry, Ranger. I promise I'll do better next time." She dismounted with care, following her teacher's instructions to keep her weight on her hands on the saddle until she had taken her foot out of the left stirrup. This time she dropped to the ground and landed safely on her feet.

She grinned.

"*Muy bueno*." He grinned back. "Now, up again."

Virginia complied, landing like a feather in the saddle this time.

Filipé smiled and nodded. "Good. Now I lead you around a little." He suited his actions to his words, and they circled the corral a few times so that Virginia could find and get used to her seat.

"You know," she said pensively, "I think I'm going to like riding western. I feel a lot closer to my horse and I don't have my knee in the way of my bridle hand."

"Now I show you how to use the reins."

Virginia learned to neck rein the horse in no time. "This is so simple. I just move my hand in the direction I want to turn. Wonderful. No shortening of the reins, no trouble."

"Please do not cross the mane." He spoke sharply. "Is no trouble if you do it right. Just lay the rein on the neck of the horse—do not try to push him over with it."

"Oops." She laughed. "Maybe it's not so simple, after all."

He relented. "You do good. A little practice, and you can go on your own. Practice here at the barn, so that I can keep a watchful eye on you."

"Are you afraid I'll hurt myself?" she asked as she dismounted.

"No." His eyes twinkled at her. "I fear you will hurt the horse."

They parted laughing.

Maria met her at the door. "Did you learn?"

"Yes. Filipé proved to be an excellent instructor, and I really enjoyed my lesson. I found riding astride much easier than riding sidesaddle, too. It was a lot more comfortable."

Maria appeared to enjoy Virginia's telling of it as much as Virginia had enjoyed her lesson. "And when do you go again?"

"Tomorrow, of course. I intend to master riding astride as quickly as possible." She looked out across the ranch. "There is so much to see. I can't wait to get started."

"And you will ride over the ranch when you have learned how?"

"Oh, yes."

"Then I will have to get someone to look after you."

"Nonsense. I'll be fine on my own."

Maria looked unconvinced.

The next day, Virginia got to the barn while the morning was still cool. "Filipé?"

He came out of the dimness at the far end of the aisle. "*Señora*?"

"I came to see if we could continue my riding lessons."

Filipé smiled. He seemed pleased at her enthusiasm. "Yes. We can ride again today. This time I go with you, and we leave the coral."

"I'd like that."

He selected horses and had them both tacked up and ready to go in ten minutes. "I did not groom them, except under the saddles. It is not nice. A horse likes to be properly groomed. That is the reward he expects for letting you ride him."

"Will you teach me how? I was never allowed to do any grooming at home in Boston."

"I will teach you. But now we ride." He led both horses out of the barn and handed the reins to Virginia.

She carefully watched him mount to be sure she hadn't missed anything yesterday, then duplicated his movements. Ranger was patient, and she mounted with no trouble.

They rode for an hour or so. By the end of that time, Virginia had found her seat and was as comfortable as she had ever been riding at all three gaits.

Filipé evidently recognized that Virginia was an excellent horsewoman. He seemed to have decided she was certainly skilled enough, now that she was comfortable riding astride, to handle a younger horse.

When they got back to the barn, he disappeared for several minutes. Then, as Virginia watched, full of curiosity, he brought out the mount David had chosen for her, already tacked up.

The moment she saw her, Virginia fell in love with the little mare. A bright chestnut he'd fittingly named Rosy for her glowing red coat, she was every bit as sweet-natured as she was pretty.

"Oh, Filipé, isn't she beautiful?"

He grinned to see her so pleased. "*Si, Señora. El Patrón* chose very carefully. And he chose well."

It didn't take long for Virginia to decide to rename the mare 'My Fancy,' for she certainly did fancy the lovely mare. She thought that 'Fancy' was close enough to 'Rosy' to save the animal any confusion in switching over.

"Thank you, Filipé. I can't wait to go adventuring around the ranch."

Smiling broadly, he answered her comment by opening the gate for her to ride Fancy out.

The boy Maria had assigned to watch over her kept a safe distance behind.

Soon, Virginia was exploring her surroundings every day, all day. The days that she had been certain would drag by seemed to fly as she explored the ranch.

As soon as she was completely confident in her mare, she rode into town for tea with Bess Johnson. She cantered the five miles to town, with one brief walk at midpoint to let both of them catch their breath, in less than a half hour. She made a point of walking the last quarter mile to cool Fancy down.

"Mrs. Norris! What a pleasant surprise." Bess looked at Fancy. "Oh, my dear, what a beautiful horse."

"Thank you. David chose her for me before he left for the east to collect me."

"And how glad we all are that he did go east to 'collect' you." Bess led the way to the apartment she and Herb lived in over the store. "The whole town is delighted with you."

"You're just being kind."

"Well, maybe not everybody. Hal Broudy probably isn't. He's never glad to see anybody."

Virginia laughed. "That's all right. Truth to tell, I wouldn't be glad to see him again, either."

Bess wrinkled her nose. "He can be a most unpleasant man."

Virginia took the cup Bess offered her. "Does anybody know why he hates David so?"

"Everybody knows. He's jealous. David's relatively new here. That's to say, he's been here fewer than ten years, and everybody likes him and applauds his success. Broudy's been here since time began and has absolutely no friends. Not even his hired hands can stand him."

"You'd think he'd figure it out. What's that saying? 'To make a friend, you have to be one'?"

"I don't think Hal Broudy understands that. The worst of it is that he has political aspirations, and no one in power will give him the time of day. On the other hand, David, in no time at all, has become their golden boy."

"Oh, dear."

"Yes. Oh, dear. Add to that the land that David bought recently that Broudy wanted, and you can see how trouble starts." She sighed. "I'm afraid he really hates your husband."

"Do you think . . . No. That's silly."

"What?" Bess wanted to know.

"You don't think he'd do David harm, do you?"

Bess only looked at Virginia and shrugged.

They tacitly agreed to change the conversation to more pleasant topics.

Bess said, "The whole town is looking forward to the barbeque when David gets back from his drive. The town council has already made signs to hang, and every woman is planning the dishes she'll bring." She grinned. "We make a big thing of barbeques in Texas."

"I hear they do in most of the south, as well. We don't raise as much cattle in the north. I suppose that's why we have town picnics, instead."

"That sounds like fun, too."

"I imagine it would be. Boston's gotten too big to do it as a single community, so it's gone to neighborhoods."

"Glory. I can't even imagine that many people."

"It's quite a crowd, all right." Virginia glanced out at the sun and rose. "Oh, dear. I really should be going, Bess. Thank you for the tea. It was lovely."

"Please come again soon." She smiled teasingly. "Now that you've learned to ride."

They walked down the stairs and turned toward the front door of the shop. As they reached it, it opened and Hal Broudy entered.

Seeing Virginia, Broudy made a point of walking so that his shoulder slammed into her as he passed. Virginia was shoved into the wall.

Herb Johnson leaped forward. "That's no way to treat a lady, Broudy!"

Virginia grabbed his arm. "Don't make an enemy for my sake, Mr. Johnson. It doesn't matter." She glared at Broudy. "*He* doesn't matter."

While Broudy glared back at Virginia, Bess came up and took her husband's other arm. "Please, dear."

Herb Johnson looked at the two women, snorted in disgust, and walked away.

Bess escorted Virginia to her horse. "Are you all right? Did he hurt you?"

"No, I'm fine. Just a little angry." She

chuckled as her mood lifted. "I'll get over being angry, but that man is still going to be a nasty character."

Bess smiled as she was expected to, but her eyes were worried. She stood and watched Virginia until she was out of sight.

Running into Broudy, or rather having Broudy run into her, had taken all the pleasure out of the trip.

Virginia was uneasy as she rode home.

The boy trailing her finally had something of interest to report to his Aunt Maria.

Virginia decided to stay on the side of the ranch farthest from town for a while. She was on top of the butte that David had said was the farthest limit she could roam. Sitting on the lovely, well-mannered chestnut mare that David had been so thoughtful to give her, Virginia looked down on Prodigal Ranch.

This was her favorite place to come. Ever since Maria and Teresa had helped her find the split skirts for her to ride in, she had regaled them with her adventures around the ranch every night at dinner.

Turning Fancy, she rode back away from the precipitous edge of the butte, back to her secret place. She hadn't even told Maria and Teresa that, away from the well-worn trail down to the ranch, she had found another trail.

She thought of it as her trail, for obviously no one had used it for a very long time. It was no more than a narrow, brush-obscured path that ran along a taller cliff face. The way was dangerous, but Fancy was surefooted, and Virginia had every confidence in her.

Nevertheless, the very first time she'd explored it, Virginia had left the little mare behind, walking the overgrown path alone. She had to be certain it was all right to bring a horse along it. She'd never risk her precious Fancy.

Later on, she'd brought a shovel from the barn—quite a feat for a small woman on horseback—and cleared much of the low brush from the trail. She'd even cleared away all the rocks she'd been able to lift or to pry off the path, flinching as she listened to the clatter they made as they bounced and spun their way to the valley floor below.

She didn't want anything to trip her mare's feet as they walked over the narrow path. She didn't want any place for one of those awful rattlesnakes to hide, either. Just thinking about them made her skin crawl and prompted a quick prayer.

She'd thought as she'd worked in the hot arid dust that she had to get it done because she'd just die if anything happened to Fancy. So she'd worked hard to create this haven for them, rider and horse.

Physically, the work had been a reward in itself. She reveled in the new strength and firmness in her arms. Amazed, too, to find it was oddly liberating to labor, she had gone at her task with a song on her lips.

It had taken her several days to get the job done, but her persistence had been rewarded beyond her wildest dreams. She'd hoped that she might find a small plateau she could set up a day camp on for picnic lunches, or even a new way to access another part of the ranch.

Instead, at the end of the cleared trail, she'd found a wonderful surprise—a tiny, abandoned cabin, full of dust and cobwebs.

When Virginia had asked Maria about it, the cook had shrugged and told her it was probably what some called a line shack. "They use them to the east of us, where some people have put fences up on their ranches. It is a place for ranch hands to spend the night when they get far from the bunkhouses, riding the fence line. For running to if you get caught out in bad weather, too."

"It is not used here," Teresa had added. "Prodigal has no fences except the ranch road and the corrals."

Virginia was pleased to have found the line shack, and even more pleased that no one used it . . . or seemed to know about it. From the moment she'd learned that the forlorn little cabin held no interest for anyone else, she'd claimed it for her own.

Over time, she'd brought little things

from the house for her comfort. Sheets and a pillow for the narrow bunk and a blanket for warmth—should she ever need one—had been added. Those items had followed the few books of poetry she'd brought from Boston. She made it a sanctuary for the times she might like to get out of the sun in the warmest part of the day but not to ride back to the house where she wouldn't be alone to savor the freedom she'd found on Prodigal.

As it had turned out, Fancy, for whom Virginia had built a crude lean-to, spent many hours there. In the hottest part of the day, Virginia often put her mare in the shade of her crude construction. Each time she led the mare into it, she smiled to think that she had, no matter how badly, built it herself.

As she sat overlooking the ranch, Virginia felt as if she wore contentment like a cloak. Certainly she felt it now.

Loving the sun on her face, she turned to face it. Today, there was a beautiful breeze, and she tipped her head back so that her broad-brimmed hat, a copy of the low-crowned one

David had worn in Boston, slid off her hair and down to rest on her back, hanging by its thin, leather *barbe geho*.

That name, 'beard grabber,' made her want to laugh. She certainly had no beard for it to grab.

Virginia laughed a lot these days. The west was all she'd hoped it would be— a place where she could come and go as she pleased and escape all the strictures of society. Her only restriction was that she be at the house when dusk came.

After hearing a coyote or two howl as she made her way back later than usual, she didn't mind that restriction at all. She didn't mind the boy Maria had appointed to watch over her, either. If she should fall, or be bitten by a snake, he would be there to help her.

Since he tried to remain unseen, she pretended she didn't know he was there. Filipé had told her what was going on when she'd pretended nervousness at being followed and asked him who he thought it could be.

She didn't even mind David's absence anymore. Though she missed him

dreadfully, she knew that only his departure had made possible this wonderful
wandering.

Suddenly, she stood in her stirrups
and shaded her eyes. Was that a cloud
of dust approaching from the west? Yes,
she was certain it was. It was following
the rough little road that entered the
ranch from that direction, so it couldn't
be stray cattle or a herd of wild horses.
Could it be David coming home?

With a broad smile, she decided it
couldn't be anything else. She sent her
mare down the trail from the top of the
butte, her heart soaring.

David was back!

CHAPTER 17

Virginia galloped all the way to the house, never mind that she knew she ought to walk the last bit to cool her mount. The whole way, she was trying to keep an eye on the dust cloud to be sure to get there first.

Dismounting in a single leap, she called to Filipé, who waited in the doorway of the barn with a startled look on his face.

Virginia begged him please to cool out her mare. As she ran off, she apologized for the necessity. Running, she called back to him, "He's home!" She caught only a glimpse of his glad expression as she left him.

Sailing across the porch, she dashed

through the house to the kitchen to alert Maria and Teresa that David was home.

When she had, she went back out on the porch to watch for him. She was so eager to tell him of the magic Prodigal had worked on her! How it had proved to her that she was free and could take care of herself and find her way on her little jaunts all over the ranch.

Now that he was home, she could hardly wait. She felt healthier and more full of energy than she ever had, too. David would be so pleased.

She waited on the porch so David would be free to give any last minute orders . . . and so that their reunion could be private. She felt a shiver of pleasure shoot through her at the thought of being in his arms again.

Finally, the little group of men turned in at the barns, where they were no doubt giving Filipé and the other men there their horses to see to. Three came out of the barn and headed off in the direction of the bunk house, and then two more exited the barn. David!

She wanted to run to meet him, but his head was bent to Bart Hastings, the foreman. No doubt, some last minute orders were being given. Finally, Hastings turned away, and David strode in her direction.

Virginia could wait no longer. Rushing off the porch, she ran to meet him. When she got to where he had stopped to stare at her, she threw herself into his arms.

David grasped her shoulders and held her away. He was shocked. Where was his beautiful bride with the pale, creamy complexion? The woman beaming up at him was still beautiful, of course, but she had *freckles* across her patrician nose and her forearms were as tan as a farmer's. Where was his perfect hostess? "What have you done to yourself, Virginia?" The words were startled out of him.

Virginia was still so bubbling over with happiness to see him that she missed the disapproval in his tone.

"Oh, David, I've missed you so. I thought I'd die of misery when you first left, but I took your advice and used the time to explore the Prodigal." She fell into step beside him. "And I love Fancy.

That's what I named the mare you gave me. She's as good a companion as some of my Bostonian friends! We go everywhere. Thank you!"

She laughed up at him. "Oh, dear. I'm so glad you're home, and I have so much to tell you that I'm babbling. I feel so free here, David. It's so open and beautiful. It's everything I'd always hoped the west would be." She smiled radiantly. "No wonder you love it so."

He stopped walking and looked down at her.

"What is it, David? What's the matter?" At last, she'd sensed that there was something amiss. Concern for him replaced her joy. "Are you all right? Did the drive go well? What's wrong?"

He stood frowning down at her for a long moment before saying, "You are, Virginia." He said it in exasperation. "Look what you've done to yourself. You look like some poor rancher's daughter." He stared down at her with a pained expression on his handsome face. "You have . . . freckles." He said it as if she had the plague.

The wonderful happiness she'd been

feeling drained out of her. She could only stare back at him.

"I chose you so that you would be a credit to Prodigal. To the ranch, to the house. I wanted you to be the grand mistress of all I've built here. I was proud of your creamy, ladylike complexion. Now . . ." David made a visible effort to gain control of his words.

It was too late. Virginia was cut to the quick. She backed away from him.

Had she suddenly lost her value to him because she'd gotten tanned as she wandered Prodigal? She was having trouble believing that, but it seemed the case.

What did he want from her? Was she to have been some cherished china doll, always staying in the shade of the house? Or maybe, she thought as her hurt gave place to anger, was she to have been kept on a shelf, only to be taken down and put on display when she was needed to impress her husband's guests?

Her heart felt as if it had sustained a blow, and the quiet tide of anger rose in her. Couldn't he see how much freer and happier she was than she had been when he met her?

Or didn't he care?

She was momentarily crushed. His disapproval was so like the constant criticism she'd endured from her mother. Must she go through that again? Had she exchanged one sort of domination for another?

Rebellion surged through her. How dare he fail her like this? Blazing anger followed hard on the heels of resentment. First, he'd abandoned her physically, going on the cattle drive; now he'd done this—this withdrawal of moral support when she needed it.

Wanting to further shock him, she said with spite in her aching heart, "Oh, and now I eat all my meals in the kitchen with Maria and Teresa."

David turned an astonished expression her way.

Her lips tightened, and she added, "The three of us have become very good friends."

Her eyes dared him to express any disapproval. After all, he'd deserted her in a strange land without first seeing to it that she had a single friend.

She'd been a little saddened by his neglect then, but now she was grateful for it. His hurtful disapproval of her appearance had shown her beyond the shadow of a doubt that he probably would have chosen as her friend some woman who would have been sure to keep her and her so valued creamy complexion locked up in the house out of the sun!

She moved two more paces away from him. They walked into the house with the widened space between them.

Why not?

David didn't seem to mind.

When they were inside, she said stiffly to this husband who had not even kissed her hello, "I shall go and tell Maria and Teresa that you're back," she said as if she hadn't already sung the news of his return to them.

Unsmiling, David said, "I feel pretty sure they know."

"Nevertheless, I shall want to plan supper." She lifted her head high and moved away from him as regally as any queen. *Any suntanned and freckled queen,* she thought maliciously.

"I'll go bathe some of this trail dust off, then." He took the stairs two at a time.

Virginia felt as if he were running from his horror of a wife. Now, standing at the foot of the grand staircase watching him go, she didn't feel rebellious and defiant any longer.

Now she just felt ill.

The wonder and the magic that she and David had shared during their trek west was gone, and the cause of his displeasure—her new-found, hard-won, and very precious freedom—was tarnished.

She didn't feel as if she could ever forgive him for that.

CHAPTER 18

Virginia felt David leave the far side of the bed he'd slept on. Then she heard him dress and quietly leave the room, closing the door softly so that he wouldn't wake her. She slowly uncurled from the tight ball of hurt she'd been all night.

David, bone-weary after the long ride back to Prodigal at the end of the cattle drive, had done nothing to mend matters between them. Virginia wasn't even certain he realized the width of the chasm that now separated them.

Last night, she'd waited for her husband to speak or at least to kiss her goodnight, but he hadn't. She tried to tell herself that it was because he was exhausted after his long cattle drive, but lying to herself was something she made it a practice never to do.

Besides, it would have been monumentally difficult when she believed she had felt waves of disapproval emanating from him.

Hurt, she turned to the comforting Friend who never failed her.

"Lord, please. Don't You be distant, too," she prayed.

I will never forsake you.

Virginia gasped as the phrase from her Bible ran through her mind. It was a promise God had made to Joshua in the Old Testament.

"Dearest Father, I have been so remiss." Hot tears of regret ran down her cheeks. "I have been so taken with my new life and the freedom You've permitted me . . . and with my new husband . . . that I have neglected You."

I came so that you could have life abundantly.

Virginia looked around the luxuriously appointed bedroom. "Yes, Lord. But I know this isn't the abundance You mean. My marriage is the abundance

You blessed me with, and now it looks as if I've lost that." She was almost sobbing now. "I don't know if I can ever get it back."

You can do all things through Him who strengthens you.

Virginia gulped down the last of her tears. Sitting up on the edge of the bed, she straightened her back and threw her chin up. "Yes, Lord. Yes, Lord, I can!"

With a last determined sniff, she wiped her eyes on the fine lawn of her nightgown's sleeve and went to her dressing room. There she began to pull on her riding clothes as if the house were on fire. After dragging a brush through the tangle of her hair, she ran for the stairs.

When she came to the first landing on the wide staircase, she turned right instead of running left and down into the formal part of the house. Hurrying down the butler's stairs to the kitchen she muttered, "Butler's stairs. Butlers. I suppose that I must carry on with my duties, even if I am as displeased with my husband as he seems to be with me.

"Sulking is always counterproductive,

and I really must get us a butler if David is going to go on with his dratted dinner parties. I might as well get on with it."

"Yes, *Señora*, you called?" Teresa was peering up at her from the bottom of the narrow staircase. She'd obviously overheard Virginia talking to herself.

Virginia plunged down the last few steps.

Teresa leaped aside.

"Sorry, Teresa. I'm in a rush. Could I have some toast and tea, please?"

Maria looked up from the stove, startled. "*Señora!*" She laughed at her young mistress. "What energy so early!"

Virginia ran across the room and gave her a hug. "I have to get out of the house for the day." She ignored the troubled look that passed between her two friends. "Can you pack me a picnic lunch? A small one?"

"*Sí*, Little One, Maria can pack up a part of the large breakfast the *Señor* ordered me to take up to you." The cook had stopped hiding the affectionate name by which she called Virginia when Filipé had told her that Virginia had caught on to being followed and had accepted it.

Virginia whirled to look at the table, where she saw a large tray covered with a cloth. David had no doubt eaten at the crack of dawn. "Heavens," she said as she uncovered the food. "There's enough here for all three of us."

The two servants smiled, their fondness for her evident in their faces. "*Sí*," they agreed.

"Fine! Sit. We'll eat it. We'll pack me a lunch from what's left." She rushed to a cupboard and pulled out dishes for them. "Teresa," she ordered, "cups."

Maria chuckled and began to serve the three plates her mistress plunked down in front of her from the items on Virginia's breakfast tray. "Do you want eggs, Little One? They are not on your tray. They would get cold."

Virginia looked at the bounty on the overloaded tray. "I think we can manage with this, don't you?"

Both her guests agreed, and they began their breakfast of fruits, sliced ham, and toast.

"Why are you dressed for riding?" Teresa asked.

Virginia sighed. "I have to get away from this house and seek some solace."

Maria instantly smiled and nodded. Turning to Teresa, she said, "The Little One speaks of God."

Virginia rode out to her favorite place—the tall, distant butte that overlooked the ranch. They'd made good time, she and her mare.

Perched on the great rock above the ranch, she could see the house and barns and bunkhouse in the distance far away. Closer to her, she could see the huge clouds of dust from the hooves of thousands of steers being rounded up for all the things that had to be done before the next cattle drive. Very faintly, she could hear the bawling of the steers. It made her glad she wasn't closer to them.

For an instant, Virginia thought she could see her husband sitting on his big bay, Crusader. He was at a little distance from one group of his men, up on a bank from which he could look down, directing their actions.

If all had been well between them, the sight of David at work would have thrilled her. As matters stood, however, the hurt she still felt at his disappointment in her appearance kept her from admitting that she had any pride in him.

Obviously, her assumption that he returned the deep feelings she'd developed for him was in error. David didn't love her. He couldn't have spoken to her as he had if he did. Worse, he couldn't have let the sun go down on his anger, going to sleep without so much as a 'good-night.'

She had foolishly believed what her heart had wanted to believe. Now she was paying the price.

She had to brace herself against unshed tears as she admitted that she didn't have a place here as David Norris's wife. Her place—the place David had planned for her all along—wasn't as a wife. It was as a mere decoration for the magnificent house he'd built.

Determinedly, she blinked away tears

that threatened to blur the scene before her. So she'd been mistaken about David returning her love. Well, she wasn't the first woman ever to make such a mistake, and she was certain she wouldn't be the last.

She lifted her chin. She would find a way to live with her devastating disappointment. Somehow.

Turning Fancy, she sought the comfort afforded her by the dilapidated little cabin and the Bible she kept there. Time spent in that marvelous book had always proved a balm to her spirit, and she needed it now more than ever.

David was back, and all her dreams lay like broken pieces of pottery—in shards around her new-found freedom.

CHAPTER 19

Back of the butte on her private plateau, Virginia hooked her boot heels on the edge of the boulder in front of her hideaway and looked onto the great valley. *David had been right about the boots being comfortable*, she mused.

She was the one who had been wrong. Wrong about the boots, wrong about everything.

She'd thought she was escaping the strictures of Boston society by coming to the wonderful west. Instead, she found that she had also come to a society almost without laws.

Maria was always telling her to be careful of strange riders. Teresa darkly warned her about the awful Hal Broudy.

Virginia had seen him twice now— once when she arrived and again when she'd ridden into town to have tea with Bess Johnson. Hal Broudy was not only unpleasant, he was also her husband's sworn enemy. At their last meeting, she'd known that he was deliberately shoving her into walls so that she'd tell David.

David would, no doubt, take the matter up with Broudy, and things would get dangerous. Someone was sure to get hurt.

She'd sworn the Johnsons to secrecy and vowed never to tell her husband herself.

Virginia shifted on her rock and shook her head. She refused to worry. There was certainly nothing she could do about it.

There was nothing she could do but pray, and since she had left the house this morning so that she could spend time with her Creator, it seemed to fit right in.

Right now, though, she needed comfort from her Heavenly Father.

She slid off her perch and went into

the little cabin. Reaching under the pillow on the narrow bunk, she pulled out a Bible. It was one that she had found on a shelf in her husband's study. Its pristine condition told her that David must keep his personal Bible somewhere else.

She'd been unwilling to bring her own precious, well-thumbed King James to the shack, for fear that field mice might gnaw it. She'd had her Bible since she was a child. It had been an award for perfect attendance at Sunday School back when her world had been a very different place.

She sat with the borrowed Bible in her lap, her hands clasped prayerfully on it. "Dearest Father, Thank You for Your Word. Please help me understand the plan I know You have for my life."

She let the peace of sitting quietly with the inspired word of almighty God wash over her.

She'd always been awed by the fact that sixty-six men over thousands of years could pen a book so interwoven that men still sought to understand and be comforted by it.

When she thought of the many prophecies in it that had already been fulfilled to the letter, she wondered how anyone could doubt that it had been inspired by God.

"Lord," she said at last, "I'm here because I don't see what it is that You want me to do."

Part of a scripture came to her. She remembered it was from Proverbs. It was something about seeking wisdom. Well, she was certainly doing just that.

After a moment, she sighed and opened the Bible on her lap. It fell open to Psalm 100. She knew it by heart. "Make a joyful noise unto the Lord," she whispered. That would be hard to do just now, when she felt as if every hope was dashed and her life was in shards, but she'd try.

She'd try to enter His gates with thanksgiving, too. Praising Him was easy—just looking around as she rode, she found lovely flowers and beautiful vistas that sent her praising their Creator.

Now, it was time to do what she'd come up here for. Virginia bowed her head. "Thank You, Father, for David. I know that You'll solve the problem that has arisen between us, because I know You brought us together."

She felt a small twinge of conscience. Had she precipitated her fate by answering the advertisement? Should she have waited for a clearer sign from God?

She sat quietly considering the question. The thought came to her that her father had always told her that you can't steer a boat that is not underway. She just hoped that she hadn't gotten underway by her own precipitous actions.

Maybe it was time to be a little more obedient. Thanks were in order for a great many things. She took a deep breath. "Thank You for my safe arrival here. Thank You for Maria and for Teresa. And for Fancy."

The mare whickered softly at the mention of her name. The sound brought the first real smile of the day to her mistress's face. The heaviness in Virginia's heart eased a little.

Heaving a great sigh of surrender she

asked, "Lord, please. Just tell me what to do."

By the time she got back to the ranch, it was late afternoon. She remembered that they were having an early supper, and the knowledge lent wings to her feet.

Virginia left Fancy at the barn and hurried to the house. She ran up the stairs, grabbed her robe from the bedroom and headed for the bathing room.

She had taken more time to get back than she'd meant to. She always rode more slowly when she was trying to listen to her Maker. Now she knew she'd have to hurry to get to the dining room in time to have supper with David.

After her bath, which she made a hasty affair instead of the usual long soak she so enjoyed, she slipped into a simple dress that she could manage without disturbing Teresa for assistance. Tying her damp hair back with a ribbon that exactly matched her gown, she hurried downstairs to the formal dining room.

David was standing at the fireplace, one elbow resting on the mantelpiece. The expression on his face told her nothing. Without a word he walked to her chair and drew it away from the table for her.

"Thank you," Virginia said quietly.

"You're welcome."

Teresa served them. They ate without conversation, Virginia only picking at her food.

As Teresa placed slices of apple pie in front of them, David smiled. "My favorite. Thank Maria for me."

Teresa bobbed her head in ascent, then shot a troubled glance at Virginia.

Feeling she had to say something to reassure the tall maid, Virginia offered, "Yes, Teresa. Please thank Maria for our lovely dinner. And thank you for serving it."

She'd rather have eaten it in the kitchen with friends than here in all this cheerless formality with her cold husband. That wasn't possible, of course.

Teresa nodded again and left the room.

David cleared his throat. "Where were you today?"

Virginia, who had been so excitedly eager to show him all that she had accomplished in his absence, suddenly didn't want this changed David to know anything about the line shack. Her secret hideaway was just that now—her secret. And she wanted to keep it far from this cold stranger who had been her beloved David.

She really didn't want this disapproving man to come and see her pitiful efforts.

She cleared her throat in her turn. She wouldn't lie to her husband; she just wouldn't tell him the whole truth. Even if that idea bothered her, she was determined to adhere to it.

Virginia regarded her husband steadily. What could she honestly tell him without giving him access to her wounded heart? "I went exploring on Fancy. We do that a lot." It sounded flat.

It certainly didn't seem to matter. David wasn't the least bit interested. Never mind. He probably didn't care what she did, anyway. He certainly wasn't asking her to elaborate about her adventures.

"I wish you would . . ." David began and stopped when he saw the look in her eyes. Great Scott! She looked as if she thought he might confine her to the house.

Why would she think he'd do such a thing? He forced himself to consider his extreme reaction to her appearance and his tactless treatment of her from her point of view.

Maybe that *had* been what he'd started to say. He didn't know himself. He *had* been angry about her tan. Until he saw it, he'd no idea that he'd treasured her creamy complexion so much. But she was still Virginia, still bright and still beautiful.

In fact, looking at her now, with the soft glow the sun had given her skin, he felt like an utter fool. Had he really thought he could bring an intelligent, active, curious woman from Boston's cool, damp climate to the sun-filled southwest and have her stay as pale as she had been back east?

Shocked at the change when he'd

first seen her, he'd behaved badly and now, he didn't know how to fix it. That made him uncomfortable. He didn't consider helplessness a masculine trait.

He felt like the meanest cad who'd ever been born to have upset her as much as he obviously had.

Virginia, unaware of David's inner turmoil and determined to be polite, tried to ease the moment. "How did your cattle drive go?"

"It went well." He cast about in his mind for something to add. "Things were pretty bleak on the reservation by the time we got the beeves there."

"Reservation?" Virginia was truly puzzled.

"Yes. I drove the herd west, not east to the railhead market. Meat was badly needed on the reservation by those who used to roam free on this land."

He was speaking so casually! Virginia could hardly take in his words.

David didn't notice. "The prices aren't as good from the army, of course, but it is the least I can do for the people who might have been driven off Prodigal."

"Driven off Prodigal!" Virginia was shocked.

"The government had the army remove them so they could be better taken care of and so this part of the west could be opened up for settlement." It was David's turn to look puzzled. "I thought everyone knew that."

Virginia's eyes were blazing. Latent hurt and anger blended with this fresh outrage. "Possibly. I don't know."

Clearly, she was very badly rattled. "I certainly never thought I'd be living on land stolen from the people who had lived on it for centuries! I never thought I'd be married to someone who profits from their misery!" She was standing now and threw her napkin down on the table as men used to throw down a glove to challenge an opponent to a duel.

"Profits from their misery!" David was on his feet now. "For God's sake, Virginia, didn't I just tell you I was instrumental in seeing them fed?"

Virginia gasped, appalled. "David!" His name was a shocked cry. "Christians," she said with heat, "do *not* take the Lord's name in vain!"

David lost his temper. "And just who in the blazes told you I was a Christian?" He threw his napkin on the table, as if answering her challenge.

Virginia's mouth dropped open. Knees buckling, she fell back into her chair. Her eyes were wide, shocked and accusing.

She couldn't catch her breath. When she could finally speak, her words came out in a choked whisper, her words separated by gasps. "You . . . aren't . . . a Christian?"

Her distress took every vestige of anger from David. Wishing with all his heart that there was some way he could soften what he knew was a blow, he said quietly, "No, Virginia, I'm not."

CHAPTER 20

Virginia told David she planned to sleep in one of the guest rooms that night. She'd left the dining room in a flurry of skirts, running in pain and distress from what she couldn't yet grasp.

She couldn't believe it. As many times as she'd read the warning against it in the Bible, she was unequally yoked. David wasn't a Christian! And she'd foolishly thought that the man who advertised for a Christian wife would have to be a Christian, himself. There hadn't been the slightest doubt in her mind. She'd been so *sure* that he was a Christian.

She fought her confusion. David behaved like a Christian!

She forced herself to consider the

matter as calmly as she could manage. He wasn't a Christian, but he had been raised in a Judeo-Christian society, of course. And he was a gentleman. That was why he'd always bowed his head when she said grace over their campfire meals on the trail.

She'd suspected nothing when he'd insisted she be the one to offer their thanks to God. She realized at that moment that it was his way of avoiding to offer thanks for their meals as he properly should have done as the head of their household.

No wonder he'd been embarrassed at that first dinner! She'd forced him to say grace in front of his guests. What a fool she had been!

She'd been deceived . . . But wait! Even though it hurt, she had to be fair. Hadn't she helped in that deception? Hadn't she believed it because she wanted to? Because she wanted to escape Boston and her domineering mother?

When David had come to Boston, hadn't she taken one look at the tall, handsome Texan with the sun-streaked hair and laughing gray eyes and counted herself lucky?

Lucky. She had counted herself lucky. Not *blessed,* but lucky. That had been her first misstep.

Had she even once asked God if she was doing the right thing to marry David? Had she asked if this was *His* plan for her? Had she waited for the Father to give her His peace to tell her she was making the right choice?

For that matter, had she even consulted Him before she answered the advertisement that Dorothy had torn out of the newspaper and given to her?

No, no and no! *No to all of it.*

She had been deceived, all right. Self-deceived!

She buried her head in the pillow of her strange bed and wept hot, quiet tears. Her heart actually hurt, and it didn't help to realize that every bit of the pain she was feeling was of her own making.

There was no one to blame but herself. She had known that she should pray before making important decisions. She knew she should always wait to see if she would be granted peace from her Maker concerning them.

And why hadn't she?

The truth smashed into her mind with the force of a locomotive. Ever since William had been killed, she—Virginia Anne Davenport Warner Norris—had been angry with God.

She cringed inside at that realization. She'd been remiss in everything pertaining to God, but she continued to want Him to bless her. What hypocrisy!

"Oh, Father, I am so sorry!" she cried aloud. "Please forgive me and come back to me."

I never left you.

At this answer, spoken in the recesses of her heart, Virginia vowed never to forget again that her first love should always be Jesus. She'd been embittered by William's death, embittered to the point of rebellion, and then she'd been distracted by David. And all of it had brought her to the point of neglecting her God. "Oh, dearest Lord, can You forgive me?"

She felt Him smile. It was the oddest, most wonderful sensation. He *did* forgive her—had already forgiven her. She thought she could feel Him laugh with triumphant joy. Hadn't He come and died to forgive the sins of those who did and would believe in Him?

"Of course," she murmured, "that's what You do best, isn't it?"

With the ear of her heart she heard her Lord say, *There is no condemnation for those who are in Me.*

Happy tears streaming down her face, she slid off the bed. "I'm coming to talk to You, Lord. Please be there in the line shack for me."

Lo, I am always with you.

A long minute later, hoping to keep David from hearing her, she ran barefoot down the great staircase, her riding clothes and her boots clasped to her chest. Sitting down on the first chair she came to, Virginia dressed in her riding clothes as quickly as she could. As soon as she was fully clad, she drifted to the front door, her boots again clamped to her chest.

Outside, she thrust her feet into them and ran for the barn. She knew that all the barn men, having finished their work for the day, would be at supper. She'd be able to make her escape unnoticed.

Inside, she went straight to Fancy's stall. Fancy hung her head out over the door and greeted her with a low whicker.

"Shh!" Virginia held a finger to her lips to hush her. She didn't want anyone to hear the mare. She wanted to leave without being noticed.

Thanks to the length of the summer days—and the fact that David had wanted an early supper so that he could work on the ranch payroll—she and Fancy would be safely up on the butte and in their hideaway before darkness came. Virginia still didn't feel quite safe riding on the ranch after nightfall, and Maria and Teresa strictly forbade her to do it.

"Coyotes and snakes are out at night, Little One," Maria had told her solemnly. Shaking her finger at Virginia she had ordered her mistress, "So you should not go."

Fancy took a quick turn around her stall, then came back to the door where

Virginia stood. Virginia had her tacked up in no time.

Mounting, she sent the little mare out of the barn at a trot, ducking as she rode through the door. When they were clear of the building, they galloped off in the direction of the butte and their hide-away, hurrying to beat the sunset.

David looked up from his desk. The sound of galloping hooves sent him to the porch. There was no sign of a horse-man, and all looked peaceful.

Yawning, he stretched, checked the tall clock in the foyer, and started back to his desk. It was still an hour or so be-fore sunset. Maybe one of the men was trying out a new mount.

Then he startled to a halt. Virginia! He'd no idea if she was all right.

She'd been dreadfully upset at dinner by his declaration that he was not a Christian. She'd gone so far as to tell him she intended to sleep alone tonight. He'd understood that she was disconcerted and hadn't tried to interfere with her intention.

He hadn't tried to make matters right between them, either. Surely, though, she hadn't been upset enough with him to leave the house without a word, had she?

Now *he* was upset.

Nothing would do but that he go up to check on her. He headed for the guest wing. All the doors stood open as usual, and one of them showed a bed with rumpled bedclothes, but there was no sign of his wife.

"Virginia!" he bellowed.

Silence answered.

David ran down to the servants' quarters. "Maria!"

"*Sí, Señor*?" Maria appeared in answer to his shout.

Teresa stuck her head out of the door across the hall from Maria's. "*Qué pasa*?"

"*Señora* Norris is not here," David told them. "She's left the house. Do you or Teresa have any idea where she could have gone?"

The women looked at each other. Finally, Maria spoke. "*La Señora* tells Teresa and me about a place she has made for herself."

"A place for herself?" He was incredulous. "Where?"

David fought down his impatience. Anxiety gnawed at him. Virginia had left the house. Soon, she'd be out in the night, and he didn't know where. He cast a glance out the window. The sky was darkening.

The ranch was perfectly safe during the day, with the men scattered over it working cattle and the sun hot enough to keep snakes from appearing. Night, though, was a different matter.

Anything could happen to her, and he couldn't protect her. Cougars, snakes, even having her horse step in a prairie dog hole—the hazards on Prodigal were multiplied by darkness, and darkness was on its way.

"We don' know where, *Señor* David," Teresa told him. "Maria let Miguel stop following her when he told us everywhere she went she was safe."

Maria offered reluctantly, "*Sí, es verdad*. That is true. But the *Señora* was asking us about deserted cabins." She shot a look at Teresa. "Is that not so, Teresa?"

"*Sí.*"

"She said no more than that?"

The women shook their heads.

"Thank you." He turned away and hurried off.

How would he find Virginia, though? He'd never known of a cabin on Prodigal. With no fences, they'd had no need to build line shacks. Where could she be?

He was past worry and coming up on frantic by the time he headed for the old ranch house that had become his foreman's place. Pounding on the door when he reached it, he told himself that Virginia was no foolish girl to run off into the evening without some safe haven in mind. The thought did nothing to calm his nerves, however.

Finally, Hastings opened the door, a fork in his hand. "Is something wrong, boss?"

"Mrs. Norris and I had a quarrel, and she's gone off. I have to know if you can remember any cabin or line shack on Prodigal."

Hastings took only an instant to think. "No, I can't say that I've ever seen one. Never heard tell of one, either."

David's heart sank. Where could she be? He didn't even know in which direction to look for her.

"Get the men mounted," he ordered. "Send them out in parties to look for my wife. It'll be dark soon. I can't have her out in the night alone."

"Yes, sir!"

"Have whoever finds her fire three shots."

"Yes, sir."

David ran to the barn for Crusader. He didn't know what he'd do if any harm came to Virginia.

He'd planned to apologize to her at dinner. To tell her she was beautiful tan and that he'd been a prime idiot to have acted the way he did.

He'd intended to take her in his arms and tell her how much he'd missed her while he was on the drive and to smother her with the kisses he should have given her when he arrived and first saw her. Saw her all shining and full of joy—joy that he'd driven out of her lovely eyes by acting like a churlish moron.

Then at dinner they'd had that stupid quarrel.

"Blast it!" he said aloud, and Crusader turned his head around to look at him as he tightened the latigo on his saddle.

"Crusader," he spoke to the animal, "tonight, a jackass is going to ride a horse, because that's exactly what I've been." He swung up into the saddle and trotted the big bay out of the barn.

"When I find her, I'm going to kiss every one of those freckles," he promised himself grimly.

Unaware of the teams of men out searching the ranch for her, Virginia arrived safely at her cabin. The last bit of daylight had begun to fail as she navigated the path to it, and when she had finished making Fancy comfortable in the lean-to it was almost gone.

When she opened the door, it was quite dim inside. She went to where the oil lamp sat on its tiny table and lifted the chimney.

She struck a match and applied it to the wick. Immediately, the cabin was filled with a warm glow. Then she turned the wick down and put the chimney carefully back on the lamp.

Sitting on the edge of the narrow cot, she reached under the bunk's pillow and pulled out the Bible she kept there. Here she was again, in need of comfort.

Folding her hands, she bowed her head and prayed. "Lord, I really need You to tell me what it is You want me to do.

"I don't know what my place is, or even whether I'm to stay here. It seems to me that David doesn't want me any-more, and now that I know that he's not a Christian and that we're unequally yoked, I simply don't know what You want me to do. Please guide me, Lord."

David had ridden like a madman over the whole front part of the ranch without finding any sign of Virginia. Finally, he decided to go up on the big butte over-looking the ranch to see if he could catch a glimpse of Virginia and her mare.

Daylight had almost faded, and his anxiety for her safety rose in direct pro-portion to the rate at which the sun was setting. If he had any chance of seeing her, it would have to be soon.

As he approached the butte, he saw a dim glow in the distance, and then it had receded. He turned Crusader and rode back to where it had appeared.

Yes! There was an even tinier light showing on the face of the cliff at the back of the butte. He didn't know how that could be, as there was no real con-nection between the butte and the cliff that rose behind it and the cliff had a sheer face. Nevertheless, he had no in-tention of letting that soft bit of light go uninvestigated.

He pushed Crusader hard to get to the top of the butte. If there was a chance that Virginia was up there with a small camp fire, or just a candle, then he was going to find her.

Arriving at the top, he was at a loss as to where to go next. The problem was solved when Crusader whinnied so hard it shook him in the saddle.

A whinny answered from somewhere in back of the butte.

Puzzled and elated, David let his horse have his head, and Crusader began to pick the way. Soon, David was riding the narrow path Virginia had cleared.

He was amazed that he'd never seen it before. Someone had done a great deal of work to open it. At the end of the rough trail, he was astonished to find a plateau hidden against the cliff face.

The dilapidated cabin Maria and Teresa had told him about stood in its center. There was a ramshackle lean-to beside it.

Crusader showed an eagerness to join the horse standing in it, and after a moment, David recognized Fancy. Relief flooded him.

Dismounting, he let the big horse go and walked quietly to the line shack's door. It was open to the balmy night, and inside, in the gentle glow of an oil lamp, was his wife.

Kneeling at the side of a narrow bunk, her dark head bowed over her clasped hands, she was praying. So intent was she on her prayers that she never heard him until he was standing at her side.

"Virginia," he said quietly.

She leaped up. "David!"

He opened his arms and said, "I'm sorry," in a ravaged whisper.

Virginia, who had learned in her prayer time just what it was that the Lord wanted her to do, walked into them.

Many words and kisses later, they found the bunk was not too narrow, after all.

Chapter 21

When she awoke in the morning, Virginia found David fully clothed and lying beside her on the narrow bunk. He was wide awake and leaning on his elbow, simply looking down at her. His blond hair was ever so slightly tousled, and his silver gray eyes were full of love.

"Good morning." Virginia's greeting was full of joy.

"Yes, it's a beautiful morning." He smiled. "Would you like to go exploring today?"

Virginia could hardly believe her ears. Was David actually going to take time off and go wandering with her? Her answering smile was radiant.

"Shall I take that for a yes?"

"Yes! I would love to explore Prodigal with you."

"Good. Let's start with a swim."

"You don't even know if I can swim."

"I'd be willing to bet."

"Umm. Suppose you just wait and see." She gave him a pert look and rose, pulling the sheet with her and wrapping it around herself.

"All right, I will." With that he caught her up in his arms and, holding her tightly against his chest, left the cabin.

"David," she screeched, "I'm not dressed."

"You're dressed just right for a swim."

"David! Put me down this instant."

"What? And have you running around out here, wrapped in a sheet? Never! What if somebody saw you?"

"Now you're being silly. Who in the world could possibly see me out here?"

"Well, I'm taking no chances." He walked purposefully toward the lean-to where the horses waited.

Virginia was surprised to see both mounts saddled and bridled and eager to go. She was tremendously relieved to see her clothes slung behind David's saddle.

He called Crusader and the big bay came to them. Seemingly without effort, David stepped up into the saddle with Virginia in his arms.

Virginia was through worrying about dressing. It was too pleasant to rest against David's chest and listen to the slow steady beat of his heart.

Today was going to be a wonderful day. Her own heart was beating faster with the expectation of it.

David rode down from the butte. Instead of going toward the house and the river, though, he turned and rode back alongside it.

Virginia felt a little thrill of excitement. David was going to take her into the part of Prodigal that he'd told her he didn't want her to explore without him.

Before long, the terrain changed from the open pastures and wide vistas of the land in front of the butte reaching toward the house. There were more trees here and the grass was greener and softer, and got even greener as it sloped down toward the river that flowed through Prodigal.

"Where are we going, David?" Virginia asked, not really caring as long as she could go there as she was, carried in her husband's arms.

"You'll see."

Soon she heard water splashing down as if they were approaching a waterfall. "David? Do I hear a waterfall?"

"Uh-huh. I thought you might like to bathe before you dress."

"Are you serious?"

"Never more so. This is one of the reasons I didn't want you going past the butte until I could come with you."

She shot him a coy look. "You didn't want to share this with me? You told me I couldn't go any farther than the butte. Were you keeping something as wonderful as a waterfall from me all this time only because you wanted me to see it with you?"

"No."

"Why then? And while I'm asking questions, what were the three shots I heard last night after we'd gone to sleep?"

He grinned at her. "You must really have gone to sleep if you didn't realize that I was the one firing the shots. I left the cabin so I wouldn't startle you with them. I only went as far as the butte to fire 'em, though. The shots were to tell the other men hunting for you that they could give up the search and go to bed."

"Oh." Suddenly she was concerned for the men who were worried for her and lost their rest so they could hunt for her. She wondered if she could have saved them their trouble and decided there was no way she could have come off by herself as she had if she had told anyone she was going.

She had a pretty good idea that David wouldn't have permitted her to escape the house so close to dark. Still, she regretted keeping Bart and the rest of the men up searching for her.

Of course, David could have fired those three shots a good deal earlier.

"And," David was saying, "the reason I didn't want you to explore this area alone and enjoy the waterfall and its pool is that I didn't want to share *you* with the cougars that drink at it."

Virginia lunged up out of his arms so quickly that she nearly slid off the horse. "Cougars!"

"Well, some people call 'em mountain lions, but I always think of lions as having manes, don't you?"

"David!" She still hadn't settled back into his arms and was regarding him with a mixture of disbelief and mild resentment. "Are you joking?"

"No, Bride." He shifted her closer, securing her against him again. "There are all sorts of wild life back in here where there are more trees for their cover and the waterfall's pool to drink from."

"What sort of wild life?"

"Deer, an occasional bear, lots of smaller animals like rabbits and such. The combination of water and animals to feed on means cougars." He looked down at her. "I don't want you out here alone."

"I must admit, with all that to worry about, I'm glad to have you here with me."

At that moment, Fancy, who had been

patiently trailing Crusader, broke into a trot and passed them, pushing her way through the brush toward the water. Crusader, given his head, trotted after her.

They arrived almost immediately at a small area of sand that made a little beach. It was a lovely spot next to the wide pool into which the waterfall was splashing.

The horses dropped their muzzles into the sparkling water and began to drink.

"Oh, David, this is lovely."

David dismounted with her in his arms, and moved to the edge of the pool. He stood there a while, just holding her against his chest, then he began to grin.

Virginia felt the subtle change in his body. "Oh, no!" Reading his intent, she wrapped her arms around his neck in a fierce grip. "Don't you dare even think of throwing me in there!"

David gave a huge sigh. "Bride, you just don't want me to have any fun."

"No, I don't. Not when it involves throwing me into a pool." Seeing she

wasn't changing his mind, she tried
something else. She looked up at him
through half-closed eyes, hoping to hide
her intended deception from him. "You
don't even know whether or not I can
swim."

He looked at her through his own
hooded eyes. He set her gently away
from him, and kissed her softly. Then
she saw his grin turn evil.

Before she could react, he whipped
the sheet off her. "Time we found out."
He gave her a shove.

Virginia hit the water with a splash
and disappeared.

After a long moment, when she hadn't
resurfaced, David's grin was gone. Panicked, he cried, "Virginia!" He dropped
his gun belt and plunged in after her.

The minute he was under water, Virginia grabbed him and took him to the
bottom. He retaliated by crushing her to
him.

David got his feet under him and
pushed off mightily, sending them
shooting up into the light again. Virginia
was laughing so hard she couldn't catch
her breath.

David treaded water, holding her up, enjoying her laughter. "Looks like you can swim after all, Bride."

"Race you across." She bent her knees and brought her feet up. Before David knew what she was doing, she placed them on his chest and straightened her legs. Shoving off from her husband not only gave her a head start but also knocked the wind out of David. She was halfway across the pool before he struck out in pursuit.

Swimming strongly, David caught her just as she was about to touch the bank at the other side of the pool. He grabbed her ankle and pulled her backwards before she could. Then he slammed a hand into the bank signifying his win, while Virginia cried, "No fair!"

"Oh, and I suppose using me to push off to get a head start was?"

"Umm."

"There goes that sound again. What does it mean this time?"

"It means that every husband should be happy to help his wife get ahead."

He laughed at her, but didn't disagree. Turning lazily away, he smiled at

her over his shoulder, reached out, and
took a stroke, leaving her.

Virginia watched him as he moved
through the water as sleekly as a seal.
Then she pushed herself away from the
bank and swam after him.

He was waiting when she got to the
other side of the pool, standing there in
his soaking wet jeans. He was watching
her as she reached the bank.

"Turn your back so that I can come
out, David."

He stood still, grinning.

"David!"

Finally, he turned and walked to the
horses. Taking her clothes from behind
his saddle, he waited for her to call him,
knowing she would. She would want
him to keep his back turned to preserve
her modesty as she rose from the water.
He sighed and muttered, "But I sure
don't want to."

Virginia caught up the sheet he'd
snatched from her and wrapped it
around herself. Going to him, she slid
her arms around his waist and rested
her cheek on the firm muscles of his
bare back. "Oh, David. This is so won-

derful. I can't tell you how much I'm enjoying today."

"Are you, Bride?" He turned so he could see her face.

"You know I am." She smiled up at him. "We're together for the first time to do something that is just for us. Usually, if you're even home, you're worrying with something about the ranch." Her smiled faded. "Or worse still, thinking up ways to further your ambitions."

For an instant, Virginia looked as if she regretted her last statement, then she took a breath and plunged on. "David, isn't Prodigal enough?" Her eyes took on a sadness that almost broke his heart as she whispered, "Aren't *I* enough?"

He stood looking down at her, his face expressionless. Then he bent down and kissed her softly. "I love you, Virginia."

"And I love you, David. With all my heart, I love you. My whole happiness rests in you . . . and in God."

David flinched as if she'd hit him. "Let's not bring Him into it."

"But . . ." She stopped speaking

when he laid a gentle finger across her
lips.

"Don't try to take me there, Bride.
Don't spoil our day."

She surrendered. She felt as if he'd
thrust a knife in her heart. "I'll go dress,"
she told him, reaching for her clothes.

David handed them to her, and she
was able to turn away before the tears
came. Walking into a stand of young
trees, she started to dress.

Her heart was crying out for answers.
Why couldn't she talk with David about
God? Surely, he knew that the Lord was
central to her life.

She had no choice but to honor his
request that she not bring God into their
day. How could she not, though, when
every beautiful thing David was showing
her was His creation?

She wept quiet tears as she dressed.
When she had finished, she wiped them
away.

Straightening her clothes, she ran her
fingers through her hair, took the ribbon
out of the pocket of her skirt, and tied
it back as neatly as she could. She
pinched her cheeks to bring color into

them, in case her sorrow had made her pale. Without a mirror, she could do no more.

She came out of the trees with a smile on her face. Today, she was determined, was going to stay a special day.

David had said that today was their day.

Virginia was going to savor it to the full, this—almost—perfect day.

CHAPTER 22

Virginia was terribly glad that things between David and her were resolved. Things weren't *mended,* but they *were* resolved.

Now, too, they had shared a perfect day.

Unfortunately, still there remained a very great difference standing between them. The resolution made it possible for them to live together harmoniously, and although Virginia was far from content, David was pleased and relaxed.

With all her heart, Virginia wished that David were a Christian. That would have mended everything. It broke her heart that she couldn't discuss the joy of knowing God with him. She prayed fervently that he would soon accept Jesus as his Lord and Savior.

God had given her instructions during her prayer time up in the cabin. God expected her to live with David as his helpmate, and that had made going into her husband's arms when he found her at the cabin the most natural and pleasant thing in the world.

Knowing that they were truly one flesh in God's eyes gave her peace. Regardless of her dismay on learning that she had married a nonbeliever, that fact was of great comfort to her.

Nor, she realized, had any of the rest of the time she had spent poring over her Bible been wasted as she'd sat there in the cabin behind the butte. In reading, she had gleaned much to help her understand what the Lord expected of her as David's wife.

The most comfort of all came to her when she found in First Peter that she was instructed to live with David in harmony and in hopes that her example would lead him to the Lord. That couldn't be hard. She knew now that she truly, deeply loved him. No power on Earth could change the way she felt. She was certain, too, that David loved her in return.

Virginia was willing to bloom where God had planted her.

She also prayed every night, as well as every time during the day that she thought of him, that David would come to get to know the Lord. She wanted him to experience the peace and happiness she had always felt, knowing that she belonged to Him.

She also spent a great deal of time praying for his safety. She couldn't shake the feeling that Hal Broudy was a real threat to him.

Even though she didn't eat her meals with Maria and Teresa now that David was home, she did make it a habit at least to have tea with them every afternoon.

This afternoon was no exception. While she sipped her tea, Maria reminded her to be careful of strange riders, but especially Hal Broudy.

"With half of our men away on the cattle drive to Lubbock, Teresa and I will be watching that *hombre*, you can bet."

Virginia smiled to think the women

thought they could be much of a deterrent if Hal Broudy decided to act up, but she took their warnings to heart. Even so, she didn't let that curtail her activities.

Today, she decided to ride into town to check on the mail and visit with Bess Johnson. Fancy's canter, or lope as she'd found people out here called the gait, ate up the miles, and within the hour, she had arrived at the distance she knew she must walk her precious friend to cool her out before she reached the hitching post in front of Johnson's Mercantile.

David's insistence that the fenced ranch road be kept in near-perfect condition made the trip a real pleasure. Gates at either end made sure it stayed that way.

Virginia hadn't the knack of opening the gates from Fancy's back and was doubly glad she wasn't riding sidesaddle, since she had to dismount and remount after each gate.

Thanks to the gates and the fencing, though, no rider had to wait for a herd of cows to get out of the way, nor have his mount trip in some hole carved in the road by one. There were no bumps for those who drove carriages or wagons on it, either.

Such thoughtful care made for a peaceful and speedy passage, and Virginia was glad that it was her David who had made it possible. He spared no effort to make Prodigal a wonderful place to be, and she was becoming as proud of the ranch as he was.

In town, Bess was delighted to see her. "Come in, Mrs. Norris."

She smiled. "Virginia. I thought we'd settled that on my last visit."

"Virginia, then." Bess was pleased as punch to have been given permission to use her new friend's first name, and it showed in the glow of her welcoming smile. "Go get your mail, then come on up. I'll go put water on for our tea." She ran to the stairs that led up to the Johnsons' apartment over the store, stopped at their foot and turned to say, "I'm so glad you could come."

"So am I."

Bess ran up the stairs, and Virginia said hello to Herb as she retrieved the mail from the cubbyhole marked in Bess's neat printing, 'Norris/Prodigal Ranch.' She went through it as she climbed the stairs. She was delighted to find an answer to the letter she'd sent her mother requesting her help in finding a butler.

"Look, Bess," she exclaimed as she waved the letter at her friend. "A letter from my mother."

"Oh splendid! Did she find you a suitable candidate to be your butler?"

"Umm." Virginia finished reading to the end of her mother's letter before telling Bess, "She writes that she's found the perfect butler and that she's sent him on his way to me."

Bess smiled and poured their tea. "How nice." She looked up, "Why, he could be here in a few weeks."

"Yes, and imagine this. Mother says that I will be surprised and delighted with the man." Virginia frowned pensively. "Isn't that curious? Mother never speaks in enigmas. Directness has always been her forte."

"That still sounds wonderful."

"Yes." Virginia's brow furrowed. "But I

wonder who it could be? Maybe one of her friends' butlers that I knew vaguely, I suppose."

"Speaking of servants for Prodigal, how are your four new boys working out?"

Virginia threw up her hands. "Two are to be gardeners. We have to show them the difference between flowers they aren't familiar with and weeds. Carlos and Juan are excellent workers, but if they haven't seen it before, they think it must be a weed."

Bess laughed. "That doesn't bode well for anything that isn't a native plant."

"True." Virginia joined in. "That's the worst of it, though. Diego and Manuel are learning to serve, which is a great help to Teresa, and Maria is quite pleased with the help they are in the kitchen.

"They are all so eager to please. It's impossible to be out-of-sorts with them."

Bess smiled. "I'm so glad. They really are nice boys. They're always polite when they come in the shop."

"Thank heavens I have Maria and

Teresa! I must praise them to the skies for all they've done with the boys. I fervently hope the butler, when he comes, will be able to cope better than I have."

Then Virginia started telling of all the dinners David had planned that they would have to serve at while Bess listened with fascination. When the new butler arrived and took on the task of organizing it all, he'd certainly have his hands full.

"The very first thing we want to do is the barbeque David promised the town, though." Virginia was aglow with that idea. "David says he and the town council have planned it for Saturday after next." She laughed, "We don't need a butler for that, I'm glad to say."

Though she certainly didn't voice it, she'd much rather meet more people like Bess and Herb Johnson than to entertain the rather pompous crowd that had come to that first dinner.

Bess was excited, too. "I'm so glad you're happy at the idea of having a barbeque," she told her friend. "And I'm not the only one. The whole town is looking forward to it."

The rest of the morning passed swiftly. Before they knew it, Virginia had to go, and Bess walked her down to Fancy.

An instant later, they both lost the happy glow of their visit when they came face-to-face with Hal Broudy.

The man never tipped his hat, nor gave Virginia a greeting of any kind. He merely scowled and told her, "Tell that husband of yours we still have a debt to settle." Then he pushed rudely past her, jostling her aside as he did.

"Mr. Broudy!" Bess was outraged by such behavior.

Herb Johnson rushed forward, ignoring Broudy as the girls had asked him to. "Is everything all right, Mrs. Norris?" He inquired of Virginia, but his stern gaze was riveted on Broudy.

Virginia put her hand on his arm. "I'm fine. Don't trouble yourself, Herb." She certainly didn't want bad feelings between her friends and Broudy on her account. Especially since he seemed to have a sixth sense about when she would be at the mercantile so that he might just come and shove into her.

The man was uncanny. This was her second visit with Bess, and it was also the second time Broudy had happened by to collide with her.

It was obviously intentional. She was beginning to think that he was abusing her to try to provoke a quarrel with David.

Well, she'd block that ambition! There was no law demanding that she run to her husband to whimper about her mistreatment by a boor!

She gave Bess a quick hug. "Thank you for a lovely tea. I'll see you again soon." Smiling brightly at them, she turned Fancy toward home, but a lot of the pleasure had gone from the day.

The last thing she wanted was to have Broudy decide to start trouble for the Johnsons. Most of all she prayed that David would never hear of Broudy's treatment of her.

She truly feared what David might do.

Back at the ranch, David was having a serious conversation with his foreman, Bart Hastings, on that very subject.

"I've been hearing some nasty rumors about Hal Broudy, Mr. Norris. And it's worse than he usually is. A lot worse."

"In what way?"

"Well, like he always does, he's cussing you. That's nothing new, and he's still telling people he's gonna get even with you over that last parcel of land you added to Prodigal." Bart's brow was deeply furrowed. "But I'm telling ya', the way he's saying it all has changed. Before he was just making chin music, but now it sounds like he's cooking up a plan to do something about his gripes. I don't like the sound of it."

"Neither do I. Broudy is a nasty piece of work, and he can hold a grudge longer than any man in the territory." David's own brow was marred by a scowl. "Bart, I keep worrying about my wife. If he should strike at her, I'd be forced to kill him. In light of that, the day I go to Dallas, I want you and the men to stick close to the house."

Just the idea that any harm might come to Virginia was more than David could bear. If he couldn't be beside her himself, then he'd just have to make sure she was surrounded by men he could trust to keep her safe. It was the best he could do.

"Make any excuse you need for sticking around if she gets curious," he told his foreman. "Mend harness, groom horses. Cut each other's hair if you have to." Both men laughed at that, but the grimness never left their faces. "Just be sure you keep Mrs. Norris in the house and be sure that you keep a good eye on her."

"You have my word."

"That's good enough for me."

He wished he didn't have to go to Dallas, but papers were being brought to him from the east that had to be signed to secure the very parcel of land Broudy was so upset about. Papers were being prepared from his end, as well.

His meeting with Eaton couldn't be postponed. Eaton had no other time open for the rest of the year. The banker was doing him a favor to come west at all.

He strove to reassure himself. Anyway, who could say that Broudy had anything in mind for now, or even that he might have something up his sleeve for later?

Wishing he were a mind reader, or that at the very least he'd been smart enough to put a spy on Broudy's ranch, David turned and went into the house to prepare the documents he needed to take to Dallas.

Though he felt better after his conversation with his foreman, he was not completely relieved. He had every confidence in Hastings and in the rest of his men. All the same, caring as deeply as he did for Virginia, he wouldn't be completely at rest until he got back and could watch over her himself. He intended to ride hard and get back as soon as possible so that he could.

At least they could look forward to having an enjoyable time together at the barbeque Saturday after next. David was pretty sure Broudy wouldn't pull anything there.

Just in case, he'd made it a point to ride into town and see the sheriff. He'd ascertained that the man and his deputies would be ready to quash any unpleasantness that might occur.

David was familiar with the sheriff's ability to take care of things. Even so, he had carefully briefed his own men on what to do, should the need for action arise. Nothing was going to happen that might spoil Virginia's pleasure in meeting the townsfolk if he could help it.

Still uneasy about having to leave Virginia, he faced another weighty problem. He had to tell her he was going. That was another matter that could take the pleasure out of the event.

Heaven help him if anyone mentioned that he had to be in Dallas shortly after the barbeque before he told her about the trip himself. Virginia would be more than upset.

He sighed. "Then you'd better tell her yourself, Norris," he told the wall opposite his desk. "And you'd better get it over with."

The slowness with which he rose from his chair would have told anyone watching how he felt about telling his wife he was going away again. Squaring his shoulders, he went to do it.

He found Virginia in the kitchen having tea with his servants and discussing different ideas for the dinner parties he had scheduled. By now, he'd gotten used to the sight of Virginia with Maria and Teresa and their obvious friendship, and rather than feeling the momentary criticism he'd experienced at first learning of her habit, he felt a deep sense of approval.

Never would he have expected the wife he advertised for in the Boston paper to make friends of her servants, nor had his visit to the east done anything to disabuse him of that opinion. He'd seen his hosts at various houses there treat the help as if they weren't even human.

Just looking at Virginia sitting there, going over something on her list with Maria and Teresa, made his heart swell with pride.

She was a treasure. *His* treasure, and he fully intended to guard her as such.

"Virginia."

She looked up, surprised to see him there. The radiance of her smile staggered him. "Yes, David?"

He stood just looking at her, smiling.

"David?" She laughed up at him. "What is it?"

"I need to talk to you."

She rose from the table, her smile fading slowly.

David held out his hand.

Virginia slipped hers into it. "I'm not going to like this talk, am I?"

"No."

They walked in silence to the library and settled together in the big chair by the simple expedient of David pulling her down on his lap. He placed a kiss on the nape of her neck.

Virginia shivered once, and then pushed herself away from his chest. "Now, David," she told him, "don't try to distract me with kisses. And don't keep me in suspense."

"I have some business I must take care of in Dallas."

She regarded him solemnly for a long moment. "And how long will you be gone?"

"Only a few days. No more than four, counting hard riding. Less, if I can do it without killing a horse."

"When?"

"After the barbeque. I just wanted to give you plenty of warning this time. I remember how upset you were with me springing the cattle drive on you almost the day we arrived here."

"Umm." She scowled down at him. "Yes, you certainly did spring it on me. I remember that, too. Thank you for telling me about Dallas now."

"Virginia, I don't want to leave you any more than you want me to go."

She leaned down to put him out of his misery with a kiss. She'd intended it to be brief, just a little reassurance, but he caught her to him and added an emphasis of his own.

They were both breathless by the time Teresa appeared at the library door and announced, "Maria ask me to come inquire what you would like for supper."

Sometimes David felt as if they could get along with no servants at all.

This was one of those times.

CHAPTER 23

The day of the barbeque dawned bright and clear. Even the wind was cooperating and there was no more than the gentlest of breezes to stir the banners and flags along the main street.

The committee of townsmen that Herb Johnson had gotten together to decorate had clearly outdone itself, and the street sported two banners, one at either end, that proclaimed 'Barbeque, Picnic, Games and Fun!' and a lesser banner under that which read, 'Everybody Welcome!'

In addition, there were streamers of red, white, and blue hanging everywhere. Texas was glad to be a part of the United States and wasn't shy about showing its colors.

The women of the little town had done their share, as well. Large pots of red geraniums sat along the boardwalks in front of the stores, and blue flags appliquéd with the Lone Star of Texas flew from every post.

The town's whole population and all of the ranchers within an easy ride had turned out for the barbeque. People were everywhere.

Even old Mrs. Ennis, who rarely left her daughter's house, was there in her wheelchair. In her lap, she had a basket full of hard candies she had carefully ordered from Herb Johnson weeks ago, just for this occasion. She was giving them out to the little children who crowded around her.

The older children ran in the streets, calling to one another. Dogs, as ready to play as any of them, were hard on their heels.

Many of the people from the Mexican village were there, too. They stood grouped together, holding themselves back a little, not quite sure they were welcome.

Virginia and David arrived with Maria and Teresa in the back of the well-sprung dark green wagon that had brought the couple from Kansas. Greetings filled the air and many of the townspeople came up to offer their thanks to David for the steers roasting under the shade of a tent erected in the church yard. Beside it was a tent for all the food the ladies of the town had brought.

David lifted Virginia down from the wagon, watched as she was surrounded by friends, and then helped Maria down. Teresa jumped down unaided and hurried off to greet her friends from the village.

"The sauce," David heard their plump cook muttering to herself as she bustled off toward the open-sided cook tent, "I must see to the sauce. It must not burn." Obviously, she was determined to see that Roy, who had been basting the steers since late last night from the huge buckets of sauce she'd spent all day yesterday preparing, was doing it right.

When she had spoken to all the townspeople, Virginia went over to the isolated group of Mexicans. The headman greeted her in halting English. She smiled and asked Teresa, "Will you please tell them all we are so glad they have come?"

Teresa complied and smiles broke out. They all began talking at once. Virginia had no idea what they were telling her, but she smiled back and asked Teresa to be sure to encourage them to participate in the picnic.

Virginia hadn't been in Texas long, but she had quickly become aware of the tension that sometimes existed between peoples there. She didn't want anyone to feel strained today. With all her heart, she wanted everybody to have the time of their lives.

To be certain they and the others understood her wishes, she linked arms with one of the young women who seemed a little less shy and walked with her over to the group of women standing around Bess Johnson. As they walked, she asked the girl's name as well as she could without one of her faithful interpreters.

There was a moment of hesitation when they got to the group, but Virginia smiled brightly. "This is Consuéla. She lives in the village, and I know we all want to make her welcome. Do any of you speak Spanish? I have to confess that I'm at a loss."

Bess smiled and stepped forward. "I do, a little." In response to Bess's effort, Consuéla attempted to speak a little of her broken English.

A minute later, they were both admitting the difficulty of getting to know people when you couldn't easily converse and laughing about the mistakes they made, trying to use the other's language. Their laughter lured more of the townsfolk to them.

Virginia moved off when she saw others trying to use their limited Spanish to put the girl at ease, as well. Soon the ice was broken, and everyone was mingling freely.

Virginia's heart was light. This was a good town. These were good people.

Seeing their effort, she had to fight a lump in her throat. Her own Boston, she well remembered, had not been as kind to the people who came over from Ireland, and there hadn't been any language difficulty with them.

Thank You, Father, for bringing me to such a good place. She had to blink back happy tears.

David came over to her. "Are you all right?"

"Yes, of course. Thank you." She smiled up at him. "Aren't people nice?"

"Are you happy, Bride?"

Virginia's heart soared. She loved it when he called her 'Bride,' and all that time that he hadn't, she had sorely missed it. "Yes," she told him. "And thank you for calling me 'Bride' again. I can't tell you how much I have really missed that."

"You're mighty easy to please, Bride."

After the tiniest hesitation Virginia asked him, "Aren't you glad?"

"Yes, I am glad." He was looking at her closely.

"What?" she asked him, smiling.

David had seen the fleeting veiling of

her thoughts in her eyes when she hesitated, however. "Yes, what. What is it, Virginia? What is it that's interfering with your happiness?"

Tears welled in her eyes. She didn't want to say it. Surely he must know.

"Virginia," he insisted, "tell me."

There was a long silence between them. People saw their serious faces and left them alone. They were a solitary island in a swirling river of celebrating townspeople.

"Virginia, you know I love you more than . . ."

Before he could finish answering her plea, Bart Hastings came up to them. The foreman wore a worried look. "Pardon my interrupting, Mrs. Norris, Boss, but there's something coming into town that's raising a lot of dust."

Knowing that he'd commanded his men to be on the alert, David could hardly ignore this. He squeezed Virginia's hand in apology, then drew her tight against him so that she stood in the circle of his arm.

David's gaze went beyond the edge of town to where he could just make out

360 MARRIED IN BLACK

a distant dust cloud. "Not all of them,"
he muttered, going back to finish what
they had originally been talking about.
"Not all people are nice." He was
steadily watching the cloud of dust.

Out loud he said, again referring back
to their earlier remarks, "Yes, the folks
here in town are nice, Virginia. I'm glad
you've made friends with so many of
them."

"Me, too." The words weren't as relaxed as they might have been. She had
sensed the tension in David. Turning
away from him to look in the direction
his attention was fixed, she tried to
make out whatever it was that her husband was watching.

Seeing nothing but a little cloud of
dust way beyond the edge of town she
asked, "David, what are you watching
so intently?"

He brought his gaze back to her face.
"There's something coming. Could be
the stage that stops here every other
week. Could be riders."

"The stage. Oh, good." She relaxed
visibly. "Perhaps I'll have word of the
butler we're expecting." Now she re-

garded the approaching dust cloud with a great deal of interest.

Her mother's promise in her last letter that Virginia was going to be pleased with the man she was sending her had kept Virginia in a high state of curiosity. Watching now, she could just make out the horses and a hint of the stage behind them.

"Oh, David. It *is* the stage. How exciting! I've never seen a stagecoach arrive before. We'll have to invite everyone on it to the picnic."

David had relaxed visibly, too. Clearly it hadn't been the imminent arriving of the stage that had made him tense.

"We might make up packets of food for them to take along." He gave her an approving look. "It's a kind idea. I'm sure they'll have a schedule to keep and won't be able to stop long though."

Turning to one of his men he asked him to go ask Maria and Teresa to make up the packets. Then he took Virginia's arm and drew her up onto the boardwalk in front of the general store. "He'll stop here. Best keep out of the way."

Parents were gathering children out of

the street. Boys were whistling for their dogs, and everyone was avidly looking at the approaching coach. Except for today's festivities, the arrival of the stagecoach was the most excitement the town had had since the last time it had come through.

"Whoa! Whoa, there!" The driver, fully aware that all eyes were on him, wasn't above a little drama. As the horses responded to his cry and his pull on the long reins, he kicked the brake forward and locked the wheels. The coach skidded to a halt, exactly in front of the Johnsons' general store.

Virginia fanned the dust away from her face and watched the proceedings through squinted eyes. When the driver looped the lines around the brake and jumped down to open the door, she was as eager as everyone else to see who was actually going to get out of the coach.

When she saw, she felt her mouth drop open.

Grissom! It was Grissom! Her mother had sent her Grissom to be her butler!

Throwing decorum to the winds, she

leaped off the boardwalk and flung her arms around his neck. Tears began as she hugged him fiercely. "Grissom! Oh, how wonderful it is to see you!"

Blushing brightly, the recipient of her enthusiastic greeting tried to pull her arms from around his neck. "It is wonderful to see you, too, Miss Virginia."

Then he whispered, "Miss Virginia, everyone is watching, and one does not hug one's butler. It is simply not done."

She backed away, laughing delightedly. "Oh, Grissom. This is the best surprise. I can hardly believe mother sent you to me. I doubt she will be able to get along without you there."

Smoothing his lapels, he informed her firmly, "I have been training my replacement since the day your letter arrived. I can assure you that you have no need to worry about Mrs. Davenport. I have taken great pains to see that she is in competent hands."

Virginia just stood and grinned at him, waves of pleasure washing through her.

David was standing at her elbow. "David, isn't this the most wonderful surprise?" Virginia looked up at him, her eyes glowing. "But he's come such a long way." Suddenly she was all concern. "We must get Grissom to the ranch so that he can rest."

Smiling his own welcome, David stuck out his hand to shake his and looked at the tall man critically. "No, I think he's had enough travel for the moment. And if I recall the food he must have had on the trip, I'd be willing to bet he'll gladly fight off fatigue for a few hours to have a good meal. What do you say, Grissom?"

"Why, sir, I'd have to say that a little time without motion and some palatable sustenance would be a more than welcome change."

"Good. You can rest all day tomorrow and the next day, once we've fed you and gotten you back to the ranch."

"Very good, sir."

David and Virginia introduced Grissom to the Johnsons, and except for Grissom's obvious surprise and discomfort at being treated like an equal and a guest, all went well.

The picnic was well begun, with people filling their plates from the vast array of dishes on the tables in the food tent and lining up for a slice or two of beef when Virginia saw Bart Hastings hurry to David's side again.

David walked out into the street and stood with his legs spread, as if he braced for something. His arms were crossed over his chest.

Virginia followed him, stood on the boardwalk, and watched as he looked to the edge of town again with the same intensity he'd shown when the stagecoach had appeared. Now, though, he was even more alert.

Hastings stood at his side, as watchful as David. It couldn't be the stage this time. Their expressions were grim.

The cloud of dust rapidly grew larger, and in another minute, Virginia could make out horses bearing riders this time. Tension mounted in her as she watched them come. These men were anything but considerate of their mounts, and she clearly remembered Hal Broudy's last arrival. He and his men were in the habit of treating their horses cruelly.

They swept into the town like a whirlwind, hooves pounding the dirt of the street and raising even more dust than the stagecoach and its team had. Hal Broudy rode at the head of the group, his quirt flailing his lathered horse's flanks. Disgust and dread filled Virginia at the man's appearance.

She watched in shock as he whipped his horse even more viciously and charged the frantic animal straight toward David. Throwing herself off the sidewalk into the street, she stepped in front of her husband.

Startled, David drew her to his side.

With a string of curses, Broudy stopped his horse only feet from running them down. "Hiding behind your wife's skirts now, Norris?"

David met his taunt with a level gaze.

With a sneer Broudy hauled his horse's head around and rode to the nearest hitching post. Dismounting, he tied the lathered horse there and stalked past David and Virginia. "Come on, boys." He gestured his men to follow him. "Let's see what Prodigal beef tastes like."

David was clenching his teeth so

tightly that a muscle jumped in his jaw. Virginia put her hand on his arm. "Don't respond to him, David. That's what he wants you to do."

David looked down at her with a tight smile. "You're right, of course."

He drew a deep breath. Finally he gave a brittle laugh. "Let's try to keep him from ruining the picnic for everybody else, shall we?"

"Yes, but how?"

"By playing least-in-sight." Turning to his foreman, he asked, "Bart, would you get Mr. Grissom and bring him to the mercantile? I noticed he was wearing wool. We need to look at clothing for him that will make him more comfortable in our climate."

Hastings grinned as he nodded his awareness that his employer was going to vanish into the store before Broudy finished heaping his plate—and spewing his venom—and could look around for David Norris to attack. Moving off to go in search of Grissom, he permitted himself to relish thinking about the dose of frustration he knew the angry Broudy would soon experience.

David took Virginia's elbow and steered her into the general store. A few minutes later, Hastings escorted Grissom in and shut the door firmly behind him. Then he and several of the crew from Prodigal settled down to eat their barbeque on the steps that rose up from the street to the store.

David smiled at the dusty butler from Boston. "I thought you'd like to select a few things to wear before we left town for the ranch. Our climate is a far cry from the northeast's and something lighter would be a lot more comfortable for you."

Seeing Grissom's shock at the idea that he dress in anything other than the traditional garb of a proper butler, Virginia hastened to add, "Just until we get your usual clothing ordered in lighter fabrics, of course." She smiled persuasively. "You really will be miserable if you try to wear wool here just now."

Bess slipped into the store at that moment, laughing low and breathlessly. "Oh, David, it was so clever of you to come in here and remove Hal Broudy's reason for staying. He's absolutely seething!" She was plainly delighted. "Everyone is just waiting for him to take his men and leave so we can enjoy the rest of the picnic."

She turned her attention to the few articles of clothing David had been able to force the taciturn Grissom to choose. "I'll just wrap your things for the trip to the ranch, Mr. Grissom. That's easily done and will keep the dust out." She smiled at Grissom. "You'll find that dust is a problem here in Texas. We have a lot more than you could ever have seen in Boston."

She moved off to where she had counter space to wrap the parcel and brought out a roll of paper to do the job. As she smoothed out the paper, Bess told Virginia in a whisper, "I think Broudy is about to leave. What a dreadful man. You must tell David to be careful of him."

Virginia answered in a low voice, "I certainly shall. I think he's more than dreadful, though, Bess. I think he's dangerous." She shivered involuntarily.

Just then David came up with more

clothing for Grisson draped over his arm. "Am I missing something?"

"Just the thought that both Bess and I want you to be very careful of that awful Hal Broudy."

David dismissed their fears casually. "His bark is worse than his bite. He's been blustering ever since I came here." He walked away to where the hats hung and invited Grissom to select one.

Virginia and Bess exchanged troubled glances. Obviously David didn't share their fear of Broudy.

That was understandable. He was a man, of course, and lacked the intuition they had.

Virginia whispered to Bess, "I wish he'd at least worry."

Bess shook her head slightly to warn Virginia that David was coming back to where they stood at the counter.

Smiling to Bess, David handed her the hat that he'd chosen for his new butler. Grissom had protested vigorously that his bowler would do, but David had ignored him. "Would you put these on the ranch account, please, Bess?"

"Certainly." Bess smiled her best merchant's smile.

Outside, there was a sudden commotion. With loud shouts and shrill whistles, Hal Broudy and his gang sped by the store, their horses already at full gallop, leaving the children and dogs playing in the streets to look to their own safety.

Grissom stood stiffly looking toward the window, eyes wide.

Undaunted, David grinned and told him, "Welcome to the wild west."

CHAPTER 24

Finally the festivities began to wind down. The sun began its slow descent, sliding toward the hills to the west of town. The day of the town barbeque was coming to a satisfying close. Children were beginning to find their parents and a quiet place to sit down close by them to recuperate from the rowdy games they'd played all day.

Even their dogs were quiet now. Happily worn out by their rough-and-tumble racing in pursuit of their young masters, they'd stopped sniffing for possible treats of left-over barbeque, plopped down, and curled up beside their owners.

David turned to Virginia. "Tired?"

"Deliciously. It's been a wonderful day, in spite of Hal Broudy." She smiled up at him. "I'm very proud of the way you handled that situation, David. It could really have gotten ugly if you'd stayed where he'd been able to pick a fight with you."

Her husband grinned down at her. "One of the greatest pleasures of life is foiling people like Broudy." He sobered. "Besides, what earthly good could have been served by staying outside and trading insults with him?"

"No good at all. It would have ruined the picnic for everybody."

"Right."

Virginia reached up and brushed back a lock of hair that had fallen down on his forehead. "You knew that, and you cared. That's why you took Grissom and me into the store and made me so proud of you."

David caught her hand as she took it down from his hair and kissed it. "I thought you might want me to."

Virginia's breath caught. For a moment, she couldn't speak for the emotions raised in her by the tenderness in his eyes. "Thank you," she whispered.

David lowered his face to hers.

She waited for his kiss.

Just then, Bart Hastings came up to them. "Missus," he touched the brim of his hat to Virginia, then turned to David. "Boss, the boys and me think we'll just ride home alongside the wagon, if that's all right with you."

David looked at him for a moment, then turned his attention back to Virginia. "Why don't you go round up Grissom and Maria and Teresa and meet me at the wagon."

Virginia glanced from one man to the other. It was obvious to her that they had something to say that they didn't want her to hear. Obediently, she left without a word. There was no way she could miss the tension in the air between the two men and it troubled her.

She found all three she'd been sent for and led them to the wagon. Grissom stopped at the side of it. "So this is the conveyance that brought you to Texas from Kansas, Miss Virginia."

She grinned at him. "Yes, it is. It was my home for over a month."

Used to the impassive face he habitually wore in his capacity as butler, Virginia noted the smile in his eyes. "Yes, I know," she told him. "You think it was a lot more comfortable than the stage. Well, it was, I'm sure. The stage passengers always look so cramped."

She looked at him earnestly. "Stagecoaches don't stop for you to sleep either, do they?"

"If I may say so, I am indeed glad to have gotten off it at last. One rather felt as if it were going to go on forever. A punishment for one's sins, no doubt." He turned away to help Maria up into the wagon bed.

Maria thanked him nicely. *"Gracias, Señor Grissom."*

Teresa shot him a sour look and climbed in without his assistance. Evidently, she was still not certain she liked the idea of having a butler at the ranch house.

David lifted Virginia to the seat and came easily up beside her. He took up the long reins, and the team moved off.

An instant later, men from Prodigal appeared from several directions to gather around the wagon for all the world like an honor guard.

The journey home was uneventful, except for once when Hastings pointed out a small cloud of dust that seemed to parallel their course for a while. Finally, it disappeared, and he relaxed a bit.

Virginia asked David. "What was it you and Bart Hastings had to say to each other that I couldn't hear?"

"What makes you ask a question like that, Bride?"

"The fact that you sent me away to gather our group. David, don't attempt to fob me off." She looked at him steadily, her lips firm. "I want to know."

"Bart thought maybe Broudy was going to try to make trouble."

"Trouble? But he left."

"He evidently didn't go far."

"How do you know that?"

"Bart had some of the men keeping an eye on him."

"And?"

"And Broudy and his men went just out of town and hunkered down in a draw so that nobody'd know they were still around."

"But what could they have meant to do?"

David's patience was wearing thin. "Just leave it alone, Virginia. We men will take care of it."

Virginia wasn't about to leave it alone. "What do you and Bart think he'll do?"

David sighed in exasperation. "Virginia, he's not going to do anything. We have forty or fifty of our own men riding around us. What . . ." he swallowed an expletive, "could he possibly do?"

She was aggravated by his refusal to tell her what he thought was going on. "Obviously, he intended to make a problem for us on the way home. How wonderful that Bart realized it and that the men have foiled him by accompanying us home."

She folded her hands in her lap, satisfied that she had let David know that she was aware of what 'we men' were 'taking care of.' Maybe he wouldn't keep things from her in the future.

David only grinned.

Even with their cowboy escort, or

possibly because of it, Virginia was more than glad to arrive safely at the house. She waved and called her thanks to the hands as they peeled off from escorting the wagon and headed for the barn and the corrals.

Entering the house, they turned their attention to taking care of Grissom. They settled him in the biggest room in the servant's wing, bade him ask for anything he needed, and went up to their own bed.

As she brushed her hair, Virginia asked, "Was Bart really worried about us?" She turned on the bench of the dressing table toward David.

He came over and took the brush from her hand. Slowly, he stroked it through her hair, his gaze locked with hers in the mirror. "Why do you think that?"

"David." She gave him a stern look. "I will not let you avoid my question, no matter how nice it is to have you brush my hair."

"Do you really like it? I shall have to do it more often."

"David! Stop that."

He stopped brushing, in his reflection his eyebrow rose as if inquiring of her whether to stop brushing her hair.

"David Norris, you know perfectly well what I mean. I mean you are to stop avoiding my question. I'm not an empty-headed ninny, you know. You can tell me if there was any reason the men rode home all around us as if they were guarding us."

His expression grew grave. "Bart is a bit of a worrier. He seems to think that Broudy would have tried to make trouble."

Her own face was grave. "And you, David? What do you think?"

David resumed brushing her hair, but the strokes were slower and his face was thoughtful. "I think he'd like to make trouble, but he's a small man, and unless he can find an advantage over me, I don't think he'll try anything." He grinned at her in the mirror. "There." He brushed more quickly. "Now are you satisfied?"

"Umm." She nodded.

He bent and kissed her gently on the

neck just under her ear. "Ah. There's that 'umm' I've been missing."

Virginia turned on the bench and reached up. "Oh, David. I do love you so."

He claimed her mouth as her arms encircled his neck and tightened. Instantly, he scooped her from the bench into his arms and carried her across the room to their bed.

Suddenly, Virginia found she wasn't as tired out from the day's events as she had thought she'd been.

CHAPTER 25

Virginia lay in bed late the next morning. David had left her there after kissing her awake to insist that she rest longer after the strenuous day of the barbeque.

She stretched luxuriously and knew a contentment that she had seldom felt before. The sun was high in the sky, and all was right with her world.

Her mother had sent Grissom to her and proved by doing so that she truly did love her daughter. So very often Virginia had doubted that. Now she realized that when her mother had been harsh in her criticisms, it was just her way of rearing a child. She'd known no other way, as that was the way her own parents had reared her.

When she realized that, she'd found that she had to ask God to forgive her for her distrust, yes, and even dislike, of her mother. It was such a blessing to be rid of those resentful feelings. It was as if she had gotten rid of a millstone that had been hanging around her neck.

She couldn't help wondering if there were other women who had the same problem as she had with her mother. After thinking seriously about it for a while, she decided that perhaps it was something that had existed between mothers and daughters throughout the ages.

Virginia vowed to herself that when she had her own children, she would raise them with much love and tell them daily how very much she cared for them. If she spoiled them, there would always be David to see that they turned out all right.

With all those thoughts behind her, the only 'fly in her ointment,' as Grissom might say, was a truly heartbreaking one. She was devastated by her husband's lack of faith.

She could see in him now, as she had from the very beginning, that he behaved as if he were a Christian. He was brave and kind and true. There was no doubt in her mind that he'd been raised in a God-fearing atmosphere.

She could only hope that the First Peter passage would quickly come to pass in their lives, and David would be brought to salvation. When, she told herself, not *if*, but *when* that came to pass, she would be the happiest woman alive.

Not that she wasn't very close to that now. With David's love wrapped around her like a cloak, how could it be otherwise?

Her only other problem was a very small one. She'd had to change her habit of saying her prayers every night before she got into bed to saying them every morning, kneeling beside the bed after David had left it. Every time she did, her heart almost burst with yearning for the day when they would say them together, side by side.

Now she had to put all such thoughts aside and be patient. She was well aware that God worked in His own perfect time, no matter how much one wished for something to happen sooner.

She just needed to keep busy. She intended to do this today by making plans for the party David had scheduled before his trip to Dallas.

There was a great deal to do, and having Grissom to do most of it was wonderful. He was surely the most patient man alive.

Watching Grissom trying to train Manuel and Diego to serve was a source of great amusement for the entire household. The two boys who had been chosen to work in the house were proud not to have been relegated to gardening as their friends Juan and Carlos had been. As a result, they were trying so hard that they made more mistakes than they would have if they could have relaxed about it.

Grissom was exceedingly kind with them, however, his only frustration being the language barrier. Maria helped with that cheerfully; Teresa, a little less so. Things were beginning to shape up, though, as David was fond of saying.

Now, however, the day of the party

was fast approaching. Life at the house had become a whirlwind. Grissom had been flabbergasted to find that Virginia and David were expecting forty-five guests for the weekend. "Miss Virginia!" he admonished. "I have hardly trained your staff!"

"Nevertheless, Grissom, this party is unavoidable. It was planned some time ago, and there is just no help for it." She smiled winningly at him. "What is it you used to say to me when I was a little girl? Do your best; angels can do no better."

"I trust madame is not comparing my feeble efforts with those of celestial beings." Grissom turned up his nose and walked off in a huff.

It might have upset Virginia if she hadn't heard him chuckle.

The night of the party, Virginia selected the moonlight blue gown that David had first sent to her. Having refused to wear it for their wedding and having worn at their first dinner party the glamorous

black gown that told her David respected her mourning for William, she
wanted to wear this gown tonight to
honor her beloved.

David came into her dressing room,
resplendent in his evening clothes. "You
look especially lovely tonight." His cool
fingers closed around her neck. He
tilted her face up for his kiss. "I have
something for you."

She watched as he drew a jeweler's
case out of his breast pocket. Opening
it for her, he took out a necklace of diamonds and sapphires to complement
the gown she wore. "I thought you
might like this."

"Oh, David, it's lovely. Thank you."

He laughed. "You're very welcome,
Bride."

She smiled up at him, her eyes aglow.

"Do you like that?"

She touched the gems at her throat.
The sapphires and diamonds caught the
light from the oil lamps flanking her
dressing table and shot fire. "Of course
I like it. It's beautiful."

"That's not what I meant," he dismissed the small fortune as if it were of

no importance. "I meant do you like being called 'Bride'?"

Virginia answered softly, "As long as it's you who calls me that."

David took her in his arms. "I planned and searched for you." He began to grin. "And I braved the dragon in her very own Boston lair to wrest you forth to be my own."

Virginia laughed breathlessly and entwined her arms about his neck. "Yes?"

"So you are my very own, Bride. And since you like it, you will always be my Bride." He lowered his head to kiss her.

Virginia lifted her face for his kiss, her fingers caressing the hair at the back of his neck.

There was a pounding at their door, and they both looked in that direction, startled.

Manuel poked his head around the edge of the door. "Butler say come now."

With that, he was gone.

So was the tender moment they'd been about to share. They both sighed.

Virginia's sigh was wistful.

David's was exasperated.

Both of them were laughing as they walked obediently to the door, hand-in-hand.

Hours later, dinner was over, and the guests drifted into the large room designed for dancing. Chandeliers there sparkled, and the musicians played softly enough for the assembled guests to converse.

Several couples danced. Most of the guests stood talking in small groups.

The French doors on the outside wall were open to the cool night breezes. To add to their guests' comfort, Grissom directed the two boys to offer cooling glasses to the guests.

All was going well.

David looked across at his wife where she stood talking to several of the other wives and smiled. Alert to his gaze, Virginia smiled back.

Then, suddenly, he saw her expression change to one of shock. Following the direction of her stare, he saw Hal

Broudy and two of his men standing in one of the open doors.

"Norris!" Hal Broudy weaved a little on his feet. David wondered if he were drunk. Moving forward, David called out, "What do you want here, Broudy." It was a challenge, not a question.

"Ah! There you are."

"Where would you expect me to be? It's my party."

"An' you sure didn't invite me."

David didn't reply to the obvious. "What is it you want?" Out of the corner of his eye, he saw Grissom send Diego out of the room. The musicians stopped playing, dwindling off, one after another.

"I want you to give over that land you snuck out from under me. I figure you'll have to stick to your word to return it to me if you promise to give it to me in front of all your fancy friends."

"Not only did I not get it from you, but I also have no intention of ever promising to give you Prodigal land, Broudy," David responded reasonably, certain now that the man was drunk. "Now, please leave quietly. You're upsetting the ladies."

Behind Broudy, the men of Prodigal Ranch were gathering.

Broudy began to rant, his coarse voice rising to a shout. "I don't care who I upset . . ."

Bart Hastings shoved the muzzle of a six-shooter into Broudy's ribs. "Time to go, Hal. Like you said, you ain't invited."

With immense dignity, Grissom walked to the open door in which the little drama was being played and closed it firmly in Broudy's face, saying, "Thank you, Mr. Hastings." Then the butler turned and signaled for the musicians to resume playing.

David smiled and went to Virginia. "Remind me to write my own note of thanks to your mother. She has truly sent us a jewel."

"Oh, David. That awful man. Are you certain he doesn't mean you harm?"

"As I said, he's harmless. And tonight he's drunk. Put him out of your mind."

She looked at him with wide, troubled eyes, and he realized that she couldn't ignore Broudy. He could see the enjoyment had gone out of the evening for her. Sadly, he noted that the rest of the party had become only a duty to her.

As he surreptitiously watched, she spoke the proper platitudes and smiled at the right witticisms. "Good, brave girl," he whispered to himself.

He wished he could reassure her. It was clear to him that her mind, unfortunately, was really on his safety and just how much of a threat Hal Broudy was to it.

CHAPTER 26

"Virginia." David tried again, still speaking softly, "Virginia." He placed a kiss on her shoulder, then gave it a little shake.

Virginia stirred and snuggled deeper into his arms. "Umm."

He laughed and shook her gently again. "Bride, I need to talk to you."

"Don't want to talk. Sleepy."

"It's time for our talk. I have to go to Dallas for a few days."

"What?" She was fully awake, now, his startling statement having shocked her awake. He couldn't be leaving today!

Twisting out of his arms, she sat up. "Oh, David. So soon? Why do you have to go to Dallas, anyway?" She was feeling petulant and didn't bother to keep that out of her voice.

"As I told you, just on business. I'll be as fast as I can. I have to leave at first light tomorrow, and I'll do my best to finish early enough the day after I get there so I can start back to you." He grinned lazily up at her. "After all, I don't want to be gone away from you any longer than I have to."

"Well, I suppose that's some consolation." She settled back against him. "I just wish you didn't have to go at all."

He kissed her neck where it joined her shoulder. "I wish I didn't have to go either."

"I can't help it, David. I know I'm being morose, but I have this unreasoning fear that you won't come back to me. No matter how hard I pray, I just can't shake it."

"Of course, I'll come back to you." He hugged her tightly, unused to seeing her like this. "I'll always come back to you, Bride."

She was quiet for a moment. Then she told him softly, "William promised he would come back to me, but he didn't. Things aren't always under our control."

Gently grasping her chin, he turned her face toward him. With his thumb, he wiped away her tears.

"I'll come back to you, Bride. I'll come back to you if I have to walk through fire to do it."

That solemn promise given, David kissed her quickly and rose to dress. He'd much to do today before he could leave the next day.

In spite of all his reassurances, Virginia's heart was still troubled. She was inconsolable and burdened with feelings of dread—feelings that persisted in spite of her prayers.

As the door closed behind David, she slipped from the bed to kneel beside it. Clasping her hands, she bowed her head. "Dear Father, please make his journey safe and cause his business to go quickly. I know he's only going to be gone for three or four days, but I do miss him so.

"And Father, I keep having these awful feelings. Feelings that I'm about to lose him as I lost William. I couldn't bear that. Please protect him."

She swiped impatiently at her tears.

"But most of all, dear Lord, I want You to cause my David to accept Your Son's sacrifice—to accept Him as his Savior."

Before she'd finished the prayer, more tears were forming. "Dearest Lord. I know that You've told me to stand by him, and I do, gladly, because I love him so. So please keep him safe and please grant me this prayer. In Jesus's name." Then, with a big, indrawn breath she added, *"No matter what it takes."*

Outside the big ranch house, David headed toward his foreman.

He got right to the point. "What do you hear, Bart?"

"I hear Broudy is gathering extra hands." Bart gave his boss a look full of meaning. "Seems to me he has enough men to handle that herd of his. Makes me wonder why he needs any more."

"Makes me wonder, too."

"Seems like a lot of Broudy's new men are a rough bunch."

David was quiet, thinking. "Bart, he's up to something, and I don't like it any more than you do." The expression on his face was grave. "He's slow to get started on plans, so I don't think he'll do anything right away. Just in case, though, I want you to keep the men close around the house, as we discussed.

"I'll get my business done as quickly as I can. Eaton can only be in Dallas at this time then he's got to be heading back east, or I'd change my appointment with him. Two days should see the end of it, less time if I can manage it. In all, I make it not more than four days, and maybe just three."

"Okay, Boss. You can count on me and the men about looking after Mrs. Norris."

"I know I can, Bart." Still, he felt faintly troubled, so he said again with more firmness. "I know I can."

That night, David packed his saddle bags with a change of clothes and the papers that were the reason for his trip. Then he made up his bedroll, just in case he might need it, and placed it near the front door.

When he looked up from that task, he saw Virginia watching him with a longing that took his breath away. "I won't be gone long, Bride. I promise."

Her eyes told him that any absence was too long just now. He could see, too, that clearly she was deeply worried about him. "You're taking some of the men with you, aren't you, David?"

"Why? I'll make better time alone."

"I . . . I'd feel better if you took someone to . . . to watch your back. Isn't that what you say?"

He laughed and took her in his arms. "Yes, that's what men say when there's a gunfighter after them or a range war. I don't have a gunfighter after me."

"But Broudy constitutes an insipient range war, all the same."

That struck him as amusing. "Hal Broudy hasn't the stomach for a range war, Bride, believe me."

Virginia didn't voice it, but she thought, *No, he's more apt to make some sort of a sneak attack*. Aloud she said, "I just couldn't bear it if anything happened to you, David." She shook her head and repeated, "I couldn't bear it. Please take at least two of the men with you."

"Would that really put your mind at ease?"

She settled for what she recognized as all she was going to get. "Yes."

"All right. I'll take one of the men with me. I'll take Clint. He can ride, and he's the best shot on the ranch." He bent down and kissed her gently. "Does that make you feel better?"

Virginia clung to him desperately. Nothing made her feel better.

David hugged her tightly, then moved slowly back from her to hold her at arm's length. He grinned down at her. "Now, can we go up to bed?"

CHAPTER 27

David had barely been gone three hours when Hal Broudy attacked. He and his gang arrived at full gallop, whooping and firing off their six-shooters.

Broudy yelled, "Circle them wagons, boys!"

His men and the thugs he'd added to their number obediently encircled the ranch house while Broudy yanked his mount to a standstill, opposite the front door of the ranch house.

"Come on out, Mrs. Norris!" he shouted. "It's Hal Broudy, come to get you."

"I don't think so, Broudy." Bart Hastings appeared in the front doorway, a rifle cradled in his left arm.

Cursing, Hal Broudy spun his horse in a tight circle. He was surprised and furious to find the house defended.

Virginia watched from the hall behind the foreman, her heart in her throat. Words, had she been able to voice any, could not have expressed how relieved and grateful she was for Bart's presence. Obviously, he'd made preparations in case this sort of thing happened.

She sincerely thanked God that Bart had not been as casual about the threat Broudy posed as David had been. She shuddered to think what might have happened if Bart hadn't been here.

Determined to take the responsibility of his boss's wife seriously, Bart had taken every precaution and a good deal of joshing from the men. Nevertheless, he'd sternly informed the hands of what he thought might be danger from Hal Broudy, armed every one of them, and told them to be ready to run into the ranch house at a moment's notice.

All chores had been suspended and the men forbidden to leave the immediate area of the house. Some of them had found the orders vastly amusing.

No one was laughing now.

Bart had begun by posting lookouts as soon as David Norris had left. When one of them had signaled that trouble was on the way, he'd been able to call the men into the ranch house the minute Hal Broudy and his men arrived on the edge of Prodigal.

Virginia had been amazed when only five minutes ago she'd responded to Bart's knock and opened the door. She could have been knocked over by a feather when almost all the Prodigal hands had tramped silently into the house after him, carrying guns.

Now Bart had stepped out of the door on to the porch and his rifle was pointed in Broudy's direction. "What do ya want, Broudy?"

"I've come to collect me that pretty little wife of Norris's. I figure when I have her, Norris is gonna get real agreeable."

"Is that so? Well, *we* figure *you're* gonna get real disappointed."

Broudy cursed and pulled his gun out of the holster on his hip. By the time he'd freed the weapon and pointed it at Hastings, Bart had stepped back into the house and slammed the door. Prodigal men appeared at every window.

Bart shook his head and told Virginia, "Ma'am, I sure hope you'll be able to get your husband to forgive us if the place gets shot up a mite."

Virginia's laugh was just short of hysterical. At one time, she'd feared she might be in Texas in the middle of a gunfight. She remembered, as well, a verse in the Word that said, 'That which you feared has come upon you.'

"Do what you must, Mr. Hastings. I have the utmost confidence in you and your men."

"Thank you, Miz Norris. Now if you will, please go upstairs and take the other women with you. Meaning no disrespect, but me an' the boys'll have easier minds if we know you're safe up there."

"Of course, Mr. Hastings." She gestured to Maria and Teresa to accompany her.

Grissom came forward and took up one of the rifles Bart had stacked in the foyer the minute David had left. "I believe I will see to the women a bit better if I go armed, Mr. Hastings. However, if you should need an extra man down here, you have only to call me."

"Will do, Mr. Grissom. Thanks." Bart smiled at the butler. When Grissom had walked away, Virginia heard Bart mutter, "Good man, in spite of them fancy duds."

Grissom shepherded the three women up the sweeping staircase and left Broudy to Bart Hastings.

Out in front of the house, Hal Broudy bellowed, "Send her out, Hastings. We ain't gonna wait all day."

"Guess you've heard people tell of hell freezing over, Hal. I sure hope so, 'cause until we hear that's actually happened, ain't none of us giving up our boss's wife to the likes of you."

In reply, Broudy's men started shooting. Then bullets were flying from all the riders around the house. The noise was deafening. Splinters flew everywhere.

Upstairs, Virginia heard glass breaking out of all the windows.

Putting her fingers over her ears, Virginia looked, wide-eyed, toward Grissom.

Grissom shrugged elaborately. "Glass can be replaced, Miss Virginia."

"Oh, Grissom, I don't care about the glass. I'm only worried for the men. What if one of them gets hurt defending me?"

Grissom went to her and put an arm around her shoulders. "Virginia," he said, speaking to her as he had when she'd been a small child, "the men are fighting as much for Prodigal and their honor as they are to keep you safe. Their injuries, should they sustain any, will be in a cause they have willingly—and I must add, rather joyously—embraced." He smiled one of his rare smiles. "Truth to tell, I think that they're welcoming this exciting change from cattle care."

"Surely you're mistaken."

From downstairs, they was a whoop of triumph and a shouted, "Got him!"

Grissom gave her a satisfied look as his surmise was proven correct. "I think not, madame."

Virginia responded a little breathlessly, "I suppose you are right, Grissom." Realizing she could serve no useful purpose in a gunfight, she turned away and asked Maria and Teresa, "Would you like to come into the dressing room and pray with me?"

The two women joined her in the interior room instantly.

"This is good," Maria pronounced with great satisfaction.

"Yes," Teresa agreed. "No windows."

As if to underscore her remark, a bullet splatted into the wall above the big four-poster across the room from the window wall. In the smaller dressing room, the three women took it as a signal and knelt to pray.

Evening came at last, with no let-up in Broudy's attack. Virginia was frantic with worry about the men defending the ranch house and her, and was more than willing to become Broudy's hostage if it would spare the men bloodshed. She told Grissom so.

"Miss Virginia. The men are fighting

for their battle flag, or if it would be easier to understand, a prize. Like it or not, you are that prize." He paused to let his words sink in, and then continued, "Would you take the very thing they hold with such pride and freely give it to their enemies?"

As she absorbed his words, she stared at him as if he were from another world. Men, she decided, were incomprehensible. She would, however, accept Grissom's evaluation. She was certain he was speaking the truth, just as he had all her life.

Sighing, she got back to her prayers. At least that was useful.

Evening lengthened into night, and the shooting finally stopped. The attackers built temporary camps rather than leave. There was a bright campfire flaring at each corner of the house. Hal Broudy's men tore down corral fencing to keep them burning bright.

Prodigal was under siege.

Virginia thought that the campfires were a bad sign. What if Broudy and his men were still there when David rode home? Uneasiness drew her nerves taut.

Since the shooting had stopped, after sending Maria and Teresa to find something for the men to eat, she went downstairs to confer with Bart Hastings. She had to feel her way, as Bart sensibly permitted no lights in the house.

"Mr. Hastings, do you think those men mean to be here tomorrow as well?"

"Looks like it, ma'am."

She thought hard for a moment. "What do you think our chances are of getting word to the sheriff?"

"Pretty slim." His expression was grim with determination. "But I could try if you wanted."

"No!" She was appalled that her question might have sent him out among the enemy. She felt foolish to have asked and hastened to tell him so. "It was silly—no, it was downright stupid—of me to even ask that question," she castigated herself. "Quite obviously, Hal Broudy will have men to stop us from doing just that."

"I reckon so."

She was silent a long moment, then asked, "Should I be worried about our supply of ammunition?"

Hastings grinned at her. "No, ma'am. You just let us fellows worry about that." When he saw her look as if she mildly resented being put off, he added, "Mr. Norris keeps a healthy supply of such around Prodigal, ma'am. Didn't used to be real peaceful 'round here when he first came. A man had to hold his claim to this land or lose it."

Seeing curiosity struggling with distress in her face he reassured her. "Nothing too serious, ma'am. Was only a few hostiles—Comanches mostly— and they were glad to settle for a guarantee of so many beeves a year.

"They knew the boss always plays fair, and they needed him, too, after all the buffalo got killed off."

Again Virginia looked as if she wanted to know more.

"The Comanches are like them Arab nomads. They'd go up to the great plains to hunt buffalo and make jerky and pemmican to last them through to the next hunt.

"Then, lots of people back in the east got to wantin' buffalo heads for their walls and white men made fortunes massacring the buffalos.

"Made for a lot of hungry families here, you see. They were plenty glad to be given beef in exchange for peace on Prodigal."

"Thank you," she told him sincerely. "There's so much I don't understand about the west." She offered a smile. "I have a lot to learn."

"Just takes time."

"I'll go see how supper is going."

When she returned from the kitchen, she saw that Hastings had divided the men into two groups—one to sleep, and one to stay alert and stand guard. Helping Maria and Teresa get both groups fed almost took her mind off worrying about her beloved David.

Almost.

CHAPTER 28

In the middle of the night, Virginia was awakened from a light sleep by the sound of galloping hooves. She ran downstairs, skidding her hand along the wall to guide her. She went to Bart to see if they were about to be rescued by the sheriff and some of the men from town.

"No, ma'am. Broudy's men've just driven the horses out of the barn so we can't use them to run for it or to send anybody for help."

"Oh."

"Don't you worry, Miz Norris." He smiled at her gently. "It's a good thing."

"How?" How could it be a good thing to send their horses tearing off into the night?

He considered the wisdom of telling her for a moment before answering her. Then he said, "Well, because I don't have to worry about Broudy burning the barn. Now it's only a building. We can rebuild that easy if we have to, but there's no way I could get you another Fancy, ma'am."

Tears welled in Virginia's eyes to the point that Bart's kind face became a blur. Obviously he had seen and noted how much her little mare meant to her.

She'd had no idea the men even paid attention to her once they'd looked her over and decided it would be all right to go on and accept her as the mistress of Prodigal, yet Bart had known how much she loved Fancy. Now he'd told her the little mare was safe.

Her voice was choked with tears of gratitude as she told the foreman, "Thank you, Bart. Thank you very much."

It was the first time she had ever used his Christian name. He grinned his appreciation of the new relationship between them that it signified. "Try to get back to sleep, Miz Norris. This is gonna take a while, looks like."

She turned obediently and went back upstairs, careful not to stumble against the first step in the dark. She'd love to stay down here where she would know what was happening but was unwilling to add her hovering presence to Bart's burdens.

They were all doing so much already, these men who served her husband so loyally. She wished there was something she could do to help them.

She went back to her makeshift bed in the dressing room, prayed for the safety of the men and of David and for the end of Broudy's attack, and finally dozed fitfully. As she tossed and turned, she even prayed that the men delegated to sleep at this time were finding it an easier task than she was.

The next day dawned bright and clear. Men shot at the house. The men in the house shot back. Virginia, Maria, and Teresa cooked and prayed, thankful that there were no wounded men among those in the house.

The shooting went on. It looked like Broudy was hoping the men holding the ranch house would run out of ammunition, or get hungry enough to give up Virginia Norris.

Neither was about to happen.

Virginia became more uneasy about David as the time wore on. She hoped against hope that Broudy would give up and go away by the time David came back.

That wasn't happening either. It was a stalemate.

Virginia looked out cautiously. The cloudless sky burned with a merciless blue glare. There wasn't even a dust devil playing on the prairie.

Bright sun beat down on the attackers of Prodigal Ranch, and Virginia found herself struggling not to hope they got heat stroke. She did permit herself to hope they were all hot, sweaty, and thoroughly miserable.

Virginia wished there were something to mask David's approach to the ranch, should he come. Even though she knew he'd intended to be gone for three or four days and couldn't possibly have started back yet, she was already straining her eyes to see if she could discover any sign of his return.

The anxiety she felt for David was almost more than she could bear. Somehow, dread kept invading her heart.

As the day wore on, it was almost as if she were sensing that he was on his way to her. If he were, he would be walking right into Hal Broudy's trap!

The thought of her beloved David riding into a hail of gunfire tore through her very being, and she was so nervous she couldn't stay still. Never in her life had she wrung her hands before. Now she paced the floor doing it.

Surely David would hear the guns and stay away from Prodigal. Or, better yet, he'd circumvent the fight and ride for the sheriff and the townsmen to rescue them.

He'd have sense enough to avoid the conflict here at the ranch house once he heard all the shooting. After all, what could one man expect to do against a dozen?

She sought refuge in prayer. "Dearest Father, please keep David safe."

No matter what. The words ghosted through her mind.

Instantly, she felt a bone-deep chill. It penetrated her mind and filled her every thought. David coming. Her heart began pounding as if it would beat its way out of her chest. David in danger. And the words, *no matter what* ran through her head, over and over.

She clapped her hands over her ears as if that would stop the words. It was true she had prayed those words. She had meant them at the time.

But there hadn't been any bullets flying then.

God must know she didn't really mean it if it meant physical harm to David!

She had prayed those very words about David's salvation. Surely, though . . .

Suddenly, the firing started again. She clamped her hands more tightly over her ears again and walked back into the dressing room. There, she could at least hear herself think. She was joined by Maria and Teresa almost immediately.

"We have fed a good breakfast to all of the men," Maria told her.

Teresa added, "*Si,* and we have left with each one a cup and the jug of coffee."

"But," Maria said, "I must warn you, *Señora*, the kitchen is a very big mess. Some *muy malo perros* was shooting at the windows."

"So we left," Teresa concluded with a firm shake of her head.

"Of course you did." Virginia was distracted. She couldn't rid herself of the terrible foreboding that clawed at the edges of her mind, filling her soul with dread.

Giving herself a hard mental shake, she said, "Thank you both for all you've done." She smiled. "Stay here and try to get some rest. You'll be safest here with no windows for the 'very bad dogs' to shoot through."

The two women laughed at her translation of Maria's comment. Then they began settling themselves comfortably in the windowless dressing room, chatting quietly in Spanish.

Virginia was watching the two women when another stab of fear hit her. It tore through her like a bolt of lightning.

David!

Panicked, she left them then and ran lightly down the stairs to the front door. Bart and the men in the front hall were intent on the men outside. No one noticed Virginia.

Throwing the locks off, she gripped the double handles of the doors.

One of the hands saw her. "Stop! Miz Norris!"

"Miz Norris! Get back!" Bart was running toward her from the post he'd assigned himself. "They're shooting!"

Driven by her awful premonition, Virginia threw open the big, front double doors. Bullets hit the door jamb.

Broudy howled, "Don't shoot her, you fools. We want her alive!"

She rushed to the edge of the porch. David! She could feel him near.

She ran to the steps leading down from the porch, Bart in hot pursuit. "Miz Norris! Stop!"

The shooting changed direction as Virginia leaped from the porch.

Shots echoed everywhere, but they weren't aimed at her now. They weren't even aimed at the house. They were aimed at the lone rider galloping toward her. There was no way she could miss seeing that the horse was Crusader.

Immediately, the scene slowed for Virginia until every action took long seconds. David! She saw David.

He was coming to her.

Even as she watched, the tall figure in the saddle jerked as the first bullet hit him. He grabbed the saddle horn to steady himself and came on. Then a second bullet found its target, and he began to fall.

"David!" Virginia screamed as he fell from his horse. He lay still in the dust like a broken doll. Crusader stopped and stood beside his fallen master.

Virginia's world exploded.

"David!" Desperately sobbing his name, Virginia ran toward her husband. It seemed to take her forever to reach him. When she did, she threw herself to the ground beside him. Gathering him into her arms, she curled around him to protect him with her own body.

"Bride," he gasped, forming the words with great difficulty, "didn't I tell you I'd ride through fire to come to you?"

"Oh, darling," she wailed. "Not *gun-fire*."

He tried to laugh for her. It didn't work, and he smiled a crooked smile instead. "It was . . . the only kind of fire I could . . . find." Then he fainted. His head fell back over Virginia's supporting arm.

Seeing David helpless, Broudy whooped with glee. Instantly, he and his men began to converge on the couple from all sides.

Bart ran forward from the house and slid to his knees beside them. He crouched there beside Virginia, shooting repeatedly to keep their attackers away.

Broudy's men slowed but kept shooting from whatever cover they found.

Suddenly, out of nowhere, there was a volley of gunfire. Some of Broudy's men were hit. Cursing, the attackers scattered.

They hadn't planned on any resistance, much less a flank attack. Unnerved, they broke and ran, as a large
group of men rode toward them from
the direction David had come, firing as
they came.

Those of Broudy's men still capable
of standing threw down their weapons.
Their hands shot skyward in surrender.

In short order, the newcomers surrounded Broudy and his men. Pointing
rifles from horseback, they roughly
herded Broudy and his thugs off, victors
by virtue of superior arms.

Virginia sat sobbing in the dirt and
tried to staunch the flow of blood from
David's shoulder. Men swirled around
her as the battle ended.

Someone touched Virginia's shoulder
and a deep voice said, "Let us have him,
girl. We need to get him inside and take
care of those wounds."

Virginia looked up without really seeing. David needed help, and she
couldn't lift him. She was utterly helpless. Tears streamed down her face.

The man spoke again, his voice

strained, "Let us have him. We'll help him."

Slowly Virginia understood. She relinquished her desperate hold on her husband.

Two men picked David up and started for the house. Carrying him as gently as they could, they walked up the steps and across the porch, leaving a trail of blood behind them.

David's blood.

The stranger lifted Virginia to her feet, put a steadying arm around her, and guided her after David. Over his shoulder, he ordered, "One of you ride for the doctor."

Instantly, a man spun his mount and took off for town at full gallop.

Virginia tore her gaze from David's limp form long enough to glance at the man helping her.

Startled, she looked again. This was the man she had seen at the train station in Boston the day of her wedding!

She and David had been about to board the train when he'd appeared in one cloud of steam from the locomotive, then disappeared in the next!

This was the man David had denied recognizing.

Her bewildered eyes must have asked the question, because he told her quietly, "I'm your father-in-law, Virginia. David is my son."

CHAPTER 29

Gently they carried David into the house, but not up the stairs. Virginia was shocked to see them place him carefully on the long dining room table. In her distressed state, she could only stare and wonder why they weren't taking him up to their bed.

Powerless to help him and fearing she'd get in the way, she moved to the wall. Once there, she found she was glad to have it for support. Her knees had somehow turned to jelly and threatened to give way.

As she watched, David's father and another tall, gray-haired man bent over him and began cutting away David's coat and shirt.

Virginia's heart almost stopped as she saw how thoroughly the clothing was soaked with blood.

Maria and Teresa peered timidly around the doorjamb of the servant's entrance into the room. It didn't take them long to understand the situation.

Quickly, they turned back to the kitchen. Teresa boiled water, and Maria ripped clean dish cloths into bandages. Some of these cloth strips, she folded into pads. Then she piled them in a basket and rushed into the dining room.

The man working over David grunted approval as she passed him the pads. He snatched one up and pressed it to the bullet hole in David's shoulder. "Hold this firmly, Charles."

David's father, his face almost as pale as his son's, put his fingers where the other man had indicated and held the pad firmly in place.

It was soaked through immediately. Pressure alone failed to staunch the blood flow.

"Heat a skewer," the gray-haired man told Maria.

She nodded, spun around, and rushed back into her kitchen.

Virginia could hear the clatter of utensils flying everywhere as Maria made a hasty search for the skewer.

Teresa, eyes wide, came in with a huge bowl of boiled water, moving cautiously so as not to spill it. Her usual boldness was missing as she stared at the still form of her employer.

"Soap," the gray-haired man barked as he accepted the bowl of water.

Maria, leaving the skewer to heat on the coals in the big kitchen wood stove returned, heard his request for soap, and flew from the room. She was back in an instant with a fresh bar of kitchen soap.

Virginia would never have guessed that portly Maria could move so fast.

Emboldened, Virginia moved away from the wall and stood as close to the table as she dared. She still feared she might get in the way of the man franticly working to stem the flow of David's blood. Nevertheless, she felt a compulsion to reach out and touch her husband. She had to touch him.

Standing on his unwounded side, she took his hand. Already she was praying desperately. When she felt the chill in his long fingers, she redoubled her pleas for his recovery.

When Maria came back with a red-hot skewer, Virginia let go of David's hand and stepped back again to make room for her.

The man she didn't know took it. "Good." Grasping the skewer like a sword, he removed the pad from David's shoulder and ran the metal into the wound.

Virginia would have fainted and fallen, had Maria not grabbed her and kept her on her feet.

David writhed against the hands that held him and cried out but didn't regain consciousness. After a moment, the wound stopped bleeding. The cauterization had been a success.

Charles let go an immense sigh of relief. "Thank God."

Virginia echoed him in her heart.

A moment later, her haggard-faced father-in-law touched the shoulder of the man working over David.

"Brian," her father-in-law asked his friend, "is my son going to be all right?"

"I don't know. It's too soon to tell. A lot is going to depend on what damage the other bullet has done."

Drying his thoroughly washed hands, he turned his attention to the wound in David's side.

"I shall be forever grateful that you came with us," Charles Norris told him. "I had no idea that your services would be needed."

Brian merely grunted. He was too busy with David to spare time for talk.

Charles Norris looked around as if in a daze. He needed something to do to steady himself.

Sensing that his son's bride could do with a little reassurance, Charles turned to Virginia to tell her, "Brian was a surgeon in the army before he retired."

Relief washed over Virginia. Well aware that it would take at least an hour or more to get the doctor from town, she'd been lost in despair. Now she felt as if David might have a chance.

She went to a chair and sat down, quietly thanking the Lord that Broudy and his men's bullets hadn't killed her beloved David.

David's father could do no more to help his friend Brian. With nothing to do, his desperate worry about his son was unnerving him. Totally unused to feeling helpless, he sought something that would take his mind off the dread that threatened to unman him.

Seeing how tense Virginia was, he went to her. "Shall we go find a pillow for David's head? I think we can make him a little more comfortable."

Virginia looked up at him, "Wouldn't it be better to put him in our bed?" Quick tears came to her eyes, and she made a helpless little gesture. "The table is so hard."

Charles Norris held out his hand and spoke with a gentleness that he hadn't used since his beloved wife had died. He spoke slowly, knowing that would be the only way to get through to the dazed Virginia. "We will have to leave him there on the table long enough for the bleeding to well and truly stop. Even then, we will have to be very careful with him, but we mustn't chance it now."

He took her hand and all but lifted her from her chair. "All we can do now is to try to make him a little more comfortable where he is."

"Yes. Yes, of course." Having been given a purpose, Virginia was slowly recovering from the shock of seeing her husband gunned down.

At that moment, Grissom, who had spent the night firing in his shirtsleeves from the post that Bart Hastings had assigned to him during the fight, appeared. The sweat-streaked gunpowder he'd worn earlier had been bathed away and he was again perfectly attired. He was also wearing what Virginia used to call his 'butler face' when she'd been a child. He took one look at her and said, "You look distracted, Mrs. Norris. Shall I see to the gentleman?"

His 'Mrs. Norris' jolted her back to herself. It was the final reminder she needed to pull herself together.

Straightening her shoulders, she said, "You're quite right, Grissom, I don't seem to be myself just now. Thank you."

Despite her distress, Virginia made a visible effort to be hostess to the gallant men who had come to their aid. "Please ready rooms for our rescuers, and please tell Maria there will be . . ." She turned inquiringly to her father-in-law.

"There are twelve of us," he supplied.

"Twelve guests for dinner."

"Very well." Grissom bowed and went on his errand.

Virginia was left with the austere man she had only known for perhaps half an hour—this man who had told her he was David's father!

CHAPTER 30

Virginia and her father-in-law settled in chairs at the big preparation table in the kitchen. It was here that Virginia had shared so many pleasant meals with Maria and Teresa in David's absence. Those memories served to give her comfort.

Heaven knew she needed comfort. Already she had bombarded God with a multitude of desperate prayers for David's recovery. It was all she could do, and having done all, she was standing, as the scriptures instructed her to do.

She was calm, even with the clinking and grating sounds made by Maria and Teresa sweeping up the shattered glass from the broken kitchen windows.

She smiled at Charles Norris and asked, "Does the noise bother you here? We could find a quieter place."

Norris could plainly see that his daughter-in-law was comfortable here in her kitchen. He'd like to keep her that way if he could.

His heart quailed with the knowledge that the hopeful look in her eyes was shortly to be replaced with one of utter grief when David died. Just before he came in here to be with Virginia, Brian had told him there was little hope.

"No," he told her with a forced smile. "This is fine. I welcome this opportunity to talk with you undisturbed."

Virginia raised an eyebrow and glanced back at the work being carried on behind her.

Norris chuckled, glad to see she had her sense of humor intact. "At least my friends will have less chance of finding us here, and I'd like a little while alone with you."

His expression sobered and he leaned toward her. "I hope I won't be trespassing, but I would very much like to learn everything I can about all the recent events in my son's life. I want to know so badly that I'm willing to risk being rebuffed. Won't you please tell me your story?"

She hesitated. "It's a rather strange one, you know."

He settled back in his chair and waited expectantly.

Virginia took a minute to marshal her thoughts. She wondered where it was best to begin. Realizing that brevity would, no doubt, please Mr. Norris, she began at the point that concerned David. "My best friend had seen an advertisement in the Boston paper from your son for a bride and had torn it out. She showed it to me . . . gave it to me, in fact . . . and urged me to answer it."

Norris smiled at her. "You can be a little less terse, you know. We have time on our hands."

Instantly, he regretted his remark as he saw a shadow in her eyes that told him he'd brought her fears for his son back to the surface of her thoughts.

Virginia made a supreme effort to

keep her mind on what she was telling her new father-in-law. All the same, her heart was with David. Taking a deep breath, she continued her narrative. "I just put the advertisement in my pocket, rather than offend my friend Dorothy by my lack of interest.

"When I got home and my mother quizzed me on my whereabouts and chastised me as if I were a small child for taking so long on my errand, in an act of rebellion, I answered David's advertisement for a wife." She smiled a little, remembering. "I still can't believe I did that. Even so, I was perfectly certain nothing would come of it."

She looked a little sheepish. "Then everything happened so quickly. First, the telegram came saying he was on his way, and then he was there with us in Boston." She smiled again. "And, as they say, the rest is history. He was wonderful. He swept me off my feet, and he charmed my mother." Her smile broadened. "That last was no easy feat, believe me."

Charles Norris smiled encouragingly.

He seemed to be enjoying the tale, and glad for the distraction.

"David just swept everyone along before him by sheer force of personality." She laughed a little. "I was married before I quite expected it and was on my way here to the ranch.

"David had worked so hard to get this land, you know. He'd been a hired hand for other ranchers, and then he'd gotten just a little land and built his own herd. With money from the herd, he got more land and more and better cattle, and slowly he built the ranch to what it is now. It took him the better part of ten years. The ranch now has three hundred and fifty acres, and David is fiercely proud of Prodigal."

She looked up sharply, her tone changing. "Prodigal! He named the ranch Prodigal."

"Yes." Norris saw that she had guessed David's reason for naming the ranch and met her accusing stare steadily.

"You could tell me a great deal more, Mr. Norris." Her tone was distinctly cooler than it had been. "I think I have a right to know, don't you?"

Norris sighed. "Yes, my dear, I suppose you do." He offered a small smile. "Pardon an old man while he gathers his thoughts, won't you?"

Virginia had to contain herself to keep from giving an unladylike snort. *Pardon an old man, indeed.* Seldom had she seen a more vital man his age, and she was no longer in charity with this one.

He began as slowly and carefully as she had, feeling his way through the labyrinth of years gone by. Finally, he spoke, "I was happily married to the most wonderful and beautiful woman God ever made. She died when David was still a boy, and I was inconsolable.

"First, I completely neglected him, which was bad enough, but then I turned all my unreasonable, demanding attention on him, full blast.

"He tried to please me, but it was impossible. No matter what he achieved, I expected—demanded—more. Every time I looked at the boy, I saw Katherine.

"Pushing him away was all I could do

to keep the terrible pain of having lost her out of my mind."

He passed a hand over his eyes. "I never thought David might need consoling for the loss of his beloved mother. In my own selfish grief, I never cared. Then suddenly, he was seventeen, a man grown, and I'd driven him away from me by my impossible expectations and continual disapproval, as surely as if I'd used a whip."

"Please," Virginia reached out a hand in sympathy, wanting him to stop because she could see how he was suffering. Her woman's heart was touched by his pain and she promptly forgot that she'd decided she wasn't in charity with him only a few minutes ago.

"No. Let me go on." He straightened. "He left. I liked to say he ran off. That was what I told all our friends, but he didn't. He came to me and told me he was leaving . . . that he was going to make his own way in the world."

His voice broke. "He told me that he was sorry he had failed me and failed to be part of my life."

He hung his head. After a long moment, he went on. "And I let him go. I gave him nothing with which to start a new life. Nothing. No money, no letters of introduction, not even a voiced 'good luck.' " He sighed heavily.

"So you see, in that respect David was certainly nothing like the prodigal son in the Bible. That son had received and wasted his inheritance. David had nothing." He shook his head, hating himself for what he had done to his only son. "I gave him nothing."

"Oh, Mr. Norris." Virginia ached for him.

He looked up at her, his face haggard. "I didn't even keep track of David. Years passed without word of him. Finally, some of the all-consuming grief for my wife in which I'd been wallowing eased off. Feelings for my only child, my only son, began to stir.

"One day, I faced the fact that I'd behaved abominably to the lad. Driving him to bigger and better achievements. Never satisfied with anything he did . . . always expecting more because he was my son. My only child. My son that I'd . . . driven from me."

He shook his head again. "Finally, the realization that I had done something for which my beloved wife would never have forgiven me broke some dam in my hardened heart, and I did all I could to find David again.

"I hired a group of men who specialized in locating people, and weekly I received their empty reports. After a while, I began to fear he'd been killed."

He looked up at Virginia and she could see the agony of his words in his eyes. "It never occurred to me he would be ranching in the west. He'd always had such a good head for figures, I suppose I'd imagined him in the banking world.

"At any rate, the first clue to his whereabouts finally came when one of my agents spotted your wedding announcement. I didn't have much hope that the man in it was my son. It could have simply been someone with the same name, of course, but I had to know.

"I came to Boston and saw you at the train. I was stunned. It *was* David and my search was over, and all I could do was stand there and watch the train pull out of the station and disappear.

"Frantic, I found out from your well-wishers that you were headed to Texas, and I planned to follow as soon as I could put my affairs in order.

"Unfortunately for me, Texas is a very large state." He flashed her a sardonic smile. "And certainly there were no directories for finding the people in it.

"Then, in a rare stroke of luck, while spending my last evening at my club, I learned that a David Norris of Texas had made an appointment with Henry Eaton, one of my oldest friends, a financier. They'd planned a meeting in Dallas, and I got there as quickly as possible, and I waited there to catch sight of David.

"Finding the west a lawless and wild place, I carefully gathered the eleven men you have seen.

"Brian, my surgeon friend whom you've met, recommended the other ten men to guarantee our safety. I had no idea what I was getting into, nor whether I'd need my little army, but I was taking no chances.

"When David transacted his business the very night he arrived there and left Dallas the next morning as if there was a fire under him, I was greatly relieved that I'd made such elaborate preparations beforehand. Almost instantly, we were ready to give chase.

"We couldn't catch him. He rode like a demon. Nevertheless, I was determined to follow David wherever he went.

"I'd lost my first chance to talk with him in the Boston train station; this second chance in Dallas." He smiled a bitter smile. "I wasn't going to risk losing him a third time. I was determined to trail him to his lair, so to speak. When he left Dallas, the twelve of us were right behind him."

"I shall be forever grateful that you were," Virginia said softly.

Norris took the hand she reached out to him and patted it clumsily. "So am I, dear girl. So am I. You see, the truth of it is that it's not a prodigal son coming home. It's a prodigal father hoping to get his only son back."

Sitting back in his chair, he pulled out

his handkerchief and blew his nose, hard. "Now, daughter of mine, it's your turn. Tell me. How has the young rapscallion treated you? Well, I hope."

Virginia had thought to tell him only the good part of her brief life with David, but his eyes met hers and she knew nothing but the whole truth would do. She began with slow deliberation. "We liked each other from the very first. There was never anything but the truth between us." She cocked her head to one side as if she listened to an inner voice. "I think we fell in love on the trip to Texas. At least, I thought we had. I know I did."

"But?"

"I wondered if I'd misunderstood. That maybe he didn't want a wife, but just a decoration for all he'd achieved. His ambition . . . worried me."

"I hope you understand, now, that that was from the life I'd forced on the boy. The command was to achieve, no matter what it cost him."

"We quarreled."

"What's so awful about that?" he asked gently. "People do, my dear. Even my lovely wife and I did occasionally, and she was as close to perfect as woman ever got."

Virginia looked down at her hands for an instant, then shook her head and regarded him with a directness that seemed to give him pause. "In that quarrel, I made the most disappointing discovery of my life."

Norris leaned forward in his chair.

"I learned that David isn't a Christian."

Charles Norris didn't seem surprised. He didn't even seem to understand why a thing like that would be important to her. A long moment passed before he said gravely, "Virginia, my dear, that may be my fault, as well."

When she started to speak, he held up a hand to stop her. "My wife was a practicing Christian, you see, and she raised David to be. When she died, I was so angry with God that I forbade him to go to church, or to have anything to do with church-goers." He considered his thoughts for a moment. "I guess I still had, and indeed still *do* have, a grudge against the Almighty for taking my Katherine from me."

Virginia's heart went out to Mr. Norris. The old gentleman was reliving an old agony right before her eyes. What could she do to ease his pain? There was no way she could change the past, but what if they lost David? Her breath caught at that thought, but she knew she'd have to put her own devastating pain aside and attempt to comfort him in some way.

Fearful that she might be treading on his beliefs, she said softly, "You know, Mr. Norris, God himself calls death the last enemy."

His gaze shot to her face, but he didn't speak.

"I don't think God purposefully takes our loved one from us because of that. If I did, I'd hardly dare pray that our David live, and I certainly don't intend to give up that fight, do you?"

"Of course not. What's your point?"

"Just that we have to trust in a power, an infinite wisdom beyond ourselves." She paused, praying silently that he would understand. "We must trust God. He's all we have left."

"My wife, Katherine, had that kind of faith. I haven't."

Virginia could see that she had already said too much. She kept silent.

Finally Norris said heavily, "I love my son. If that God of yours can save David, I'll try to believe you."

CHAPTER 31

Two days later, they had hope again. Though in David's short bouts of consciousness he was incoherent, both Charles's friend Dr. Brian Ward and Dr. Smith from town agreed they could safely move David upstairs to his bed.

The bleeding had stopped. When they changed the dressings on his wounds, they were clear of blood. They began to believe that David would recover.

Virginia was beside herself with joy and sang quiet praises to God in her mind the whole day.

Her step was light as she moved through the house, making sure all the guests were comfortable and seeing if

Maria and Teresa needed help cooking for them. Most of her time, of course, she spent with David.

At night, Virginia sat in a chair close beside him, praying and speaking encouragement to her unconscious husband. She refused to leave his side.

Maria, Teresa, and Grissom had tried to persuade her to go to bed so that she would be rested when David really awakened, but she'd refused. "I'm fine right here," she told them from her well-upholstered chair beside his bed. "Besides, this way I'll be here the moment he awakes."

Finally, days later, David stirred and woke up. His voice was barely a whisper. "Bride?"

"Oh, David! Yes?"

"Are you all right?"

"Yes, darling. Of course I'm all right." She could hardly think what to tell him; she was so relieved, her mind was spinning. Every word that came was a praise to God that David was awake and lucid.

She brushed his hair back from David's forehead and placed a gentle kiss there. "Oh, David. We were all so worried."

"When I heard the shooting . . . I was frantic to get to you. I sent Clint on . . . to . . . get help from town." Under the golden stubble of his beard, he was turning pale.

Virginia put a finger across his lips. "That's enough talking for now, dearest. You must rest and get well. I'll tell you all that went on, if you like."

"I like."

Virginia smiled fondly. Even weak as a kitten and flat on his back, David was taking back the reins of Prodigal Ranch.

Obeying his command, she reassured him that the man who'd accompanied him to Dallas was safe. "Clint made it safely to town and returned with the sheriff and half the townsmen. Everyone was eager to rescue us. They were wonderful."

"Good." He relaxed visibly.

"And, of course, Bart was the hero during the attack. I've no idea what you could have told him, but he took protection of the ranch very much to heart."

David looked curious.

"Bart had lookouts posted from the moment you left, and it was a good thing, because Hal Broudy attacked before you'd been gone much more than a few hours." She carefully refrained from telling him that Broudy's avowed purpose was to kidnap her.

David regarded her without blinking.

"The minute the lookout sounded the warning, Bart had all the men in the house. They had piles of guns already in the front hall, and there was enough ammunition for a war."

David grinned.

Virginia smiled. "Yes. And Bart gave you full credit for it, too."

His grin widened.

"Bart's rather worried about all the damage to the house, but I promised him you wouldn't mind."

David scowled.

"Under the circumstances, of course."

The scowl lessened.

"And Grissom reminded me that glass can be replaced. And bullet holes can be patched and walls painted, don't you agree?"

She watched the frown he still wore

for a few seconds, and then said, "They kept me safe for you."

The frown left his face and was replaced by a genuine smile.

"That's better." She rose from her chair and bent over the bed to kiss him softly on the mouth. "And best of all, you came home to me as you promised." There were tears in her eyes that she dare not let him see. They were there because she couldn't say '*safely* home to me.'

After a moment during which she saw him gain a little strength, she decided she had better tell him about his father.

"Did you know that your father had followed you from Dallas?"

"What?" His entire body tensed. "My father? *My* father, Charles Norris? What was he doing there?"

She smoothed her hand down his arm and took his hand. "He has been searching for you for a very long time, David. His hired agents found our wedding announcement in the Boston paper, and he came to see if that was truly you or merely someone with the same name." She tried not to sound accusing as she said, "He was at the train station on our wedding day."

David lay still and tense. It was as if he were shielding himself from her words. Perhaps she shouldn't have told him about his father's presence so soon.

Mr. Norris would want to talk to David as soon as he learned his son had regained consciousness. She had to prepare him. David was in no condition to handle a sudden shock.

Tenderly she told him, "Your father loves you, David. He has been searching for you for years so that he could tell you."

David made a violent sound of disbelief. It was followed by a gasp of pain.

Virginia, alarmed that he might have somehow re-injured himself, leapt to her feet. "I'll get the doctor."

David reached for her hand, rearing up slightly to grasp it. That movement elicited a grunt of pain.

"David! Be still!"

"Stay then!"

She sank back into the chair by the bed. "Your father was waiting for you in

Dallas. He knew you'd be there because Mr. Eaton is a friend of his and told him he was going to Dallas to do business with a rancher named David Norris.

"Your father was elated. He left for Dallas right away, hoping to get in touch with you after your meeting. He missed you again, he said, because you'd left so quickly."

"I wanted to get back to you, Bride."

Tears filled Virginia's eyes. "I wanted you to get back, dearest, but not like you did it."

"Promised I'd come to you if I had to come through fire." He tried a chuckle but it was a dismal failure.

Virginia dashed the tears away with her free hand. "No one, least of all me, wanted you to come through that kind of fire. My heart stopped when I saw you."

She could see David was tiring fast. "You need to sleep, now, my darling David. Sleep will go a long way toward your healing."

He smiled. "I thought you were going to pray me well."

She sent him a mock frown. "I've

been busy just praying you alive. One thing at a time, please."

He chuckled weakly. His eyes were closing.

Virginia held a glass of water to his lips. "Drink this. You mustn't dehydrate, and you've been terribly hard to get fluids down while you were unconscious, you know."

He managed a few swallows, then turned his face away, dropping off to sleep. His breathing was strong and regular.

Virginia bowed her head. "Thank You, Father. David is so dear to me. You alone know how grateful I am that You have saved him from dying."

No matter what. The words slid through her mind again.

"Yes, Father," she said, recognizing the words from her long-ago prayer for David's salvation. "I did say that, didn't I? This is a very drastic solution, I fear, and he isn't saved yet. I'll try harder, I promise."

The Apostle Paul's admonition to work out one's own salvation danced at the edges of her mind. Instantly, she shot to her feet. "Are You saying that I can't. . . . Of course, I can't save him. I can't save anybody. Only You can save him, and *he* has to ask." Her shoulders slumped. "He has to ask."

She sat back down in the chair. She felt as if her world was collapsing around her. What was she to do? She'd no idea what it would take to cause David to ask the Lord for his own salvation. She feared it might never happen.

She sighed and closed her eyes for a moment. Then she took a deep breath and thrust her worries into the back of her mind.

Her duty right now was to tell the others that David had awakened, that he had spoken coherently, and that he had even taken a few swallows of water. They would be as relieved as she was, and by tomorrow, she imagined David would feel up to brief visits from his father and Bart Hastings.

She found Mr. Norris conferring with Bart in the foyer. Something about the state of the ranch house from the way they were looking around.

Without preamble, she told them

about her success in getting water down David. "Three whole swallows at first, then a few more. And he was coherent." She smiled at the relieved men. "By tomorrow, I suspect he would welcome visits from you."

It seemed clear that David was on the road to recovery. Virginia kept giving thanks in her mind as she went about the business of the house.

Maria and Teresa wore big smiles. Even Grissom looked as if he had something to celebrate.

The entire household, including Charles Norris and his men, was beginning to be more cheerful as they went around with lists assessing the damage to the ranch house and deciding what they could do to repair it without disturbing David's recuperation.

Then the fever struck.

CHAPTER 32

Virginia had just arisen from the first good night's sleep she'd had since David had been shot. Sleeping in her bed had certainly been more comfortable than the chair beside David's bed.

She took her time dressing and then, smiling, went to check on her husband. The sight that greeted her made her blood run cold.

David had tossed and turned until his body was entangled with the sheets she had left so neatly pulled over him. Even as she watched, he groaned and threw an arm wide, the dressing on his shoulder torn off by his movement. As he tossed again, the wound began to bleed afresh.

Rushing to him, Virginia tried to stop his thrashing. Taking hold of him the best she could, she sought to get him to lie still.

He was as hot as a furnace. His skin was so dry to her touch, it seemed brittle. He lunged away from her, sprawling to the far side of the bed.

"Grissom! Maria!" Virginia shouted.

David shook his head and moaned.

Grissom ran into the room, his usual dignity forgotten. "What is it, Miss Virginia?" He saw even as he asked her. Rushing to the bedside, he put his hand on David's forehead.

David grunted and pushed Grissom's hand away like a petulant child.

Grissom told Virginia, "Go! Run for Mr. Norris and his Dr. Ward. I'll hold him to keep him from throwing himself off the bed. Tell them he's burning up."

Virginia flew from the room and down the stairs in pursuit of the two men needed. Tearing into the dining room, she found them peacefully eating their breakfasts.

They looked up, startled by her precipitous entrance. Charles Norris leapt to his feet. "What? Is it David?"

"Please come! He's burning up and tossing around and I couldn't manage him. Grissom is trying, but we need your help." She turned and dashed for the stairs.

Dr. Ward rose bellowing, "Maria!" When she appeared in the door to the kitchen, he ordered, "Cold water, lots of towels, sheets—hurry!"

"*Sí!*" She whirled around and dashed back into the kitchen yelling, "Teresa! *Rapido!*"

The men caught up with Virginia and passed her on the stairs. When she entered the bedroom, they were already repositioning David and seeing if he had done any damage to himself. It took both men and Grissom to hold him.

Maria and Teresa rushed into the room an instant later, water from the bucket and bowl they carried sloshing everywhere. They plopped them down, and left the room again to go for the sheets and towels Dr. Ward had ordered.

Brian Ward began bathing David's fever down by simply dipping his hands in the water and tossing it on David. When the water hit him, David flinched and thrashed as if from a blow. A few more applications, however, and he calmed and lay there, panting.

Maria and Teresa arrived, each with a huge stack of sheets and towels. The doctor indicated the foot of the bed, and they piled them there.

Virginia stood at the side of the big four-poster. She watched in silence, her eyes wide with worry.

"Brian! What does this mean?" Charles Norris's voice was a harsh rasp.

"Means he's got infection somewhere. Fever means the body's fighting it, but . . ."

"What can we do?"

"Just what we're doing, Charles. We want to keep him from burning up, make him as comfortable as we can and hope the fever kills the infection before it kills him."

Virginia heard an agonized little moan. It took her an instant to realize it came from her.

Charles Norris looked up. "This might be a good time to see if you can get that God of yours to step in and save David for us."

Virginia understood the strain he was under and didn't take offense. She couldn't do anything to help David that the men couldn't do better, but she could pray. She knew her Lord and what He was capable of far better than they did.

Going straight to the chair in which she'd spent several nights at David's bedside, she dropped down on her knees in front of it, placed her elbows on its seat, and clasped her hands. Closing her eyes tight, she sought the presence of God.

Remembering that she should enter His presence with thanksgiving, she began. "Thank You, Father," she murmured softly, ignoring the sounds of David's attempts to thrash and the voices of the men working to restrain him. "Thank You that we may come to You in our times of need. This is such a time, Lord, and I praise You that I can come to You now.

"You instruct us to put You in remembrance of Your Word, and I say that Isaiah fifty-three says that by Your Son's stripes we are healed. Not were, Lord, *are.* I claim that for my husband David.

"I know that You love David as much as I do. I ask for his healing. And I know that sometimes the answer to our prayers might be 'no,' even though You want us to have life more abundantly. So I have an even more fervent prayer, Lord. Please don't let him die without knowing You."

She didn't know what else to say. She sat back on her heels and took a deep breath. Very, very softly she whispered, "Save him, Lord. In Jesus's Name." She smiled a small sad smile. "I know You are going to, because I realize that this is the 'No matter what.' "

Rising, she went to the bed to be near him. She was in time to hear Dr. Ward say, "If he makes it through the night, we may save him."

Virginia bowed her head. No more

prayers came. She had done her best. Now they'd have to wait.

For now all that she could do was to accept whatever happened.

CHAPTER 33

Virginia stayed in the chair beside David's bed. There was no question of her sleeping, and she resisted every attempt from those around her to get her to go where she might rest more comfortably.

The very idea that she could rest anywhere when David's life hung in the balance was ludicrous. She knew that they meant to help her, and thanked them for their concern, but she refused to leave David's side.

For two more days she watched over him.

He had calmed down and was lying quietly for the most part.

His father and Dr. Ward had dragged

in two more chairs and sat on the other side of the bed from her. Every now and then, one of them would touch David's forehead.

Dr. Ward seemed satisfied with whatever progress David was making, but Charles was inconsolable.

When the two men drifted off to sleep and filled the room with their snores, Virginia got up and wrung out a cloth in the bowl of water Teresa kept fresh for them. Putting it on David's forehead, she left it in place until she imagined the cloth had gained heat from his head. Then she turned it to the other side before returning it to the cool water again.

It gave her a sense of accomplishment. It reassured her, as well. The cloths when she turned them were only mildly warm now. David's fever was abating.

There was so little they could do for him, and she felt so helpless. She was putting the cloth back on his head when he reached out and caught her hand.

"Bride." He looked at her for a long moment, his eyes fever-bright. The he said softly, "You've been praying."

"Of course," she answered simply.

"Thank you." His eyes closed and as she watched, his breathing evened out and he slept.

Was he sleeping normally? She prayed he was. She didn't want to wake the doctor to ask if it were so.

The man had worked so hard over David. He needed and deserved his rest.

She sat holding David's hand and changing the cold compresses on his forehead until the dawn sent rays of sunlight into the room and woke the men on the other side of the bed. Dr. Ward got up, smoothed his rumpled shirt, smiled at Virginia, and leaned over David.

Removing the last cloth she'd put on his forehead, he placed his hand there for a moment. Turning away from the bed, he nodded to her. "I think the crisis is over, Mrs. Norris. I think your husband is going to make it."

"Thank the Lord," she breathed.

"Thank Him, indeed," Ward agreed. "To tell you the truth, I didn't think he was going to pull through. It was a near thing."

Virginia whispered, "I know."

"Lots of rest until he has healed completely. You'll have your hands full keeping him still."

Virginia raised her chin. "I'll manage."

"I'll bet you will." He turned toward the door. "Now if you'll excuse an old man, I'm going to freshen up and have some breakfast." Looking toward the bed, he added, "I'll tell Maria what he's to have. It'll be up to you to get it down him."

"Thank you. Thank you for everything."

He waved a dismissive hand and was gone.

Charles Norris just stood looking down at his sleeping son, his face haggard. "I nearly lost him again, Virginia. I don't think I could have stood that. Not after just finding him after so long." He looked at her with tears in his eyes and a tentative smile.

A long moment passed during which he regained the confidence that was so much a part of him. His voice strengthening, he said to Virginia, "Well. Looks as if I'll have to let you talk to me sometime about this God of yours. Seems like those prayers you said worked. Thank you."

Virginia smiled radiantly at him. "Prayers always do," she told him. To herself she added a heartfelt, *'Thank You, Lord.'*

Tired as she was, she was aware that she owed David's life to God. The enemy of his soul had tried to claim him before he could come to know the Lord, and God had answered their prayers and stopped him.

In addition, the results of those prayers had won Charles Norris's willingness to listen. Her heart was full to overflowing.

All she had still left to hope and pray for was that David would accept Jesus's sacrifice on the cross and be eternally saved. When that happened, her joy would indeed be full. She'd no longer be unequally yoked—a situation that made her uncomfortable, no matter how wonderful her husband was—but would have the common ground on which she and David could raise their family.

Mr. Norris ran a hand through his hair. "I know you'll excuse me if I follow Brian's good example and go get cleaned up."

"Of course." Virginia smiled at him. He had never left David's side, and she knew how much better he'd feel if he did as he intended.

He stopped at the door. "You'll call me?"

Knowing that he meant if there was any change, she nodded her promise, and he left, comforted.

Two hours later, David opened his eyes and smiled at her. "I think I'm going to live, Bride."

She had to stop herself from throwing her arms around him. "Oh, my darling, I'm so glad. So grateful."

"Grateful to me?" He had his wicked grin in place, and Virginia knew he was teasing her.

"No, and you know it. I'm grateful to God."

The teasing went out of his smile,

leaving one of ineffable sweetness. "Yes. We have to talk about that."

Virginia was astonished. David had always cut her off when she wanted to talk to him about God. An unbidden joy began to steal into her heart.

"First, though," David said with a little effort, "I'd like to see my father before I run out of steam."

"Oh, yes, dearest." Virginia's joy ran over. "He's just left to rest a little. He's never left your side, you know, till just now."

"Somehow, I've been aware of that."

Virginia squeezed his hand. "I'll go get him." She kissed his forehead and rose to go. "Rest until we get back. Then I'll leave the two of you to talk."

Virginia's heart was singing as she went to find David's father. "Dearest Lord," she prayed aloud, "I know that You are about to heal the awful breech between these two wonderful men, and I simply don't have the words with which to thank You." With that she burst into grateful tears. "Father, You are so good."

When she found Charles Norris, he

blanched and reached for the wall for support. "Is it David?" He could hardly choke the words out.

"No! No!" Virginia hastened to reassure him, appalled that her tears of gratitude had led him to fear the worst where his son was concerned. "David is awake and wants to see you."

Tears started in Mr. Norris's own eyes. "Thank God!"

They hurried to David's bedside.

"Son!" His father dropped into the chair beside the bed. His voice was beyond his control, and he reached for David's hand as tears of relief spilled down his cheeks.

David smiled and lifted his hand to grasp the one his father proffered.

Virginia was overwhelmed by the feelings she was experiencing at witnessing their reunion. Knowing she was one person too many in the room, she left it, quietly closing the door behind her.

CHAPTER 34

Days later, David was much recovered. He spent most of his time propped up against many pillows, complaining that he'd do just as well sitting in a chair.

Virginia, of course, refused to let him.

Right now, he was sleeping peacefully.

Today, the room was so quiet that Virginia could hear birdsong and even the buzz of bees outside. She sat in her customary chair beside his bed and pretended to read the book in her lap. Her mind was so completely on her husband that she could not have told anyone what the book was about. Virginia was standing guard as David slept.

And while she did, she was reliving

every precious moment of their perfect day.

Then David opened his eyes.

"Bride."

"You're awake." Virginia smiled and put her book aside. "Did you sleep well? Is it easier for you to rest now?"

"Yes. I still feel as if I've been trampled in a stampede, but I'm sleeping better every night." He laughed and winced only slightly. "And every day, too, for that matter."

Virginia winced with him. She so hated to see him hurting. "Sleep is the best thing for you, you know. Brian, our Dr. Ward, says that the body heals itself better than any physician, but it does its best work while we're asleep."

"Well, with the amount of sleep I've been getting, I should be completely well. Why can't I be allowed up?"

Virginia rose from her chair and smoothed his tousled hair back off his forehead. Leaning over him, she spoke as a mother might to a small child. "Because you can't. You simply aren't all the way well yet."

He grinned at her, grabbed her hand

and pulled her down on the bed beside him. "See, I'm getting my strength back."

David," she scolded, "you'll hurt yourself."

He kissed her on the forehead. "I want to talk."

"What about?" She reached for some of the extra pillows Teresa had left in case David should need them and made herself comfortable. She was thrilled that he'd had the strength to pull her down next to him and equally thrilled that he wanted to.

As she settled herself beside her husband, she breathed a silent. *'Thank You, Father.'* She was almost giddy with joy that David had been spared and that he was doing so well, now that the terrible fever had passed.

He really was recuperating beyond her wildest expectations. She was certain that his reunion with his father had a lot to do with it.

Brian Ward had said that David's recovery fell into the ranks of the miraculous, after all. Thanking God again, she turned her full attention to David.

David told her earnestly, "I wanted you to know that, half the time I seemed to be unconscious, I could hear you praying for me. It was as if you threw me some kind of lifeline. A line not only keeping me safe, but a line holding me to this life. I wanted to thank you."

"Oh, David."

"That's the honest truth. When I could feel the dark waves trying to pull me under, I'd hear your voice praying for me, and it somehow buoyed me up again."

Silent tears started to flow down Virginia's cheeks. Gratitude to her Maker swelled in her heart. To think that David had been aware of her prayers for him was a quiet joy that threatened to send her into noisy sobs of happiness.

David went on. "Once, I was certain it was all over, and I knew a dread that I can't even describe. It was then, Bride, that I knew beyond the slightest shadow of a doubt that there was a very real hell, and I knew I didn't want to go there. I seemed powerless to do anything about it, though. It was as if my chance to avoid it had passed me by."

Virginia clutched him tight, as if there

were still some chance he might slip away, that she might lose him forever.

"Then, as if from far, far away, I could hear you praying for me. Some of the words were words that any wife might say over a wounded husband." He kissed her brow by way of apology for words that might have hurt her. "But most of them ran through my mind as if written there in letters etched by fire."

She was watching him steadily, her eyes soft and drowned by her tears.

He went on. "I know this all seems strange, and I know I lack the power to convey to you just what it was like, but it was as if a battle was raging, and your fire-marked words were the weapons that were the only protection I had against a horror that words can't describe." He looked steadily at her. "Can you understand all that?"

"Yes, David, I can." And she could, but she wanted to hear so much more. She wanted to hear that the words from the Bible were more than just protection to him. She wanted to hear that they were the very breath of life to him. She was holding her own breath as he continued.

"Then, even though I felt as if I myself were on fire . . . that was the fever, I suppose . . . it was as if some wonderful being came to my rescue." He was regarding her as if he thought she might not believe him.

"Someone like an angel from my Bible story books in my long-ago nursery entered the fray and . . . Oh, glory, Virginia, I know I sound like a madman. No doubt, it was the fever, and I was delirious with it to the point that I was seeing dreams and fables from my childhood, but it was real. As real as you are right now. And that angel wielded a huge sword and vanquished all the dark forms that were trying to drag me down into what I have every certainty was hell."

Virginia held him even closer.

"Virginia, it was your prayers that kept me. Your prayers and the words you read about healing from your Bible kept me safe from that terrible, dark force that would otherwise have taken me forever." He held her tight for a long moment in silence. Then he said, "Thank you."

"I love you, David." It was a simple reply, but it was the only one she could think of to make. There was so much more she wanted. She wanted to hear him say that he was God's own, even more than she wanted to draw her next breath and the others that should follow.

He lay holding her for a long time without a word. Then he asked her, "Bride, would you please pray with me? I'd like to make peace with God."

Hearing at last the words she had longed for, Virginia was stunned with joy. Her heart overflowed with it.

For a moment she couldn't speak—she could only look up at David with eyes filled with incredible love. Then, very softly, she began to lead her beloved husband in the prayer that would finally make him one of Almighty God's very own children.

When they had finished, there was so much light and joy in David's eyes, Virginia couldn't stop her own tears of gratitude to God.

David took her in his arms, and they

clung to each other with a new understanding of all that life had become for
them.

Finally, David pulled back and grinned
at her. "I suppose now that we have
Grissom, we should at least entertain
our friends. If they want me for governor, though, they'll just have to come
and get me."

With the words came the realization
that at last she was enough for David.
She'd thought that he would never put
his ambition aside for her. Now he had.
She hadn't believed it possible.

In her heart she heard the quiet voice
of her Lord. *With God all things are possible*.

Virginia threw her arms around her
beloved husband's neck. Tenderly,
David gathered her back into his arms,
held her close and buried his smiling
face in her hair.

Flooding in through the bullet-
shattered windows, sunlight formed a
halo around them as curious, loving
faces appeared at the door of the room.
Virginia saw David's father standing

there, met his gaze, and mingled quiet, joyful laughter with her happy tears.

In the doorway, Charles Norris smiled back at her. Then he took a long, slow, deep breath. Looking skyward, he sighed, closed his eyes, and whispered a reverent, heart-felt "Thank you, God."